Alice Walker was born in Eatonton, Georgia. She has received many awards, including The Radcliffe Fellowship and a Guggenheim Fellowship. Her hugely popular novel, *The Color Purple* (The Women's Press, 1983), won the American Book Award, plus the Pulitzer Prize for Fiction in 1983, and was subsequently made into an internationally successful film by Steven Spielberg.

Alice Walker's other novels are *Meridian* (The Women's Press, 1982), of which CLR James said 'I have not read a novel superior to this'; *The Third Life of Grange Copeland* (The Women's Press, 1985); *The Temple of My Familiar* (The Women's Press, 1989), which appeared in the *New York Times* bestseller list for four months; and *Possessing the Secret of Joy* (1992). She is also the author of two collections of essays and memoirs: *In Search of Our Mothers' Gardens: Womanist Prose* (The Women's Press, 1984), and *Living by the Word* (The Women's Press, 1988). Alice Walker has published four books of poetry, all of which have been published by The Women's Press: *Horses Make a Landscape Look More Beautiful* (1985), *Once* (1986), *Good Night, Willie Lee, I'll See You in the Morning* (1987) and *Revolutionary Petunias* (1988); her complete poetry is now collected together in one volume, *Her Blue Body Everything We Know: Earthling Poems 1965–1990 Complete* (The Women's Press, 1991).

D0418122

Also by Alice Walker from The Women's Press:

Fiction and poetry

Meridian
The Color Purple
The Color Purple: Special 10th Anniversary Limited Edition
Horses Make a Landscape Look More Beautiful
The Third Life of Grange Copeland
Once
Good Night, Willie Lee, I'll See You in the Morning
Revolutionary Petunias
The Temple of My Familiar
Her Blue Body Everything We Know: Earthling Poems 1965–1990 Complete

Essays

In Search of Our Mothers' Gardens: Womanist Prose
Living by the Word: Selected Writings 1973–1987

Alice Walker

The Complete Stories

First published by The Women's Press Ltd, 1994
A member of the Namara Group
34 Great Sutton Street, London EC1V 0DX

This paperback edition published 1995

You Can't Keep a Good Woman Down © Alice Walker 1982
In Love and Trouble © Alice Walker 1984
Preface copyright © Alice Walker 1994

Some of the stories in this volume previously appeared in *The Best Short Stories by Negro
Writers, Black World, Brother, The Denver Quarterly, Freedomways, Harper's Magazine, Ms, Red
Clay Reader*

British Library Cataloguing-in-Publication Data
A catalogue record for this book is available from the British Library.

ISBN 0 7043 4435 1

Printed and bound in Great Britain by
BPC Paperbacks Ltd

CONTENTS

AUTHOR'S PREFACE

The first short story I wrote, or that I remember writing, was never published. It was "The Suicide of an American Girl", and was deeply influenced by the stories of Doris Lessing. Not even her stories, actually, though I adored them, but *The Golden Notebook*, by which I was enthralled as a senior at Sarah Lawrence College where I began seriously writing. A copy of this story languishes in the archive in the basement of my house, perhaps. I'm actually not sure where it is. Having written it, I apparently decided to live on. And so I wrote my second short story, at the age of twenty, and that has become known as my first short story. It is called "To Hell with Dying", and is included in this collection.

I have enjoyed writing short stories from the very first. While in college I was delighted to discover a story could be completed over a weekend, as was "To Hell with Dying". As an activist I was happy to realize I could dream up and write one, even during a period of political activity, while registering voters in Mississippi, for instance, or dodging bottles during a sit-in in front of the Georgia State Highway Patrol. As a lover I was amused to see how stories could come to mind even as my every emotion seemed trained on the beloved. Best of all, short stories could be completed while one brought up a child. I remember icy winter days at the Radcliffe Institute in Cambridge, Massachusetts, where I had a sunny room to work in for over a year, a respite from Mississippi, and of working all morning on a story, perhaps "The Revenge of Hannah Kemhuff", or "Roselily", and of dashing off just before lunch to check on my two-year-old at the Radcliffe nursery school. Feeling not harried and unfinished, as I might have felt with a novel, but rather fulfilled, accomplished. I have loved as well the experimentation that is possible with the short story. All that is really required, no matter how it is written, is that it works. There is a tremendous well of creative energy to be drawn from, once the writer realizes this. There is the freedom that always comes when one is prepared to honor the singularly individual permutations of one's own experience and mind. It never concerned me if my stories looked like no one else's. On the contrary, this made me happy. Stories are, after all, rather like a thumbprint. Unique to the soul and heart they are by creation attached.

The stories in this book were inspired by my life in the South, as a child and young adult, and by my life as activist, lover, mother, teacher and *wife* (always the easiest role to overlook, in my experience) wandering and dreaming across many parts of the world. All my life I've been fascinated by the lives around me, whether in the fields or in the streets, in academia or in my bed; short stories provide a form for the deep longing I feel to know human beings better. I become them for the duration of my scrutiny of their lives. Often forgetting entirely that I am responsible for their existence; that I am making them up.

And I have outlived the telling of these tales! I don't believe I ever thought I would. The story "Laurel", for one, I thought would kill me. Or someone reading it would. The same is true of "Advancing Luna—and Ida B. Wells", "Coming Apart" and "Porn". The excitement of writing the forbidden has always sustained my passion to survive what I've come to know. But it is only in retrospect that I realize this. At the time of writing each of these stories I remember agonizing over my right to speak every step of the way, then going on anyhow.

It is satisfying to see the two collections *In Love and Trouble* and *You Can't Keep a Good Woman Down* together. The first volume concerned with the lives of women who barely realize they have a place in the world, the second filled with women who are finding or have found where they belong. And who have in any event freed their imaginations and their tongues.

In Love and Trouble

for Muriel Rukeyser and Jane Cooper,
who listened to what was never said,

and in loving memory of Zora Hurston,
Nella Larsen, and Jean Toomer:
the three mysteries,

and for Eileen, wherever you are

Wonuma soothed her daughter, but not without some trouble. Ahurole had unconsciously been looking for a chance to cry. For the past year or so her frequent unprovoked sobbing had disturbed her mother. When asked why she cried, she either sobbed the more or tried to quarrel with everybody at once. She was otherwise very intelligent and dutiful. Between her weeping sessions she was cheerful, even boisterous, and her practical jokes were a bane on the lives of her friends . . . But though intelligent, Ahurole could sometimes take alarmingly irrational lines of argument and refuse to listen to any contrary views, at least for a time. From all this her parents easily guessed that she was being unduly influenced by agwu, her personal spirit. Anyika did his best but of course the influence of agwu could not be nullified overnight. In fact it would never be completely eliminated. Everyone was mildly influenced now and then by his personal spirit. A few like Ahurole were particularly unlucky in having a troublesome spirit.

Ahurole was engaged to Ekwueme when she was eight days old.

—Elechi Amadi, *The Concubine*

... People have (with no help of conventions) oriented all their solutions toward the easy and toward the easiest side of the easy; but it is clear that we must hold to what is difficult; everything in Nature grows and defends itself in its own way and is characteristically and spontaneously itself, seeks at all costs to be so and against all opposition.

—Rainer Maria Rilke, *Letters to a Young Poet*

ROSELILY

Dearly Beloved,

She dreams; dragging herself across the world. A small girl
in her mother's white robe and veil, knee raised waist high
through a bowl of quicksand soup. The man who stands
beside her is against this standing on the front porch of her
house, being married to the sound of cars whizzing by on
highway 61.

we are gathered here

Like cotton to be weighed. Her fingers at the last minute
busily removing dry leaves and twigs. Aware it is a superficial
sweep. She knows he blames Mississippi for the respectful
way the men turn their heads up in the yard, the women
stand waiting and knowledgeable, their children held from

7

mischief by teachings from the wrong God. He glares beyond them to the occupants of the cars, white faces glued to promises beyond a country wedding, noses thrust forward like dogs on a track. For him they usurp the wedding.

in the sight of God

Yes, open house. That is what country black folks like. She dreams she does not already have three children. A squeeze around the flowers in her hands chokes off three and four and five years of breath. Instantly she is ashamed and frightened in her superstition. She looks for the first time at the preacher, forces humility into her eyes, as if she believes he is, in fact, a man of God. She can imagine God, a small black boy, timidly pulling the preacher's coattail.

to join this man and this woman

She thinks of ropes, chains, handcuffs, his religion. His place of worship. Where she will be required to sit apart with covered head. In Chicago, a word she hears when thinking of smoke, from his description of what a cinder was, which they never had in Panther Burn. She sees hovering over the heads of the clean neighbors in her front yard black specks falling, clinging, from the sky. But in Chicago. Respect, a chance to build. Her children at last from underneath the detrimental wheel. A chance to be on top. What a relief, she thinks. What a vision, a view, from up so high.

in holy matrimony.

Her fourth child she gave away to the child's father who had some money. Certainly a good job. Had gone to Harvard. Was a good man but weak because good language meant so much to him he could not live with Roselily. Could not abide TV in the living room, five beds in three rooms, no Bach except from four to six on Sunday afternoons. No chess at all. She does not forget to worry about her son among his father's people. She wonders if the New England climate will agree with him. If he will ever come down to Mississippi, as his father did, to try to right the country's wrongs. She wonders if he will be stronger than his father. His father cried off and on throughout her pregnancy. Went to skin and bones. Suffered nightmares, retching and falling out of bed. Tried to kill himself. Later told his wife he found the right baby through friends. Vouched for, the sterling qualities that would make up his character.

It is not her nature to blame. Still, she is not entirely thankful. She supposes New England, the North, to be quite different from what she knows. It seems right somehow to her that people who move there to live return home completely changed. She thinks of the air, the smoke, the cinders. Imagines cinders big as hailstones; heavy, weighing on the people. Wonders how this pressure finds it way into the veins, roping the springs of laughter.

If there's anybody here that knows a reason why

But of course they know no reason why beyond what they daily have come to know. She thinks of the man who will be her husband, feels shut away from him because of the stiff severity of his plain black suit. His religion. A lifetime of black and white. Of veils. Covered head. It is as if her children are already gone from her. Not dead, but exalted on a pedestal, a stalk that has no roots. She wonders how to make new roots. It is beyond her. She wonders what one does with memories in a brand-new life. This had seemed easy, until she thought of it. "The reasons why . . . the people who" . . . she thinks, and does not wonder where the thought is from.

these two should not be joined

9

She thinks of her mother, who is dead. Dead, but still her mother. Joined. This is confusing. Of her father. A gray old man who sold wild mink, rabbit, fox skins to Sears, Roebuck. He stands in the yard, like a man waiting for a train. Her young sisters stand behind her in smooth green dresses, with flowers in their hands and hair. They giggle, she feels, at the absurdity of the wedding. They are ready for something new. She thinks the man beside her should marry one of them. She feels old. Yoked. An arm seems to reach out from behind her and snatch her backward. She thinks of cemeteries and the long sleep of grandparents mingling in the dirt. She believes that she believes in ghosts. In the soil giving back what it takes.

together,

In the city. He sees her in a new way. This she knows, and is grateful. But is it new enough? She cannot always be a bride and virgin, wearing robes and veil. Even now her body itches to be free of satin and voile, organdy and lily of the valley. Memories crash against her. Memories of being bare to the sun. She wonders what it will be like. Not to have to go to a job. Not to work in a sewing plant. Not to worry about learning to sew straight seams in workingmen's over-alls, jeans, and dress pants. Her place will be in the home, he has said, repeatedly, promising her rest she had prayed for. But now she wonders. When she is rested, what will she do? They will make babies—she thinks practically about her fine brown body, his strong black one. They will be inevitable. Her hands will be full. Full of what? Babies. She is not comforted.

let him speak

She wishes she had asked him to explain more of what he meant. But she was impatient. Impatient to be done with sewing. With doing everything for three children, alone. Impatient to leave the girls she had known since childhood, their children growing up, their husbands hanging around her, already old, seedy. Nothing about them that she wanted, or needed. The fathers of her children driving by, waving, not waving; reminders of times she would just as soon forget. Impatient to see the South Side, where they would live and build and be respectable and respected and free. Her husband would free her. A romantic hush. Proposal. Promises. A new life! Respectable, reclaimed, renewed. Free! In robe and veil.

or forever hold

She does not even know if she loves him. She loves his sobriety. His refusal to sing just because he knows the tune. She loves his pride. His blackness and his gray car. She loves his understanding of her *condition*. She thinks she loves the effort he will make to redo her into what he truly wants. His love of her makes her completely conscious of how unloved she was before. This is something; though it makes her unbearably sad. Melancholy. She blinks her eyes. Remembers she is finally being married, like other girls. Like other girls, women? Something strains upward behind her eyes. She thinks of the something as a rat trapped, cornered, scurrying to and fro in her head, peering through the windows of her eyes. She wants to live for once. But doesn't know quite what that means. Wonders if she has ever done it. If she ever will. The preacher is odious to her. She wants to strike him out of the way, out of her light, with the back of her hand. It seems to her he has always been standing in front of her, barring her way.

his peace.

The rest she does not hear. She feels a kiss, passionate,

rousing, within the general pandemonium. Cars drive up blowing their horns. Firecrackers go off. Dogs come from under the house and begin to yelp and bark. Her husband's hand is like the clasp of an iron gate. People congratulate. Her children press against her. They look with awe and distaste mixed with hope at their new father. He stands curiously apart, in spite of the people crowding about to grasp his free hand. He smiles at them all but his eyes are as if turned inward. He knows they cannot understand that he is not a Christian. He will not explain himself. He feels different, he looks it. The old women thought he was like one of their sons except that he had somehow got away from them. Still a son, not a son. Changed.

She thinks how it will be later in the night in the silvery gray car. How they will spin through the darkness of Mississippi and in the morning be in Chicago, Illinois. She thinks of Lincoln, the president. That is all she knows about the place. She feels ignorant, *wrong*, backward. She presses her worried fingers into his palm. He is standing in front of her. In the crush of well-wishing people, he does not look back.

"REALLY, *DOESN'T*
CRIME PAY?"

(Myrna)

SEPTEMBER, 1961

page 118

I sit here by the window in a house with a thirty-year
mortgage, writing in this notebook, looking down at my
Helena Rubenstein hands ... and why not? Since I am not
a serious writer my nails need not be bitten off, my cuticles
need not have jagged edges. I can indulge myself—my
hands—in Herbessence nailsoak, polish, lotions, and creams.
The result is a truly beautiful pair of hands: sweet-smelling,
small, and soft. ...

I lift them from the page where I have written the line
"Really, *Doesn't* Crime Pay?" and send them seeking up my
shirt front (it is a white and frilly shirt) and smoothly up the

13

column of my throat, where gardenia scent floats beneath my hairline. If I should spread my arms and legs or whirl, just for an instant, the sweet smell of my body would be more than I could bear. But I fit into my new surroundings perfectly; like a jar of cold cream melting on a mirrored vanity shelf.

page 119

"I have a surprise for you," Ruel said, the first time he brought me here. And you know how sick he makes me now when he grins.

"What is it?" I asked, not caring in the least.

And that is how we drove up to the house. Four bedrooms and two toilets and a half.

"Isn't it a beauty?" he said, not touching me, but urging me out of the car with the phony enthusiasm of his voice.

"Yes," I said. It is "a beauty." Like new Southern houses everywhere. The bricks resemble cubes of raw meat; the roof presses down, a field hat made of iron. The windows are narrow, beady eyes; the aluminum glints. The yard is a long undressed wound, the few trees as bereft of foliage as hairpins stuck in a mud cake.

"Yes," I say, "it sure is a beauty." He beams, in his chill and reassured way. I am startled that he doesn't still wear some kind of military uniform. But no. He came home from Korea a hero, and a glutton for sweet smells.

"Here we can forget the past," he says.

page 120

We have moved in and bought new furniture. The place reeks of newness, the green walls turn me bilious. He stands behind me, his hands touching the edges of my hair. I pick up my hairbrush and brush his hands away. I have sweetened my body to such an extent that even he (especially he) may no longer touch it.

I do not want to forget the past; but I say "Yes," like a parrot. "We can forget the past here."

The past of course is Mordecai Rich, the man who, Ruel claims, caused my breakdown. The past is the night I tried to murder Ruel with one of his chain saws.

MAY, 1958

page 2

Mordecai Rich

Mordecai does not believe Ruel Johnson is my husband. "*That* old man," he says, in a mocking, cruel way.

"Ruel is not old," I say. "Looking old is just his way." Just as, I thought, looking young is your way, although you're probably not much younger than Ruel.

Maybe it is just that Mordecai is a vagabond, scribbling down impressions of the South, from no solid place, going to none . . . and Ruel has never left Hancock County, except once, when he gallantly went off to war. He claims travel broadened him, especially his two months of European leave. He married me because although my skin is brown he thinks I look like a Frenchwoman. Sometimes he tells me I look Oriental: Korean or Japanese. I console myself with this thought: My family tends to darken and darken as we get older. One day he may wake up in bed with a complete stranger.

"He works in the store," I say. "He also raises a hundred acres of peanuts." Which is surely success.

"That many," muses Mordecai.

It is not pride that makes me tell him what my husband does, is. It is a way I can tell him about myself.

page 4

Today Mordecai is back. He tells a funny/sad story about a man in town who could not move his wife. "He huffed and puffed," laughed Mordecai, "to no avail." Then one night as he was sneaking up to her bedroom he heard joyous cries. Rushing in he found his wife in the arms of another woman! The wife calmly dressed and began to pack her bags. The husband begged and pleaded. "Anything you want," he promised. "What *do* you want?" he pleaded. The wife began to chuckle and, laughing, left the house with her friend.

Now the husband gets drunk every day and wants an ordinance passed. He cannot say what the ordinance will be against, but that is what he buttonholes people to say: "I want a goddam ordinance passed!" People who know the story make jokes about him. They pity him and give him enough money to keep him drunk.

page 5

I think Mordecai Rich has about as much heart as a dirt-eating toad. Even when he makes me laugh I know that nobody ought to look on other people's confusion with that cold an eye.

"But that's what I am," he says, flipping through the pages of his scribble pad. "A cold eye. An eye looking for Beauty. An eye looking for Truth."

"Why don't you look for other things?" I want to know. "Like neither Truth nor Beauty, but places in people's lives where things have just slipped a good bit off the track."

"That's too vague," said Mordecai, frowning.

"So is Truth," I said. "Not to mention Beauty."

page 10

Ruel wants to know why "the skinny black tramp"—as he calls Mordecai—keeps hanging around. I made the mistake of telling him Mordecai is thinking of using our house as the setting for one of his Southern country stories.

"Mordecai is from the North," I said. "He never saw a wooden house with a toilet in the yard."

"Well maybe he better go back where he from," said Ruel, "and shit the way he's used to."

It's Ruel's pride that is hurt. He's ashamed of this house that seems perfectly adequate to me. One day we'll have a new house, he says, of brick, with a Japanese bath. How should I know why?

page 11

When I told Mordecai what Ruel said he smiled in that snake-eyed way he has and said, "Do *you* mind me hanging around?"

I didn't know what to say. I stammered something. Not because of his question but because he put his hand point-blank on my left nipple. He settled his other hand deep in my hair.

"I am married more thoroughly than a young boy like you could guess," I told him. But I don't expect that to stop him. Especially since the day he found out I wanted to be a writer myself.

It happened this way: I was writing in the grape arbor, on the ledge by the creek that is hidden from the house by trees. He was right in front of me before I could put my notebook away. He snatched it from me and began to read. What is worse, he read aloud. I was embarrassed to death.

"No wife of mine is going to embarrass me with a lot of foolish, vulgar stuff," Mordecai read. (This is Ruel's opinion

of my writing.) *Every time he tells me how peculiar I am for wanting to write stories he brings up having a baby or going shopping, as if these things are the same. Just something to occupy my time.*

"If you have time on your hands," he said today, "why don't you go shopping in that new store in town."

I went. I bought six kinds of face cream, two eyebrow pencils, five nightgowns and a longhaired wig. Two contour sticks and a pot of gloss for my lips.

And all the while I was grieving over my last story. Outlined—which is as far as I take stories now—but dead in embryo. My hand stilled by cowardice, my heart the heart of a slave.

page 14

Of course Mordecai wanted to see the story. What did I have to lose?

"Flip over a few pages," I said. "It is the very skeleton of a story, but one that maybe someday I will write."

"The One-Legged Woman," Mordecai began to read aloud, then continued silently.

The characters are poor dairy farmers. One morning the husband is too hung over to do the milking. His wife does it and when she has finished the cows are frightened by thunder and stampede, trampling her. She is also hooked severely in one leg. Her husband is asleep and does not hear her cry out. Finally she drags herself home and wakes him up. He washes her wounds and begs her to forgive him. He does not go for a doctor because he is afraid the doctor will accuse him of being lazy and a drunk, undeserving of his good wife. He wants the doctor to respect him. The wife, understanding, goes along with this.

However, gangrene sets in and the doctor comes. He lectures the husband and amputates the leg of the wife. The wife lives and tries to forgive her husband for his weakness.

While she is ill the husband tries to show he loves her, but cannot look at the missing leg. When she is well he finds he can no longer make love to her. The wife, sensing his revulsion, understands her sacrifice was for nothing. She drags herself to the barn and hangs herself.

The husband, ashamed that anyone should know he was married to a one-legged woman, buries her himself and later tells everyone that she is visiting her mother.

While Mordecai was reading the story I looked out over the fields. If he says one good thing about what I've written, I promised myself, I will go to bed with him. (How else could I repay him? All I owned in any supply were my jars of cold cream!) As if he read my mind he sank down on the seat beside me and looked at me strangely.

"*You* think about things like this?" he asked.

He took me in his arms, right there in the grape arbor. "You sure do have a lot of heavy, sexy hair," he said, placing me gently on the ground. After that, a miracle happened. Under Mordecai's fingers my body opened like a flower and carefully bloomed. And it was strange as well as wonderful. For I don't think love had anything to do with this at all.

page 17

After that, Mordecai praised me for my intelligence, my sensitivity, the depth of the work he had seen—and naturally I showed him everything I had: old journals from high school, notebooks I kept hidden under tarpaulin in the barn, stories written on paper bags, on table napkins, even on shelf paper from over the sink. I am amazed—even more amazed than Mordecai—by the amount of stuff I have written. It is over twenty years' worth, and would fill, easily, a small shed.

"You must give these to me," Mordecai said finally, holding three notebooks he selected from the rather messy pile. "I will see if something can't be done with them. You could be another Zora Hurston—" he smiled—"another Simone de Beauvoir!"

Of course I am flattered. "Take it! Take it!" I cry. Already I see myself as he sees me. A famous authoress, miles away from Ruel, miles away from anybody. I am dressed in dungarees, my hands are a mess. I smell of sweat. I glow with happiness.

"How could such pretty brown fingers write such ugly, deep stuff?" Mordecai asks, kissing them.

page 20

For a week we deny each other nothing. If Ruel knows (how could he not know? His sheets are never fresh), he says nothing. I realize now that he never considered Mordecai a threat. Because Mordecai seems to have nothing to offer but his skinny self and his funny talk. I gloat over this knowledge. Now Ruel will find that I am not a womb without a brain that can be bought with Japanese bathtubs and shopping sprees. The moment of my deliverance is at hand!

page 24

Mordecai did not come today. I sit in the arbor writing down those words and my throat begins to close up. I am nearly strangled by my fear.

page 56

I have not noticed anything for weeks. Not Ruel, not the house. Everything whispers to me that Mordecai has forgotten me. Yesterday Ruel told me not to go into town and I said I wouldn't, for I have been hunting Mordecai up and down the streets. People look at me strangely, their glances slide off me in a peculiar way. It is as if they see something on my face that embarrasses them. Does everyone know about Mordecai and me? Does good loving show so soon? . . . But it is not soon. He has been gone already longer than I have known him.

page 61

Ruel tells me I act like my mind's asleep. It is asleep, of course. Nothing will wake it but a letter from Mordecai telling me to pack my bags and fly to New York.

page 65

If I could have read Mordecai's scribble pad I would know exactly what he thought of me. But now I realize he never once offered to show it to me, though he had a chance to read every serious thought I ever had. I'm afraid to know what he thought. I feel crippled, deformed. But if he ever wrote it down, that would make it true.

page 66

Today Ruel brought me in from the grape arbor, out of the rain. I didn't know it was raining. "Old folks like us might catch rheumatism if we don't be careful," he joked. I don't know what he means. I am thirty-two. He is forty. I never felt old before this month.

page 79

Ruel came up to bed last night and actually cried in my arms! He would give anything for a child, he says.

"Do you think we could have one?" he said.

"Sure," I said. "Why not?"

He began to kiss me and carry on about my goodness. I began to laugh. He became very angry, but finished what he started. He really does intend to have a child.

page 80

I must really think of something better to do than kill myself.

page 81

Ruel wants me to see a doctor about speeding up conception of the child.

"Will you go, honey?" he asks, like a beggar.

"Sure," I say. "Why not?"

page 82

Today at the doctor's office the magazine I was reading fell open at a story about a one-legged woman. They had a picture of her, drawn by someone who painted the cows orange and green, and painted the woman white, like a white cracker, with little slit-blue eyes. Not black and heavy like she was in the story I had in mind. But it is still my story, filled out and switched about as things are. The author is said to be Mordecai Rich. They show a little picture of him on a back page. He looks severe and has grown a beard. And underneath his picture there is that same statement he made to me about going around looking for Truth.

They say his next book will be called "The Black Woman's Resistance to Creativity in the Arts."

page 86

Last night while Ruel snored on his side of the bed I washed the prints of his hands off my body. Then I plugged in one of his chain saws and tried to slice off his head. This failed because of the noise. Ruel woke up right in the nick of time.

page 95

The days pass in a haze that is not unpleasant. The doctors and nurses do not take me seriously. They fill me full of drugs and never even bother to lock the door. When I think of Ruel I think of the song the British sing: "Ruel Britannia"! I can even whistle it, or drum it with my fingers.

SEPTEMBER, 1961

page 218

People tell my husband all the time that I do not look crazy. I have been out for almost a year and he is beginning to believe them. Nights, he climbs on me with his slobber and his hope, cursing Mordecai Rich for messing up his life.

I wonder if he feels our wills clashing in the dark. Sometimes I see the sparks fly inside my head. It is amazing how normal everything is.

page 223

The house still does not awaken to the pitter-patter of sweet little feet, because I religiously use the Pill. It is the only spot of humor in my entire day, when I am gulping that little yellow tablet and washing it down with soda pop or tea. Ruel spends long hours at the store and in the peanut field. He comes in sweaty, dirty, tired, and I wait for him smelling of Arpège, My Sin, Wind Song, and Jungle Gardenia. The women of the community feel sorry for him, to be married to such a fluff of nothing.

I wait, beautiful and perfect in every limb, cooking supper as if my life depended on it. Lying unresisting on his bed like a drowned body washed to shore. But he is not happy. For he knows now that I intend to do nothing but say yes until he is completely exhausted.

I go to the new shopping mall twice a day now; once in the morning and once in the afternoon, or at night. I buy hats I would not dream of wearing, or even owning. Dresses that are already on their way to Goodwill. Shoes that will go to mold and mildew in the cellar. And I keep the bottles of perfume, the skin softeners, the pots of gloss and eye shadow. I amuse myself painting my own face.

When he is quite, quite tired of me I will tell him how long I've relied on the security of the Pill. When I am quite, quite tired of the sweet, sweet smell of my body and the softness of these Helena Rubenstein hands I will leave him and this house. Leave them forever without once looking back.

HER SWEET JEROME

Ties she had bought him hung on the closet door, which now swung open as she hurled herself again and again into the closet. Glorious ties, some with birds and dancing women in grass skirts painted on by hand, some with little polka dots with bigger dots dispersed among them. Some red, lots red and green, and one purple, with a golden star, through the center of which went his gold mustang stickpin, which she had also given him. She looked in the pockets of the black leather jacket he had reluctantly worn the night before. Three of his suits, a pair of blue twill work pants, an old gray sweater with a hood and pockets lay thrown across the bed. The jacket leather was sleazy and damply clinging to her hands. She had bought it for him, as well as the three suits: one light blue with side vents, one gold with green specks, and one reddish that had a silver imitation-silk vest. The pockets of the jacket came softly outward from the lining like skinny milktoast rats. Empty. Slowly she sank down on the bed and began to knead, with blunt anxious fingers, all the pockets in all the clothes piled around her. First the blue suit, then the gold with green, then the reddish one that he said he didn't like most of all, but which he would sometimes wear if she agreed to stay home, or if she promised not to touch him anywhere at all while he was getting dressed.

She was a big awkward woman, with big bones and hard rubbery flesh. Her short arms ended in ham hands, and her neck was a squat roll of fat that protruded behind her head as a big bump. Her skin was rough and puffy, with plump molelike freckles down her cheeks. Her eyes glowered from under the mountain of her brow and were circled with expensive mauve shadow. They were nervous and quick when she was flustered and darted about at nothing in particular while she was dressing hair or talking to people.

Her troubles started noticeably when she fell in love with a studiously quiet schoolteacher, Mr. Jerome Franklin Washington III, who was ten years younger than her. She told herself that she shouldn't want him, he was so little and cute and young, but when she took into account that he was a schoolteacher, well, she just couldn't seem to get any rest until, as she put it, "I were Mr. and Mrs. Jerome Franklin Washington the third, *and that's the truth!*"

She owned a small beauty shop at the back of her father's funeral home, and they were known as "colored folks with money." She made pretty good herself, though she didn't like standing on her feet so much, and her father let anybody know she wasn't getting any of his money while he was alive. She was proud to say she had never asked him for any. He started relenting kind of fast when he heard she planned to add a schoolteacher to the family, which consisted of funeral directors and bootleggers, but she cut him off quick and said she didn't want anybody to take care of her man but her. She had learned how to do hair from an old woman who ran a shop on the other side of town and was proud to say that she could make her own way. And much better than some. She was fond of telling schoolteachers (women schoolteachers) that she didn't miss her "eddicashion" as much as some did who had no learning and no money both together. She had a low opinion of women schoolteachers, because before and after her marriage to Jerome Franklin Washington III, they were the only females to whom he cared to talk.

The first time she saw him he was walking past the window of her shop with an armful of books and his coat thrown casually over his arm. Looking so neat and *cute*. What popped into her mind was that if he was hers the first thing she would get him was a sweet little red car to drive. And she worked and went into debt and got it for him, too— after she got him—but then she could tell he didn't like it much because it was only a Chevy. She had started right away to save up so she could make a down payment on a brand-new white Buick deluxe, with automatic drive and whitewall tires.

Jerome was dapper, every inch a gentleman, as anybody with half an eye could see. That's what she told everybody before they were married. He was beating her black and blue even then, so that every time you saw her she was sporting her "shades." She could not open her mouth without him wincing and pretending he couldn't stand it, so he would knock her out of the room to keep her from talking to him. She tried to be sexy and stylish, and was, in her fashion, with a predominant taste for pastel taffetas and orange shoes. In the summertime she paid twenty dollars for big umbrella hats with bows and flowers on them and when she wore black and white together she would liven it up with elbow-length gloves of red satin. She was genuinely undecided when she woke up in the morning whether she really outstripped the other girls in town for beauty, but could convince herself that she was equally good-looking by the time she had breakfast on the table. She was always talking with a lot of extra movement to her thick coarse mouth, with its hair tufts at the corners, and when she drank coffee she held the cup over the saucer with her little finger sticking out, while she crossed her short hairy legs at the knees.

If her husband laughed at her high heels as she teetered and minced off to church on Sunday mornings, with her hair greased and curled and her new dress bunching up at the top of her girdle, she pretended his eyes were approving. Other times, when he didn't bother to look up from his books and only muttered curses if she tried to kiss him good-bye, she did not know whether to laugh or cry. However, her public manner was serene.

"I just don't know how some womens can stand it, honey," she would say slowly, twisting her head to the side and upward in an elegant manner. "One thing my husband does not do," she would enunciate grandly, "he don't beat me!" And she would sit back and smile in her pleased oily fat way. Usually her listeners, captive women with wet hair, would simply smile and nod in sympathy and say, looking at one another or at her black eye, "You say he don't? Hummmm, well, hush your mouf." And she would continue curling or massaging or straightening their hair, fixing her face in a steamy dignified mask that encouraged snickers.

2

It was in her shop that she first heard the giggling and saw the smirks. It was at her job that gossip gave her to understand, as one woman told her, "Your cute little man is sticking his finger into somebody else's pie." And she was not and could not be surprised, as she looked into the amused and self-contented face, for she had long been aware that her own pie was going—and for the longest time had been going—strictly untouched.

From that first day of slyly whispered hints, "Your old man's puttin' something *over* on you, sweets," she started trying to find out who he was fooling around with. Her sources of gossip were malicious and mean, but she could think of nothing else to do but believe them. She searched high and she searched low. She looked in taverns and she looked in churches. She looked in the school where he worked.

She went to whorehouses and to prayer meetings, through parks and outside the city limits, all the while buying axes and pistols and knives of all descriptions. Of course she said nothing to her sweet Jerome, who watched her maneuverings from behind the covers of his vast supply of paperback books. This hobby of his she heartily encouraged, relegating reading to the importance of scanning the funnies; and besides, it was something he could do at home, if she could convince him she would be completely silent for an evening, and, of course, if he would stay.

She turned the whole town upside down, looking at white girls, black women, brown beauties, ugly hags of all shades. She found nothing. And Jerome went on reading, smiling smugly as he shushed her with a carefully cleaned and lustred finger. "Don't interrupt me," he was always saying, and he would read some more while she stood glowering darkly behind him, muttering swears in her throaty voice, and then tramping flatfooted out of the house with her collection of weapons.

Some days she would get out of bed at four in the morning after not sleeping a wink all night, throw an old sweater around her shoulders, and begin the search. Her firm bulk became flabby. Her eyes were bloodshot and wild, her hair full of lint, nappy at the roots and greasy on the ends. She smelled bad from mouth and underarms and elsewhere. She could not sit for a minute without jumping up in bitter vexation to run and search a house or street she thought she might have missed before.

"You been messin' with my Jerome?" she would ask whomever she caught in her quivering feverish grip. And before they had time to answer she would have them by the chin in a headlock with a long knife pressed against their necks below the ear. Such blood-chilling questioning of its residents terrified the town, especially since her madness was soon readily perceivable from her appearance. She had taken to grinding her teeth and tearing at her hair as she walked along. The townspeople, none of whom knew where she lived—or anything about her save the name of her man, "Jerome"—were waiting for her to attempt another attack on a woman openly, or, better for them because it implied less danger to a resident, they hoped she would complete her crack-up within the confines of her own home, preferably while alone; in that event anyone seeing or hearing her would be obliged to call the authorities.

She knew this in her deranged but cunning way. But she did not let it interfere with her search. The police would never catch her, she thought; she was too clever. She had a few disguises and a thousand places to hide. A final crack-up in her own home was impossible, she reasoned contemptuously, for she did not think her husband's lover bold enough to show herself on his wife's own turf.

Meanwhile, she stopped operating the beauty shop, and her patrons were glad, for before she left for good she had had the unnerving habit of questioning a woman sitting underneath her hot comb—"You the one ain't you?!"—and would end up burning her no matter what she said. When her father died he proudly left his money to "the school-teacher" to share or not with his wife, as he had "learnin' enough to see fit." Jerome had "learnin' enough" not to give his wife one cent. The legacy pleased Jerome, though he never bought anything with the money that his wife could see. As long as the money lasted Jerome spoke of it as "insurance." If she asked insurance against what, he would say fire and theft. Or burglary and cyclones. When the money was gone, and it seemed to her it vanished overnight, she asked Jerome what he had bought. He said, Something very big. She said, Like what? He said, Like a tank. She did not ask any more questions after that. By that time she didn't care about the money anyhow, as long as he hadn't spent it on some woman.

As steadily as she careened downhill, Jerome advanced in the opposite direction. He was well known around town as a "shrewd joker" and a scholar. An "intellectual," some people called him, a word that meant nothing whatever to her. Everyone described Jerome in a different way. He had friends among the educated, whose talk she found unusually trying, not that she was ever invited to listen to any of it. His closest friend was the head of the school he taught in and had migrated south from some famous university in the North. He was a small slender man with a ferociously unruly beard and large mournful eyes. He called Jerome "brother." The women in Jerome's group wore short kinky hair and large hoop earrings. They stuck together, calling themselves by what they termed their "African" names, and never went to church. Along with the men, the women sometimes held "workshops" for the young toughs of the town. She had no idea what went on in these; however, she had long since stopped believing they had anything to do with cabinet-making or any other kind of woodwork.

Among Jerome's group of friends, or "comrades," as he sometimes called them jokingly (or not jokingly, for all she knew), were two or three whites from the community's white college and university. Jerome didn't ordinarily like white people, and she could not understand where they fit into the group. The principal's house was the meeting place, and the whites arrived looking backward over their shoulders after nightfall. She knew, because she had watched this house night after anxious night, trying to rouse enough courage to go inside. One hot night, when a drink helped stiffen her backbone, she burst into the living room in the middle of the evening. The women, whom she had grimly "suspected," sat together in debative conversation in one corner of the room. Every once in a while a phrase she could understand touched her ear. She heard "slave trade" and "violent overthrow" and "off de pig," an expression she'd never heard before. One of the women, the only one of this group to acknowledge her, laughingly asked if she had come to "join the revolution." She had stood shaking by the door, trying so hard to understand she felt she was going to faint. Jerome rose from among the group of men, who sat in a circle on the other side of the room, and, without paying any attention to her, began reciting some of the nastiest-sounding poetry she'd ever heard. She left the room in shame and confusion, and no one bothered to ask why she'd stood so long staring at them, or whether she needed anyone to show her out. She trudged home heavily, with her head down, bewildered, astonished, and perplexed.

3

And now she hunted through her husband's clothes looking for a clue. Her hands were shaking as she emptied and shook, pawed and sometimes even lifted to her nose to smell. Each time she emptied a pocket, she felt there was something, *something*, some little thing that was escaping her.

Her heart pounding, she got down on her knees and looked under the bed. It was dusty and cobwebby, the way the inside of her head felt. The house was filthy, for she had neglected it totally since she began her search. Now it seemed that all the dust in the world had come to rest under her bed. She saw his shoes; she lifted them to her perspiring cheeks and kissed them. She ran her fingers inside them. Nothing.

Then, before she got up from her knees, she thought about the intense blackness under the headboard of the bed. She had not looked there. On her side of the bed on the floor beneath the pillow there was nothing. She hurried around to the other side. Kneeling, she struck something with her hand on the floor under his side of the bed. Quickly, down on her stomach, she raked it out. Then she raked and raked. She was panting and sweating, her ashen face slowly coloring with the belated rush of doomed comprehension. In a rush it came to her: "It ain't no woman." Just like that. It had never occurred to her there could be anything more serious. She stifled the cry that rose in her throat.

Coated with grit, with dust sticking to the pages, she held in her crude, indelicate hands, trembling now, a sizable pile of paperback books. Books that had fallen from his hands behind the bed over the months of their marriage. She dusted them carefully one by one and looked with frowning concentration at their covers. Fists and guns appeared everywhere. "Black" was the one word that appeared consistently on each cover. *Black Rage, Black Fire, Black Anger, Black Revenge, Black Vengeance, Black Hatred, Black Beauty, Black Revolution*. Then the word "revolution" took over. *Revolution in the Streets, Revolution from the Rooftops, Revolution in the Hills, Revolution and Rebellion, Revolution and Black People in the United States, Revolution and Death*. She looked with wonder at the books that were her husband's preoccupation, enraged that the obvious was what she had never guessed before.

How many times had she encouraged his light reading? How many times been ignorantly amused? How many times had he laughed at her when she went out looking for "his" women? With a sob she realized she didn't even know what the word "revolution" meant, unless it meant to go round and round, the way her head was going.

With quiet care she stacked the books neatly on his pillow. With the largest of her knives she ripped and stabbed them through. When the brazen and difficult words did not disappear with the books, she hastened with kerosene to set the marriage bed afire. Thirstily, in hopeless jubilation, she watched the room begin to burn. The bits of words transformed themselves into luscious figures of smoke, lazily arching toward the ceiling. "Trash!" she cried over and over, reaching through the flames to strike out the words, now raised from the dead in glorious colors. "I kill you! I kill you!" she screamed against the roaring fire, backing enraged and trembling into a darkened corner of the room, not near the open door. But the fire and the words rumbled against her together, overwhelming her with pain and enlightenment. And she hid her big wet face in her singed then sizzling arms and screamed and screamed.

THE CHILD WHO
FAVORED DAUGHTER

> "That my daughter should
> fancy herself in love
> with *any* man!
> How can this be?"
> —Anonymous

She knows he has read the letter. He is sitting on the front
porch watching her make the long trek from the school bus
down the lane into the front yard. *Father, judge, giver of life.*
Shadowy clouds indicating rain hang low on either side of
the four o'clock sun and she holds her hand up to her eyes
and looks out across the rows of cotton that stretch on one
side of her from the mailbox to the house in long green
hedges. After an initial shutting off of breath caused by fear,
a calm numbness sets in and as she makes her way slowly

down the lane she shuffles her feet in the loose red dust and tries to seem unconcerned. But she wonders how he knows about the letter. Her lover has a mother who dotes on the girl he married. It could have been her, preserving the race. Or the young bride herself, brittled to ice to find a letter from her among keepsakes her husband makes no move to destroy. Or—? But that notion does not develop in her mind. She loves him.

> *Fire of earth*
> *Lure of flower smells*
> *The sun*

Down the lane with slow deliberate steps she walks in the direction of the house, toward the heavy silent man on the porch. The heat from the sun is oppressively hot but she does not feel its heat so much as its warmth, for there is a cold spot underneath the hot skin of her back that encloses her heart and reaches chilled arms around the bottom cages of her ribs.

> *Lure of flower smells*
> *The sun*

She stops to gaze intently at a small wild patch of black-eyed Susans and a few stray buttercups. Her fingers caress lightly the frail petals and she stands a moment wondering.

> *The lure of flower smells*
> *The sun*
> *Softly the scent of—*
> *Softly the scent of flowers*
> *And petals*
> *Small, bright last wishes*

2

He is sitting on the porch with his shotgun leaning against the banister within reach. If he cannot frighten her into chastity with his voice he will threaten her with the gun. He settles tensely in the chair and waits. He watches her from the time she steps from the yellow bus. He sees her shade her eyes from the hot sun and look widely over the rows of cotton running up, nearly touching him where he sits. He sees her look, knows its cast through any age and silence, knows she knows he has the letter.

Above him among the rafters in a half-dozen cool spots shielded from the afternoon sun the sound of dirt daubers. And busy wasps building onto their paper houses a dozen or more cells. Late in the summer, just as the babies are getting big enough to fly he will have to light paper torches and burn the paper houses down, singeing the wings of the young wasps before they get a chance to fly or to sting him as he sits in the cool of the evening reading his Bible.

Through eyes half closed he watches her come, her feet ankle deep in the loose red dust. Slowly, to the droning of the enterprising insects overhead, he counts each step, surveys each pause. He sees her looking closely at the bright patch of flowers. She is near enough for him to see clearly the casual slope of her arm that holds the school books against her hip. The long dark hair curls in bits about her ears and runs in corded plainness down her back. Soon he will be able to see her eyes, perfect black-eyed Susans. Flashing back fragmented bits of himself. Reflecting his mind.

> *Memories of years*
> *Unknowable women—*
> *sisters*
> *spouses*
> *illusions of soul*

When he was a boy he had a sister called "Daughter." She

was like honey, tawny, wild, and sweet. She was a generous girl and pretty, and he could not remember a time when he did not love her intensely, with his whole heart. She would give him anything she had, give anybody anything she had. She could not keep money, clothes, health. Nor did she seem to care for the love that came to her too easily. When he begged her not to go out, to stay with him, she laughed at him and went her way, sleeping here, sleeping there. Wherever she was needed, she would say, and laugh. But this could not go on forever; coming back from months with another woman's husband, her own mind seemed to have struck her down. He was struck down, too, and cried many nights on his bed; for she had chosen to give her love to the very man in whose cruel, hot, and lonely fields he, her brother, worked. Not treated as a man, scarcely as well as a poor man treats his beast.

> *Memories of years*
> *Unknowable women—*
> *sisters*
> *spouses*
> *illusions of soul*

When she came back all of her long strong hair was gone, her teeth wobbled in her gums when she ate, and she recognized no one. All day and all night long she would sing and scream and tell them she was on fire. He was still a boy when she began playing up to him in her cunning way, exploiting again his love. And he, tears never showing on his face, would let her bat her lashless eyes at him and stroke his cheeks with her frail, clawlike hands. Tied on the bed as she was she was at the mercy of everyone in the house. They threw her betrayal at her like sharp stones, until they satisfied themselves that she could no longer feel their ostracism or her own pain. Gradually, as it became apparent she was not going to die, they took to flinging her food to her as if she were an animal and at night when she howled at the shadows thrown over her bed by the moon his father rose up and lashed her into silence with his belt.

On a day when she seemed nearly her old self she begged him to let her loose from the bed. He thought that if he set her free she would run away into the woods and never return. His love for her had turned into a dull ache of constant loathing, and he dreamed vague fearful dreams of a cruel revenge on the white lover who had shamed them all. But Daughter, climbing out of bed like a wary animal, knocked him unconscious to the floor and night found her impaled on one of the steel-spike fence posts near the house.

That she had given herself to the lord of his own bondage was what galled him! And that she was cut down so! He could not forgive her the love she gave that knew nothing of master and slave. For though her own wound was a bitter one and in the end fatal, he bore a hurt throughout his life that slowly poisoned him. In a world where innocence and guilt became further complicated by questions of color and race, he felt hesitant and weary of living as though all the world were out to trick him. His only guard against the deception he believed life had in store for him was a knowledge that evil and deception *would come* to him; and a readiness to provide them with a match.

The women in his life faced a sullen barrier of distrust and hateful mockery. He could not seem to help hating even the ones who loved him, and laughed loudest at the ones who cared for him, as if they were fools. His own wife, beaten into a cripple to prevent her from returning the imaginary overtures of the white landlord, killed herself while she was still young enough and strong enough to escape him. But she left a child, a girl, a daughter; a replica of Daughter, his dead sister. A replica in every way.

Memories of once
like a mirror reflecting—
all hope, all loss

His hands are not steady and he makes a clawing motion across the air in front of his face. She is walking, a vivid shape in blue and white, across the yard, underneath the cedar trees. She pauses at the low limb of the big magnolia and seems to contemplate the luminous gloss of the cone-shaped flowers beyond her reach. In the hand away from the gun is the open letter. He holds it tightly by a corner. The palms of his hands are sweating, his throat is dry. He swallows compulsively and rapidly bats his eyes. The slight weight of her foot sends vibrations across the gray boards of the porch. Her eyes flicker over him and rest on the open letter. Automatically his hand brings the letter upward a little although he finds he cannot yet, facing her strange familiar eyes, speak.

With passive curiosity the girl's eyes turn from the letter to the gun leaning against the banister to his face, which he feels growing blacker and tighter as if it is a mask that, when it is completely hardened, will drop off. Almost casually she sways back against the porch post, looking at him and from time to time looking over his head at the brilliant afternoon sky. Without wanting it his eyes travel heavily down the slight, roundly curved body and rest on her offerings to her lover in the letter. He is a black man but he blushes, the red underneath his skin glowing purple, and the coils of anger around his tongue begin to loosen.

"White man's slut!" he hisses at her through nearly sealed lips and clenched teeth. Her body reacts as if hit by a strong wind and lightly she sways on her slender legs and props herself more firmly against the post. At first she gazes directly into his eyes as if there is nowhere else to look. Soon she drops her head.

She leads the way to the shed behind the house. She is still holding her books loosely against her thigh and he makes his eyes hard as they cover the small light tracks in the dust. The brown of her skin is full of copper tints and her arms are like long golden fruits that take in and throw back the hues of the sinking sun. Relentlessly he hurries her steps through the sagging door of boards, with hardness he shoves her down into the dirt. She is like a young willow without roots under his hands and as she does not resist he beats her for a long time with a harness from the stable and where the buckles hit there is a welling of blood which comes to be level with the tawny skin then spills over and falls curling into the dust of the floor.

Stumbling weakly toward the house through the shadows of the trees, he tries to look up beseechingly to the stars, but the sky is full of clouds and rain beats down around his ears and drenches him by the time he reaches the back steps. The dogs run excitedly and hungry around the damp reaches of the back porch and although he feeds them not one will stand unmoving beneath his quickscratching fingers. Dully he watches them eat and listens to the high winds in the trees. Shuddering with chill he walks through the house to the front porch and picks up the gun that is getting wet and sits with it across his lap, rocking it back and forth on his knees like a baby.

It is rainsoaked, but he can make out "I love you" written in a firm hand across the blue face of the letter. He hates the very paper of the letter and crumples it in his fist. A wet storm wind lifts it lightly and holds it balled up against the taut silver screen on the side of the porch. He is glad when the wind abandons it and leaves it sodden and limp against the slick wet boards under his feet. He rests his neck heavily on the back of his chair. Words of the letter—her letter to the white devil who has disowned her to marry one of his own kind—are running on a track in his mind. "Jealousy is being nervous about something that has never, and probably won't ever, belong to you." A wet waning moon fills the sky before he nods.

3

No amount of churchgoing changed her ways. Prayers offered nothing to quench her inner thirst. Silent and lovely, but barren of essential hope if not of the ability to love, hers was a world of double images, as if constantly seen through tears. It was Christianity as it invaded her natural wonderings that threw color into high and fast relief, but its hard Southern rudeness fell flat outside her house, its agony of selfishness failed completely to pervade the deep subterranean country of her mind. When asked to abandon her simple way of looking at simple flowers, she could only yearn the more to touch those glowing points of bloom that lived and died away among the foliage over there, rising and falling like certain stars of which she was told, coming and being and going on again, always beyond her reach. Staring often and intently into the ivory hearts of fallen magnolia blossoms she sought the answer to the question that had never really been defined for her, although she was expected to know it, but she only learned from this that it is the fallen flower most earnestly hated, most easily bruised.

The lure of flower smells
The sun

In the morning, finding the world newly washed but the same, he rises from stiff-jointed sleep and wanders through the house looking at old photographs. In a frame of tarnish and gilt, her face forming out of the contours of a peach, the large dead eyes of beautiful Daughter, his first love. For the first time he turns it upside down then makes his way like a still sleeping man, wonderingly, through the house. At the back door he runs his fingers over the long blade of his pocket-knife and puts it, with gentleness and resignation, into his pocket. He knows that as one whose ultimate death must conform to an aged code of madness, resignation is a kind of dying. A preparation for the final event. He makes a step in the direction of the shed. His eyes hold the panicked calm of fishes taken out of water, whose bodies but not their eyes beat a frantic maneuver over dry land.

In the shed he finds her already awake and for a long time she lies as she was, her dark eyes reflecting the sky through the open door. When she looks at him it is not with hate, but neither is it passivity he reads in her face. Gone is the silent waiting of yesterday, and except for the blood she is strong looking and the damp black hair trailing loose along the dirt floor excites him and the terror she has felt in the night is nothing to what she reads now in his widestretched eyes.

He begs her hoarsely, when it clears for him that she is his daughter, and not Daughter, his first love, if she will deny the letter. Deny the letter; the paper eaten and the ink drunk, the words never wrung from the air. Her mouth curls into Daughter's own hilarity. She says quietly no. No, with simplicity, a shrug, finality. No. Her slow tortured rising is a strong advance and scarcely bothering to look at him, she reflects him silently, pitilessly with her black-pond eyes.

"Going," she says, as if already there, and his heart buckles. He can only strike her with his fist and send her sprawling once more into the dirt. She gazes up at him over her bruises and he sees her blouse, wet and slippery from the rain, has slipped completely off her shoulders and her high young breasts are bare. He gathers their fullness in his fingers and begins a slow twisting. The barking of the dogs creates a frenzy in his ears and he is suddenly burning with unnamable desire. In his agony he draws the girl away from him as one pulling off his own arm and with quick slashes of his knife leaves two bleeding craters the size of grapefruits on her bare bronze chest and flings what he finds in his hands to the yelping dogs.

Memories of once
constant and silent

like a mirror
reflecting

Today he is slumped in the same chair facing the road. The yellow school bus sends up clouds of red dust on its way. If he stirs it may be to Daughter shuffling lightly along the red dirt road, her dark hair down her back and her eyes looking intently at buttercups and stray black-eyed Susans along the way. If he stirs it may be he will see his own child, a black-eyed Susan from the soil on which she walks. A slight, pretty flower that grows on any ground; and flowers pledge no allegiance to banners of any man. If he stirs he might see the perfection of an ancient dream, his own nightmare; the answer to the question still whispered about, undefined. If he stirs he might feel the energetic whirling of wasps about his head and think of ripe late-summer days and time when scent makes a garden of the air. If he stirs he might wipe the dust from the dirt daubers out of his jellied eyes. If he stirs he might take up the heavy empty shotgun and rock it back and forth on his knees, like a baby.

EVERYDAY USE

for your grandmama

I will wait for her in the yard that Maggie and I made so clean and wavy yesterday afternoon. A yard like this is more comfortable than most people know. It is not just a yard. It is like an extended living room. When the hard clay is swept clean as a floor and the fine sand around the edges lined with tiny, irregular grooves, anyone can come and sit and look up into the elm tree and wait for the breezes that never come inside the house.

Maggie will be nervous until after her sister goes: she will stand hopelessly in corners, homely and ashamed of the burn scars down her arms and legs, eying her sister with a mixture of envy and awe. She thinks her sister has held life always in the palm of one hand, that "no" is a word the world never learned to say to her.

You've no doubt seen those TV shows where the child who has "made it" is confronted, as a surprise, by her own mother and father, tottering in weakly from backstage. (A pleasant surprise, of course: What would they do if parent and child came on the show only to curse out and insult each other?) On TV mother and child embrace and smile into each other's faces. Sometimes the mother and father weep, the child wraps them in her arms and leans across the table to tell how she would not have made it without their help. I have seen these programs.

Sometimes I dream a dream in which Dee and I are suddenly brought together on a TV program of this sort. Out of a dark and soft-seated limousine I am ushered into a bright room filled with many people. There I meet a smiling, gray, sporty man like Johnny Carson who shakes my hand and tells me what a fine girl I have. Then we are on the stage and Dee is embracing me with tears in her eyes. She pins on my dress a large orchid, even though she had told me once that she thinks orchids are tacky flowers.

In real life I am large, big-boned woman with rough, man-working hands. In the winter I wear flannel nightgowns to bed and overalls during the day. I can kill and clean a hog as mercilessly as a man. My fat keeps me hot in zero weather. I can work outside all day, breaking ice to get water for washing; I can eat pork liver cooked over the open fire minutes after it comes steaming from the hog. One winter I knocked a bull calf straight in the brain between the eyes with a sledge hammer and had the meat hung up to chill before nightfall. But of course all this does not show on television. I am the way my daughter would want me to be: a hundred pounds lighter, my skin like an uncooked barley pancake. My hair glistens in the hot bright lights. Johnny Carson has much to do to keep up with my quick and witty tongue.

But that is a mistake. I know even before I wake up. Who ever knew a Johnson with a quick tongue? Who can even imagine me looking a strange white man in the eye? It seems to me I have talked to them always with one foot raised in flight, with my head turned in whichever way is farthest from them. Dee, though. She would always look anyone in the eye. Hesitation was no part of her nature.

"How do I look, Mama?" Maggie says, showing just enough of her thin body enveloped in pink skirt and red blouse for me to know she's there, almost hidden by the door.

"Come out into the yard," I say.

Have you ever seen a lame animal, perhaps a dog run over by some careless person rich enough to own a car, sidle up to someone who is ignorant enough to be kind to him? That is the way my Maggie walks. She has been like this, chin on chest, eyes on ground, feet in shuffle, ever since the fire that burned the other house to the ground.

Dee is lighter than Maggie, with nicer hair and a fuller figure. She's a woman now, though sometimes I forget. How long ago was it that the other house burned? Ten, twelve years? Sometimes I can still hear the flames and feel Maggie's arms sticking to me, her hair smoking and her dress falling off her in little black papery flakes. Her eyes seemed stretched open, blazed open by the flames reflected in them. And Dee. I see her standing off under the sweet gum tree she used to dig gum out of; a look of concentration on her face as she watched the last dingy gray board of the house fall in toward the red-hot brick chimney. Why don't you do a dance around the ashes? I'd wanted to ask her. She had hated the house that much.

I used to think she hated Maggie, too. But that was before we raised the money, the church and me, to send her to Augusta to school. She used to read to us without pity; forcing words, lies, other folks' habits, whole lives upon us two, sitting trapped and ignorant underneath her voice. She washed us in a river of make-believe, burned us with a lot of knowledge we didn't necessarily need to know. Pressed us to her with the serious way she read, to shove us away at just the moment, like dimwits, we seemed about to understand.

Dee wanted nice things. A yellow organdy dress to wear to her graduation from high school; black pumps to match a green suit she'd made from an old suit somebody gave me. She was determined to stare down any disaster in her efforts. Her eyelids would not flicker for minutes at a time. Often I fought off the temptation to shake her. At sixteen she had a style of her own: and knew what style was.

I never had an education myself. After second grade the school was closed down. Don't ask my why: in 1927 colored asked fewer questions than they do now. Sometimes Maggie reads to me. She stumbles along good-naturedly but can't see well. She knows she is not bright. Like good looks and money, quickness passed her by. She will marry John Thomas (who has mossy teeth in an earnest face) and then I'll be free to sit here and I guess just sing church songs to myself. Although I never was a good singer. Never could carry a tune. I was always better at a man's job. I used to love to milk till I was hooked in the side in '49. Cows are soothing and slow and don't bother you, unless you try to milk them the wrong way.

I have deliberately turned my back on the house. It is three rooms, just like the one that burned, except the roof is tin; they don't make shingle roofs any more. There are no real windows, just some holes cut in the sides, like the portholes in a ship, but not round and not square, with rawhide holding the shutters up on the outside. This house is in a pasture, too, like the other one. No doubt when Dee sees it she will want to tear it down. She wrote me once that no matter where we "choose" to live, she will manage to come see us. But she will never bring her friends. Maggie and I thought about this and Maggie asked me, "Mama, when did Dee ever *have* any friends?"

She had a few. Furtive boys in pink shirts hanging about

on washday after school. Nervous girls who never laughed. Impressed with her they worshiped the well-turned phrase, the cute shape, the scalding humor that erupted like bubbles in lye. She read to them.

When she was courting Jimmy T she didn't have much time to pay to us, but turned all her faultfinding power on him. He *flew* to marry a cheap city girl from a family of ignorant flashy people. She hardly had time to recompose herself.

When she comes I will meet—but there they are!

Maggie attempts to make a dash for the house, in her shuffling way, but I stay her with my hand. "Come back here," I say. And she stops and tries to dig a well in the sand with her toe.

It is hard to see them clearly through the strong sun. But even the first glimpse of leg out of the car tells me it is Dee. Her feet were always neat-looking, as if God himself had shaped them with a certain style. From the other side of the car comes a short, stocky man. Hair is all over his head a foot long and hanging from his chin like a kinky mule tail. I hear Maggie suck in her breath. "Uhnnnh," is what it sounds like. Like when you see the wriggling end of a snake just in front of your foot on the road. "Uhnnnh."

Dee next. A dress down to the ground, in this hot weather. A dress so loud it hurts my eyes. There are yellows and oranges enough to throw back the light of the sun. I feel my whole face warming from the heat waves it throws out. Earrings gold, too, and hanging down to her shoulders. Bracelets dangling and making noises when she moves her arm up to shake the folds of the dress out of her armpits. The dress is loose and flows, and as she walks closer, I like it. I hear Maggie go "Uhnnnh" again. It is her sister's hair. It stands straight up like the wool on a sheep. It is black as night and around the edges are two long pigtails that rope about like small lizards disappearing behind her ears.

"Wa-su-zo-Tean-o!" she says, coming on in that gliding way the dress makes her move. The short stocky fellow with the hair to his navel is all grinning and he follows up with "Asalamalakim, my mother and sister!" He moves to hug Maggie but she falls back, right up against the back of my chair. I feel her trembling there and when I look up I see the perspiration falling off her chin.

"Don't get up," says Dee. Since I am stout it takes something of a push. You can see me trying to move a second or two before I make it. She turns, showing white heels through her sandals, and goes back to the car. Out she peeks next with a Polaroid. She stoops down quickly and lines up picture after picture of me sitting there in front of the house with Maggie cowering behind me. She never takes a shot without making sure the house is included. When a cow comes nibbling around the edge of the yard she snaps it and me and Maggie *and* the house. Then she puts the Polaroid in the back seat of the car, and comes up and kisses me on the forehead.

Meanwhile Asalamalakim is going through motions with Maggie's hand. Maggie's hand is as limp as a fish, and probably as cold, despite the sweat, and she keeps trying to pull it back. It looks like Asalamalakim wants to shake hands but wants to do it fancy. Or maybe he don't know how people shake hands. Anyhow, he soon gives up on Maggie.

"Well," I say. "Dee."

"No, Mama," she says. "Not 'Dee,' Wangero Lee-wanika Kemanjo!"

"What happened to 'Dee'?" I wanted to know.

"She's dead," Wangero said. "I couldn't bear it any longer, being named after the people who oppress me."

"You know as well as me you was named after your aunt Dicie," I said. Dicie is my sister. She named Dee. We called her "Big Dee" after Dee was born.

"But who was *she* named after?" asked Wangero.

"I guess after Grandma Dee," I said.

"And who was she named after?" asked Wangero.

"Her mother," I said, and saw Wangero was getting tired. "That's about as far back as I can trace it," I said. Though, in fact, I probably could have carried it back beyond the Civil War through the branches.

"Well," said Asalamalakim, "there you are."

"Uhnnnh," I heard Maggie say.

"There I was not," I said, "before 'Dicie' cropped up in our family, so why should I try to trace it that far back?"

He just stood there grinning, looking down on me like somebody inspecting a Model A car. Every once in a while he and Wangero sent eye signals over my head.

"How do you pronounce this name?" I asked.

"You don't have to call me by it if you don't want to," said Wangero.

"Why shouldn't I?" I asked. "If that's what you want us to call you, we'll call you."

"I know it might sound awkward at first," said Wangero.

"I'll get used to it," I said. "Ream it out again."

Well, soon we got the name out of the way. Asalamalakim had a name twice as long and three times as hard. After I tripped over it two or three times he told me to just call him Hakim-a-barber. I wanted to ask him was he a barber, but I didn't really think he was, so I didn't ask.

"You must belong to those beef-cattle peoples down the road," I said. They said "Asalamalakim" when they met you, too, but they didn't shake hands. Always too busy: feeding the cattle, fixing the fences, putting up salt-lick shelters, throwing down hay. When the white folks poisoned some of the herd the men stayed up all night with rifles in their hands. I walked a mile and a half just to see the sight.

Hakim-a-barber said, "I accept some of their doctrines, but farming and raising cattle is not my style." (They didn't tell me, and I didn't ask, whether Wangero (Dee) had really gone and married him.)

We sat down to eat and right away he said he didn't eat

collards and pork was unclean. Wangero, though, went on through the chitlins and corn bread, the greens and everything else. She talked a blue streak over the sweet potatoes. Everything delighted her. Even the fact that we still used the benches her daddy made for the table when we couldn't afford to buy chairs.

"Oh, Mama!" she cried. Then turned to Hakim-a-barber. "I never knew how lovely these benches are. You can feel the rump prints," she said, running her hands underneath her and along the bench. Then she gave a sigh and her hand closed over Grandma Dee's butter dish. "That's it!" she said, "I knew there was something I wanted to ask you if I could have." She jumped up from the table and went over in the corner where the churn stood, the milk in it clabber by now. She looked at the churn and looked at it.

"This churn top is what I need," she said. "Didn't Uncle Buddy whittle it out of a tree you all used to have?"

"Yes," I said.

'Uh huh,' she said happily. "And I want the dasher, too."

"Uncle Buddy whittle that, too?' asked the barber.

Dee (Wangero) looked up at me.

"Aunt Dee's first husband whittled the dash," said Maggie so low you almost couldn't hear her. "His name was Henry, but they called him Stash."

"Maggie's brain is like an elephant's," Wangero said, laughing. "I can use the churn top as a centerpiece for the alcove table," she said, sliding a plate over the churn, "and I'll think of something artistic to do with the dasher."

When she finished wrapping the dasher the handle stuck out. I took it for a moment in my hands. You didn't even have to look close to see where hands pushing the dasher up and down to make butter had left a kind of sink in the wood. In fact, there were a lot of small sinks; you could see where thumbs and fingers had sunk into the wood. It was beautiful light yellow wood, from a tree that grew in the yard where Big Dee and Stash had lived.

After dinner Dee (Wangero) went to the trunk at the foot of my bed and started rifling through it. Maggie hung back in the kitchen over the dishpan. Out came Wangero with two quilts. They had been pieced by Grandma Dee and then Big Dee and me had hung them on the quilt frames on the front porch and quilted them. One was in the Lone Star pattern. The other was Walk Around the Mountain. In both of them were scraps of dresses Grandma Dee had worn fifty and more years ago. Bits and pieces of Grandpa Jarrell's Paisley shirts. And one teeny faced blue piece, about the size of a penny matchbox, that was from Great Grandpa Ezra's uniform that he wore in the Civil War.

"Mama," Wangero said sweet as a bird. "Can I have these old quilts?"

I heard something fall in the kitchen, and a minute later the kitchen door slammed.

"Why don't you take one or two of the others?" I asked. "These old things was just done by me and Big Dee from some tops your grandma pieced before she died."

"No," said Wangero. "I don't want those. They are stitched around the borders by machine."

"That'll make them last better," I said.

"That's not the point," said Wangero. "These are all pieces of dresses Grandma used to wear. She did all this stitching by hand. Imagine!" She held the quilts securely in her arms, stroking them.

"Some of the pieces, like those lavender ones, come from old clothes her mother handed down to her," I said, moving up to touch the quilts. Dee (Wangero) moved back just enough so that I couldn't reach the quilts. They already belonged to her.

"Imagine!" she breathed again, clutching them closely to her bosom.

"The truth is," I said, "I promised to give them quilts to Maggie, for when she marries John Thomas."

She gasped like a bee had stung her.

"Maggie can't appreciate these quilts!" she said. "She'd probably be backward enough to put them to everyday use."

"I reckon she would," I said. "God knows I been saving 'em for long enough with nobody using 'em. I hope she will!" I didn't want to bring up how I had offered Dee (Wangero) a quilt when she went away to college. Then she had told me they were old-fashioned, out of style.

"But they're *priceless!*" she was saying now, furiously; for she has a temper. "Maggie would put them on the bed and in five years they'd be in rags. Less than that!"

"She can always make some more," I said. "Maggie knows how to quilt."

Dee (Wangero) looked at me with hatred. 'You just will not understand. The point is these quilts, *these* quilts!"

"Well," I said, stumped. "What would *you* do with them?"

"Hang them,' she said. As if that was the only thing you *could* do with quilts.

Maggie by now was standing in the door. I could almost hear the sound her feet made as they scraped over each other.

"She can have them, Mama," she said, like somebody used to never winning anything, or having anything reserved for her. "I can 'member Grandma Dee without the quilts."

I looked at her hard. She had filled her bottom lip with checkerberry snuff and it gave her face a kind of dopey, hangdog look. It was Grandma Dee and Big Dee who taught her how to quilt herself. She stood there with her scarred hands hidden in the folds of her skirt. She looked at her sister with something like fear but she wasn't mad at her. This was Maggie's portion. This was the way she knew God to work.

When I looked at her like that something hit me in the top of my head and ran down to the soles of my feet. Just like when I'm in church and the spirit of God touches me and I get happy and shout. I did something I never had done before: hugged Maggie to me, then dragged her on into the room, snatched the quilts out of Miss Wangero's hands and dumped them into Maggie's lap. Maggie just sat there on my bed with her mouth open.

"Take one or two of the others," I said to Dee.

But she turned without a word and went out to Hakim-a-barber.

"You just don't understand," she said, as Maggie and I came out to the car.

"What don't I understand?" I wanted to know.

"Your heritage," she said. And then she turned to Maggie, kissed her, and said, "You ought to try to make something of yourself, too, Maggie. It's really a new day for us. But from the way you and Mama still live you'd never know it."

She put on some sunglasses that hid everything above the tip of her nose and her chin.

Maggie smiled; maybe at the sunglasses. But a real smile, not scared. After we watched the car dust settle I asked Maggie to bring me a dip of snuff. And then the two of us sat there just enjoying, until it was time to go in the house and go to bed.

THE REVENGE OF
HANNAH KEMHUFF

In grateful memory of Zora Neale Hurston

Two weeks after I became Tante Rosie's apprentice we were visited by a very old woman who was wrapped and contained, almost smothered, in a half-dozen skirts and shawls. Tante Rosie (pronounced Ro'*zee*) told the woman she could see her name, Hannah Kemhuff, written in the air. She told the woman further that she belonged to the Order of the Eastern Star.

The woman was amazed. (And I was, too! Though I learned later that Tante Rosie had extensive files on almost everybody in the country, which she kept in long cardboard boxes under her bed.) Mrs. Kemhuff quickly asked what else Tante Rosie could tell her.

Tante Rosie had a huge tank of water on a table in front of her, like an aquarium for fish, except there were no fish in it. There was nothing but water and I never was able to see anything in it. Tante Rosie, of course, could. While the woman waited Tante Rosie peered deep into the tank of water. Soon she said the water spoke to her and told her that although the woman looked old, she was not. Mrs. Kemhuff said that this was true, and wondered if Tante Rosie knew the reason she looked so old. Tante Rosie said she did not and asked if she would mind telling us about it. (At first Mrs. Kemhuff didn't seem to want me there, but Tante Rosie told her I was trying to learn the rootworking trade and she nodded that she understood and didn't mind. I scrooched down as small as I could at the corner of Tante Rosie's table, smiling at her so she wouldn't feel embarrassed or afraid.)

"It was during the Depression," she began, shifting in her seat and adjusting the shawls. She wore so many her back appeared to be humped!

"Of course," said Tante Rosie, "and you were young and pretty."

"How do you know that?" exclaimed Mrs. Kemhuff. "That is true. I had been married already five years and had four small children and a husband with a wandering eye. But since I married young—"

"Why, you were little more than a child," said Tante Rosie.

"Yes," said Mrs. Kemhuff. "I were not quite twenty years old. And it was hard times everywhere, all over the country and, I suspect, all over the world. Of course, no one had television in those days, so we didn't know. I don't even now know if it was invented. We had a radio before the Depression which my husband won in a poker game, but we sold it somewhere along the line to buy a meal. Anyway, we lived for as long as we could on the money I brought in as a cook in a sawmill. I cooked cabbage and cornpone for twenty men for two dollars a week. But then the mill closed down, and my husband had already been out of work for some time. We were on the point of starvation. We was so hungry, and the children were getting so weak, that after I had crapped off the last leaves from the collard stalks I couldn't wait for new leaves to grow back. I dug up the collards, roots and all. After we ate that there was nothing else.

"As I said, there was no way of knowing whether hard times was existing around the world because we did not then have a television set. And we had sold the radio. However, as it happened, hard times hit everybody we knew in Cherokee County. And for that reason the government sent food stamps which you could get if you could prove you were starving. With a few of them stamps you could go into town to a place they had and get so much and so much fat back, so much and so much of corn meal, and so much and so much of (I think it was) red beans. As I say, we was, by then, desperate. And my husband prevailed on me for us to go. I never wanted to do it, on account of I have always been proud. My father, you know, used to be one of the biggest colored peanut growers in Cherokee County and we never had to ask nobody for nothing.

"Well, what had happened in the meantime was this: My sister, Carrie Mae—"

"A tough girl, if I remember right," said Tante Rosie.

"Yes," said Mrs. Kemhuff, "bright, full of spunk. Well, she were at that time living in the North. In Chicago. And she were working for some good white people that give her they old clothes to send back down here. And I tell you they were good things. And I was glad to get them. So, as it was gitting to be real cold, I dressed myself and my husband and the children up in them clothes. For see, they was made up North to be worn up there where there's snow at and they were warm as toast."

"Wasn't Carrie Mae later killed by a gangster?" asked Tante Rosie.

"Yes, she were," said the woman, anxious to go on with her story. "He were her husband."

"Oh," said Tante Rosie quietly.

"Now, so I dresses us all up in our new finery and with our stomachs growling all together we goes marching off to ask for what the government said was due us as proud as ever we knew how to be. For even my husband, when he had on the right clothes, could show some pride, and me, whenever I remembered how fine my daddy's peanut crops had provided us, why there was nobody with stiffer backbone."

"I see a pale and evil shadow looming ahead of you in this journey," said Tante Rosie, looking into the water as if she'd lost a penny while we weren't looking.

"That shadow was sure pale and evil all right," said Mrs. Kemhuff. "When we got to the place there was a long line, and we saw all of our friends in this line. On one side of the big pile of food was the white line—and some rich peoples was in that line too—and on the other side there was the black line. I later heard, by the by, that the white folks in the white line got bacon and grits, as well as meal, but that is neither here nor there. What happened was this. As soon as our friends saw us all dressed up in our nice warm clothes, though used and castoff they were, they began saying how crazy we was to have worn them. And that's when I began to notice that all the people in the black line had dressed themselves in tatters. Even people what had good things at home, and I knew some of them did. What does this mean? I asked my husband. But he didn't know. He was too busy strutting about to even pay much attention. But I began to be terribly afraid. The baby had begun to cry and the other little ones, knowing I was nervous, commenced to whine and gag. I had a time with them.

"Now, at this time my husband had been looking around at other women and I was scared to death I was going to lose him. He already made fun of me and said I was arrogant and proud. I said that was the way to be and that he should try to be that way. The last thing I wanted to happen was for him to see me embarrassed and made small in front of a lot of people because I knew if that happened he would quit me.

"So I was standing there hoping that the white folks what give out the food wouldn't notice that I was dressed nice and that if they did they would see how hungry the babies was and how pitiful we all was. I could see my husband over talking to the woman he was going with on the sly. She was dressed like a flysweep! Not only was she raggedy, she was dirty! Filthy dirty, and with her filthy slip showing. She looked so awful she disgusted me. And yet there was my husband hanging over her while I stood in the line holding on to all four of our children. I guess he knew as well as I did what that woman had in the line of clothes at home. She was always much better dressed than me and much better dressed than many of the white peoples. That was because, they say she was a whore and took money. Seems like people want that and will pay for it even in a depression!"

There was a pause while Mrs. Kemhuff drew a deep breath. Then she continued.

"So soon I was next to get something from the young lady at the counter. All around her I could smell them red beans and my mouth was watering for a taste of fresh-water cornpone. I was proud, but I wasn't fancy. I just wanted something for me and the children. Well, there I was, with the children hanging to my dresstails, and I drew myself up as best I could and made the oldest boy stand up straight, for I had come to ask for what was mine, not to beg. So I wasn't going to be acting like a beggar. Well, I want you to know that that little slip of a woman, all big blue eyes and yellow hair, that little *girl*, took my stamps and then took one long look at me and my children and across at my husband— all of us dressed to kill I guess she thought—and she took my stamps in her hand and looked at them like they was dirty, and then she gave them to an old gambler who was next in line behind me! 'You don't need nothing to eat from the way you all dressed up, Hannah Lou,' she said to me. 'But

Miss Sadler,' I said, 'my children is hungry.' 'They don't look hungry,' she said to me. 'Move along now, somebody here may really need our help!' The whole line behind me began to laugh and snigger, and that little white moppet sort of grinned behind her hands. She gave the old gambler double what he would have got otherwise. And there me and my children about to keel over from want.

"When my husband and his woman saw and heard what happened they commenced to laugh, too, and he reached down and got her stuff, piles and piles of it, it seemed to me then, and helped her put it in somebody's car and they drove off together. And that was about the last I seen of him. Or her."

"Weren't they swept off a bridge together in the flood that wiped out Tunica City?" asked Tante Rosie.

"Yes," said Mrs. Kemhuff. "Somebody like you might have helped me then, too, though looks like I didn't need it."

"So—"

"So after that looks like my spirit just wilted. Me and my children got a ride home with somebody and I tottered around like a drunken woman and put them to bed. They was sweet children and not much trouble, although they was about to go out of their minds with hunger."

Now a deep sadness crept into her face, which until she reached this point had been still and impassive.

"First one and then the other of them took sick and died. Though the old gambler came by the house three or four days later and divided what he had left with us. He had been on his way to gambling it all away. The Lord called him to have pity on us and since he knew us and knew my husband had deserted me he said he were right glad to help out. But it was mighty late in the day when he thought about helping out and the children were far gone. Nothing could save them except the Lord and he seemed to have other things on his mind, like the wedding that spring of the mean little moppet."

Mrs. Kemhuff now spoke through clenched teeth.

"My spirit never recovered from that insult, just like my heart never recovered from my husband's desertion, just like my body never recovered from being almost starved to death. I started to wither in that winter and each year found me more hacked and worn down than the year before. Somewhere along them years my pride just up and left altogether and I worked for a time in a whorehouse just to make some money, just like my husband's woman. Then I took to drinking to forget what I was doing, and soon I just broke down and got old all at once, just like you see me now. And I started about five years ago to going to church. I was converted again, 'cause I felt the first time had done got worn off. But I am not restful. I dream and have nightmares still about the little moppet, and always I feel the moment when my spirit was trampled down within me while they all stood and laughed and she stood there grinning behind her hands."

"Well," said Tante Rosie. "There are ways that the spirit can be mended just as there are ways that the spirit can be broken. But one such as I am cannot do both. If I am to take away the burden of shame which is upon you I must in some way inflict it on someone else."

"I do not care to be cured," said Mrs. Kemhuff. "It is enough that I have endured my shame all these years and that my children and my husband were taken from me by one who knew nothing about us. I can survive as long as I need with the bitterness that has laid every day in my soul. But I could die easier if I knew something, after all these years, had been done to the little moppet. God cannot be let to make her happy all these years and me miserable. What kind of justice would that be? It would be monstrous!"

"Don't worry about it, my sister," said Tante Rosie with gentleness. "By the grace of the Man-God I have the use of many powers. Powers given me by the Great One Herself. If you can no longer bear the eyes of the enemy that you see in your dreams the Man-God, who speaks to me from the

Great Mother of Us All, will see that those eyes are eaten away. If the hands of your enemy have struck you they can be made useless." Tante Rosie held up a small piece of what was once lustrous pewter. Now it was pock-marked and blackened and deteriorating.

"Do you see this metal?" she asked.

"Yes, I see it," said Mrs. Kemhuff with interest. She took it in her hands and rubbed it.

"The part of the moppet you want destroyed will rot away in the same fashion."

Mrs. Kemhuff relinquished the piece of metal to Tante Rosie.

"You are a true sister," she said.

"Is it enough?" Tante Rosie asked.

"I would give anything to stop her grinning behind her hands," said the woman, drawing out a tattered billfold.

"Her hands or the grinning mouth?" asked Tante Rosie.

"The mouth grinned and the hands hid it," said Mrs. Kemhuff.

"Ten dollars for one area, twenty for two," said Tante Rosie.

"Make it the mouth," said Mrs. Kemhuff. "That is what I see most vividly in my dreams." She laid a ten-dollar bill in the lap of Tante Rosie.

"Let me explain what we will do," said Tante Rosie, coming near the woman and speaking softly to her, as a doctor would speak to a patient. "First we will make a potion that has a long history of use in our profession. It is a mixture of hair and nail parings of the person in question, a bit of their water and feces, a piece of their clothing heavy with their own scents, and I think in this case we might as well add a piece of goober dust; that is, dust from the graveyard. This woman will not outlive you by more than six months."

I had thought the two women had forgotten about me, but now Tante Rosie turned to me and said, "You will have to go out to Mrs. Kemhuff's house. She will have to be instructed in the recitation of the curse-prayer. You will show her how to dress the black candles and how to pay Death for his interception in her behalf."

Then she moved over to the shelf that held her numerous supplies: oils of Bad and Good Luck Essence, dried herbs, creams, powders, and candles. She took two large black candles and placed them in Mrs. Kemhuff's hands. She also gave her a small bag of powder and told her to burn it on her table (as an altar) while she was praying the curse-prayer. I was to show Mrs. Kemhuff how to "dress" the candles in vinegar so they would be purified for her purpose.

She told Mrs. Kemhuff that each morning and evening for nine days she was to light the candles, burn the powder, recite the curse-prayer from her knees and concentrate all her powers on getting her message through to Death and the Man-God. As far as the Supreme Mother of Us All was concerned, She could only be moved by the pleas of the Man-God. Tante Rosie herself would recite the curse-prayer at the same time that Mrs. Kemhuff did, and together she thought the two prayers, prayed with respect, could not help but move the Man-God, who, in turn, would unchain Death who would already be eager to come down on the little moppet. But her death would be slow in coming because first the Man-God had to hear all of the prayers.

"We will take those parts of herself that we collect, the feces, water, nail parings, et cetera, and plant them where they will bring for you the best results. Within a year's time the earth will be rid of the woman herself, even as almost immediately you will be rid of her grin. Do you want something else for only two dollars that will make you feel happy even today?" asked Tante Rosie.

But Mrs. Kemhuff shook her head. "I'm carefree enough already, knowing that her end will be before another year. As for happiness, it is something that deserts you once you know it can be bought and sold. I will not live to see the end result of your work, Tante Rosie, but my grave will fit nicer, having someone proud again who has righted a wrong and by so doing lies straight and proud throughout eternity."

And Mrs. Kemhuff turned and left, bearing herself grandly out of the room. It was as if she had regained her youth; her shawls were like a stately toga, her white hair seemed to sparkle.

2

To The Man God: O great One, I have been sorely tried by my enemies and have been blasphemed and lied against. My good thoughts and my honest actions have been turned to bad actions and dishonest ideas. My home has been disrespected, my children have been cursed and ill-treated. My dear ones have been backbitten and their virtue questioned. O Man God, I beg that this that I ask for my enemies shall come to pass:

That the South wind shall scorch their bodies and make them wither and shall not be tempered to them. That the North wind shall freeze their blood and numb their muscles and that it shall not be tempered to them. That the West wind shall blow away their life's breath and will not leave their hair grow, and that their fingernails shall fall off and their bones shall crumble. That the East wind shall make their minds grow dark, their sight shall fail and their seed dry up so that they shall not multiply.

I ask that their fathers and mothers from their furtherest generation will not intercede for them before the great throne, and the wombs of their women shall not bear fruit except for strangers, and that they shall become extinct. I pray that the children who may come shall be weak of mind and paralyzed of limb and that they themselves shall curse them in their turn for ever turning the breath of life into their bodies. I pray that disease and death shall be forever with them and that their worldly goods shall not prosper, and that their crops shall not multiply and that their cows, their sheep, and their hogs and all their living beasts shall die of starvation and thirst. I pray that their house shall be unroofed and that the rain, the thunder and lightning shall find the innermost recesses of their home and that the foundation shall crumble and the floods tear it asunder. I pray that the sun shall not shed its rays on them in benevolence, but instead it shall beat down on them and burn them and destroy them. I pray that the moon shall not give them peace, but instead shall deride them and decry them and cause their minds to shrivel. I pray that their friends shall betray them and cause them loss of power, of gold and of silver, and that their enemies shall smite them until they beg for mercy which shall not be given them. I pray that their tongues shall forget how to speak in sweet words, and that it shall be paralyzed and that all about them will be desolation, pestilence and death. O Man God, I ask you for all these things because they have dragged me in the dust and destroyed my good name; broken my heart and caused me to curse the day that I was born. So be it.

This curse-prayer was regularly used and taught by root-workers, but since I did not know it by heart, as Tante Rosie did, I recited it straight from Zora Neale Hurston's book, *Mules and Men*, and Mrs. Kemhuff and I learned it on our knees together. We were soon dressing the candles in vinegar, lighting them, kneeling and praying—intoning the words rhythmically—as if we had been doing it this way for years. I was moved by the fervor with which Mrs. Kemhuff prayed. Often she would clench her fists before her closed eyes and bite the insides of her wrists as the women do in Greece.

3

According to courthouse records Sarah Marie Sadler, "the little moppet," was born in 1910. She was in her early twenties during the Depression. In 1932 she married Ben Jonathan Holley, who later inherited a small chain of grocery stores and owned a plantation and an impressive stand of timber. In the spring of 1963, Mrs. Holley was fifty-three years old. She was the mother of three children, a boy and two girls; the boy a floundering clothes salesman, the girls married and oblivious, mothers themselves.

The elder Holleys lived six miles out in the country, their house was large, and Mrs. Holley's hobbies were shopping for antiques, gossiping with colored women, discussing her husband's health and her children's babies, and making spoon bread. I was able to glean this much from the drunken ramblings of the Holleys' cook, a malevolent nanny with gout, who had raised, in her prime, at least one tan Holley, a preacher whom the Holley's had sent to Morehouse.

"I bet I could get the nanny to give us all the information and nail parings we could ever use," I said to Tante Rosie. For the grumpy woman drank muscatel like a sow and clearly hated Mrs. Holley. However, it was hard to get her tipsy enough for truly revealing talk and we were quickly running out of funds.

"That's not the way," Tante Rosie said one evening as she sat in her car and watched me lead the nanny out of the dreary but secret-evoking recesses of the Six Forks Bar. We had already spent six dollars on muscatel.

"You can't trust gossips or drunks," said Tante Rosie. "You let the woman we are working on give you everything you need, and from her own lips."

"But that is the craziest thing I have ever heard," I said. "How can I talk to her about putting a fix on her without making her mad, or maybe even scaring her to death?"

Tante Rosie merely grunted.

"Rule number one. OBSERVATION OF SUBJECT. Write that down among your crumpled notes."

"In other words—?"

"Be direct, but not blunt."

On my way to the Holley plantation I came up with the idea of pretending to be searching for a fictitious person. Then I had an even better idea. I parked Tante Rosie's Bonneville at the edge of the spacious yard, which was dotted with mimosas and camellias. Tante Rosie had insisted I wear a brilliant orange robe and as I walked it swished and blew about my legs. Mrs. Holley was on the back patio steps, engaged in conversation with a young and beautiful black girl. They stared in amazement at the length and brilliance of my attire.

"Mrs. Holley, I think it's time for me to go," said the girl.

"Don't be silly," said the matronly Mrs. Holley. "She is probably just a light-skinned African who is on her way somewhere and got lost." She nudged the black girl in the ribs and they both broke into giggles.

"How do you do?" I asked.

"Just fine, how you?" said Mrs. Holley, while the black girl looked on askance. They had been talking with their heads close together and stood up together when I spoke.

"I am looked for a Josiah Henson"—a runaway slave and the original Uncle Tom in Harriet Beecher Stowe's novel, I might have added. "Could you tell me if he lives on your place?"

"That name sounds awful familiar," said the black girl.

"Are you *the* Mrs. Holley?" I asked gratuitously, while Mrs. Holley was distracted. She was sure she had never heard the name.

"Of course," she said, and smiled, pleating the side of her dress. She was a grayish blonde with an ashen untanned face, and her hands were five blunt and pampered fingers each. "And this is my ... ah ... my friend, Caroline Williams."

68

Caroline nodded curtly.

"Somebody told me ole Josiah might be out this way . . ."

"Well, we hadn't seen him," said Mrs. Holley. "We were just here shelling some peas, enjoying this nice sunshine."

"Are you a light African?" asked Caroline.

"No," I said. "I work with Tante Rosie, the root-worker. I'm learning the profession."

"Whatever *for*?" asked Mrs. Holley. "I would have thought a nice-looking girl like yourself could find a better way to spend her time. I been hearing about Tante Rosie since I was a little bitty child, but everybody always said that root-working was just a whole lot of n—, I mean colored foolishness. Of course we don't believe in that kind of thing, do we, Caroline?"

"Naw."

The younger woman put a hand on the older woman's arm, possessively, as if to say "You get away from here, bending my white folks' ear with your crazy mess!" From the kitchen window a dark remorseful face worked itself into various messages of "Go away!" It was the drunken nanny.

"I wonder if you would care to prove you do not believe in rootworking?"

"Prove?" said the white woman indignantly.

"Prove?" asked the black woman with scorn.

"That is the word," I said.

"Why, not that I'm afraid of any of this nigger magic!" said Mrs. Holley staunchly, placing a reassuring hand on Caroline's shoulder. *I* was the nigger, not she.

"In that case won't you show us how much you don't have fear of it." With the word us I placed Caroline in the same category with me. Let her smolder! Now Mrs. Holley stood alone, the great white innovator and scientific scourge, forced to man the Christian fort against heathen nigger paganism.

"Of course, if you like," she said immediately, drawing herself up in the best English manner. Stiff upper lip, what? and all that. She had been grinning throughout. Now she covered her teeth with her scant two lips and her face became flat and resolute. Like so many white women in sections of the country where the race was still "pure" her mouth could have been formed by the minute slash of a thin sword.

"Do you know a Mrs. Hannah Lou Kemhuff?" I asked.

"No I do not."

"She is not white, Mrs. Holley, she is black."

"Hannah Lou, Hannah Lou . . . do we know a Hannah Lou?" she asked, turning to Caroline.

"No, ma'am, we don't!" said Caroline.

"Well, she knows you. Says she met you on the bread lines during the Depression and that because she was dressed up you wouldn't give her any corn meal. Or red beans. Or something like that."

"Bread lines, Depression, dressed up, corn meal . . .? I don't know what you're talking about!" No shaft of remembrance probed the depths of what she had done to colored people more than twenty years ago.

"It doesn't really matter, since you don't believe . . . but she says you did her wrong, and being a good Christian, she believes all wrongs are eventually righted in the Lord's good time. She came to us for help only when she began to feel the Lord's good time might be too far away. Because we do not deal in the work of unmerited destruction, Tante Rosie and I did not see how we could take the case." I said this humbly, with as much pious intonation as I could muster.

"Well, I'm glad," said Mrs. Holley, who had been running through the back years on her fingers.

"But," I said, "we told her what she could do to bring about restitution of peaceful spirit, which she claimed you robbed her of in a moment during which, as is now evident, you were not concerned. You were getting married the following spring."

"That was '32," said Mrs. Holley. "Hannah *Lou*?"

"The same."

"How black *was* she? Sometimes I can recall colored faces that way."

"That is not relevant," I said, "since you do not believe. . . ."

"Well of *course* I don't believe!" said Mrs. Holley.

"I am nothing in this feud between you," I said. "Neither is Tante Rosie. Neither of us had any idea until after Mrs. Kemhuff left that you were the woman she spoke of. We are familiar with the deep and sincere interest that you take in the poor colored children at Christmastime each year. We know you have gone out of your way to hire needy people to work on your farm. We know you have been an example of Christian charity and a beacon of brotherly love. And right before my eyes I can see it is true you have Negro friends."

"Just what is it you want?" asked Mrs. Holley.

"What *Mrs. Kemhuff* wants are some nail parings, not many, just a few; some hair (that from a comb will do), some water and some feces—and if you don't feel like doing either number one or number two, I will wait—and a bit of clothing, something that you have worn in the last year. Something with some of your odor on it."

"What!" Mrs. Holley screeched.

"They say this combination, with the right prayers, can eat away part of a person just like the disease that ruins so much fine antique pewter."

Mrs. Holley blanched. With a motherly fluttering of hands Caroline helped her into a patio chair.

"Go get my medicine," said Mrs. Holley, and Caroline started from the spot like a gazelle.

"Git away from here! Git away!"

I spun around just in time to save my head from a whack with a gigantic dust mop. It was the drunken nanny, drunk no more, flying to the defense of her mistress.

"She's just a tramp and a phony!" she reassured Mrs. Holley, who was caught up in an authentic faint.

4

Not long after I saw Mrs. Holley, Hannah Kemhuff was buried. Tante Rosie and I followed the casket to the cemetery. Tante Rosie most elegant in black. Then we made our way through briers and grass to the highway. Mrs. Kemhuff rested in a tangly grove, off to herself, though reasonably near her husband and babies. Few people came to the funeral, which made the faces of Mrs. Holley's nanny and husband stand out all the more plainly. They had come to verify the fact that this dead person was indeed *the* Hannah Lou Kemhuff whom Mr. Holley had initiated a search for, having the entire county militia at his disposal.

Several months later we read in the paper that Sarah Marie Sadler Holley had also passed away. The paper spoke of her former beauty and vivacity, as a young woman, and of her concern for those less fortunate than herself as a married woman and pillar of the community and her church. It spoke briefly of her harsh and lengthy illness. It said all who knew her were sure her soul would find peace in heaven, just as her shrunken body had endured so much pain and heartache here on earth.

Caroline had kept us up to date with the decline of Mrs. Holley. After my visit, relations between them became strained and Mrs. Holley eventually became too frightened of Caroline's darkness to allow her close to her. A week later after I'd talked to them Mrs. Holley began having her meals in her bedroom upstairs. Then she started doing everything else there as well. She collected stray hairs from her head and comb with the greatest attention and consistency, not to say desperation. She ate her fingernails. But the most bizarre of all was her response to Mrs. Kemhuff's petition for a specimen of her feces and water. Not trusting any longer the earthen secrecy of the water mains, she no longer flushed. Together with the nanny Mrs. Holley preferred to store those relics of what she ate (which became almost nothing and then nothing, the nanny had told Caroline) and they kept it all in barrels and plastic bags in the upstairs closets. In a few weeks it became impossible for anyone to endure the smell of the house, even Mrs. Holley's husband, who loved her but during the weeks before her death slept in a spare room of the nanny's house.

The mouth that had grinned behind the hands grinned no more. The constant anxiety lest a stray strand of hair be lost and the foul odor of the house soon brought to the hands a constant seeking motion, to the eyes a glazed and vacant stare, and to the mouth a tightly puckered frown, one which only death might smooth.

THE WELCOME TABLE

for sister Clara Ward

I'm going to sit at the Welcome table
Shout my troubles over
Walk and talk with Jesus
Tell God how you treat me
One of these days!

—Spiritual

The old woman stood with eyes uplifted in her Sunday-go-to-meeting clothes: high shoes polished about the tops and toes, a long rusty dress adorned with an old corsage, long withered, and the remnants of an elegant silk scarf as headrag stained with grease from the many oily pigtails underneath. Perhaps she had known suffering. There was a dazed and sleepy look in her aged blue-brown eyes. But for

74

those who searched hastily for "reasons" in that old tight face, shut now like an ancient door, there was nothing to be read. And so they gazed nakedly upon their own fear transferred; a fear of the black and the old, a terror of the unknown as well as of the deeply known. Some of those who saw her there on the church steps spoke words about her that were hardly fit to be heard, others held their pious peace; and some felt vague stirrings of pity, small and persistent and hazy, as if she were an old collie turned out to die.

She was angular and lean and the color of poor gray Georgia earth, beaten by king cotton and the extreme weather. Her elbows were wrinkled and thick, the skin ashen but durable, like the bark of old pines. On her face centuries were folded into the circles around one eye, while around the other, etched and mapped as if for print, ages more threatened again to live. Some of them there at the church saw the age, the dotage, the missing buttons down the front of her mildewed black dress. Others saw cooks, chauffeurs, maids, mistresses, children denied or smothered in the deferential way she held her cheek to one side, toward the ground. Many of them saw jungle orgies in an evil place, while others were reminded of riotous anarchists looting and raping in the streets. Those who knew the hesitant creeping up on them of the law, saw the beginning of the end of the sanctuary of Christian worship, saw the desecration of Holy Church, and saw an invasion of privacy, which they struggled to believe they still kept.

Still she had come down the road toward the big white church alone. Just herself, an old forgetful woman, nearly blind with age. Just her and her eyes raised dully to the glittering cross that crowned the sheer silver steeple. She had walked along the road in a stagger from her house a half mile away. Perspiration, cold and clammy, stood on her brow and along the creases by her thin wasted nose. She stopped to calm herself on the wide front steps, not looking about her as they might have expected her to do, but simply standing quite still, except for a slight quivering of her throat and tremors that shook her cotton-stockinged legs.

The reverend of the church stopped her pleasantly as she stepped into the vestibule. Did he say, as they thought he did, kindly, "Auntie, you know this is not your church?" As if one could choose the wrong one. But no one remembers, for they never spoke of it afterward, and she brushed past him anyway, as if she had been brushing past him all her life, except this time she was in a hurry. Inside the church she sat on the very first bench from the back, gazing with concentration at the stained-glass window over her head. It was cold, even inside the church, and she was shivering. Everybody could see. They stared at her as they came in and sat down near the front. It was cold, very cold to them, too; outside the church it was below freezing and not much above inside. But the sight of her, sitting there somehow passionately ignoring them, brought them up short, burning.

The young usher, never having turned anyone out of his church before, but not even considering this job as *that* (after all, she had no right to be there, certainly), went up to her and whispered that she should leave. Did he call her "Grandma," as later he seemed to recall he had? But for those who actually hear such traditional pleasantries and to whom they actually mean something, "Grandma" was not one, for she did not pay him any attention, just muttered, "Go 'way," in a weak sharp *bothered* voice, waving his frozen blond hair and eyes from near her face.

It was the ladies who finally did what to them had to be done. Daring their burly indecisive husbands to throw the old colored woman out they made their point. God, mother, country, earth, church. It involved all that, and well they knew it. Leather bagged and shoed, with good calfskin gloves to keep out the cold, they looked with contempt at the blood-less gray arthritic hands of the old woman, clenched loosely, restlessly in her lap. Could their husbands expect them to sit up in church with *that*? No, no, the husbands were quick to answer and even quicker to do their duty.

Under the old woman's arms they placed their hard fists (which afterward smelled of decay and musk—the fermenting scent of onionskins and rotting greens). Under the old woman's arms they raised their fists, flexed their muscular shoulders, and out she flew through the door, back under the cold blue sky. This done, the wives folded their healthy arms across their trim middles and felt at once justified and scornful. But none of them said so, for none of them ever spoke of the incident again. Inside the church it was warmer. They sang, they prayed. The protection and promise of God's impartial love grew more not less desirable as the sermon gathered fury and lashed itself out above their penitent heads.

The old woman stood at the top of the steps looking about in bewilderment. She had been singing in her head. They had interrupted her. Promptly she began to sing again, though this time a sad song. Suddenly, however, she looked down the long gray highway and saw something interesting and delightful coming. She started to grin, toothlessly, with short giggles of joy, jumping about and slapping her hands on her knees. And soon it became apparent why she was so happy. For coming down the highway at a firm though leisurely pace was Jesus. He was wearing an immaculate white, long dress trimmed in gold around the neck and hem, and a red, a bright red, cape. Over his left arm he carried a brilliant blue blanket. He was wearing sandals and a beard and he had long brown hair parted on the right side. His eyes, brown, had wrinkles around them as if he smiled or looked at the sun a lot. She would have known him, recognized him, anywhere. There was a sad but joyful look to his face, like a candle was glowing behind it, and he walked with sure even steps in her direction, as if he were walking on the sea. Except that he was not carrying in his arms a baby sheep, he looked exactly like the picture of him that she had hanging over her bed at home. She had taken it out of a white lady's Bible while she was working for her. She had looked at that picture for more years than she could remember, but never once had she really expected to see him. She squinted her eyes to be sure he wasn't carrying a little sheep in one arm, but he was not. Ecstatically she began to wave her arms for fear he would miss seeing her, for he walked looking straight ahead on the shoulder of the highway, and from time to time looking upward at the sky.

All he said when he got close to her was "Follow me," and she bounded down to his side with all the bob and speed of one so old. For every one of his long determined steps she made two quick ones. They walked along in deep silence for a long time. Finally she started telling him about how many years she had cooked for them, cleaned for them, nursed them. He looked at her kindly but in silence. She told him indignantly about how they had grabbed her when she was singing in her head and not looking, and how they had tossed her out of his church. A old heifer like me, she said, straightening up next to Jesus, breathing hard. But he smiled down at her and she felt better instantly and time just seemed to fly by. When they passed her house, forlorn and sagging, weatherbeaten and patched, by the side of the road, she did not even notice it, she was so happy to be out walking along the highway with Jesus.

She broke the silence once more to tell Jesus how glad she was that he had come, how she had often looked at his picture hanging on her wall (she hoped he didn't know she had stolen it) over her bed, and how she had never expected to see him down here in person. Jesus gave her one of his beautiful smiles and they walked on. She did not know where they were going; someplace wonderful, she suspected. The ground was like clouds under their feet, and she felt she could walk forever without becoming the least bit tired. She even began to sing out loud some of the old spirituals she loved, but she didn't want to annoy Jesus, who looked so thoughtful, so she quieted down. They walked on, looking straight over the treetops into the sky, and the smiles that played over her dry wind-cracked face were like first clean ripples across a stagnant pond. On they walked without stopping.

The people in church never knew what happened to the old woman; they never mentioned her to one another or to anybody else. Most of them heard sometime later that an old colored woman fell dead along the highway. Silly as it seemed, it appeared she had walked herself to death. Many of the black families along the road said they had seen the old lady high-stepping down the highway; sometimes jabbering in a low insistent voice, sometimes singing, sometimes merely gesturing excitedly with her hands. Other times silent and smiling, looking at the sky. She had been alone, they said. Some of them wondered aloud where the old woman had been going so stoutly that it had worn her heart out. They guessed maybe she had relatives across the river, some miles away, but none of them really knew.

STRONG HORSE TEA

Rannie Toomer's little baby boy Snooks was dying from double pneumonia and whooping cough. She sat away from him, gazing into the low fire, her long crusty bottom lip hanging. She was not married. Was not pretty. Was not anybody much. And he was all she had.

"Lawd, why don't that doctor come on here?" she moaned, tears sliding from her sticky eyes. She had not washed since Snooks took sick five days ago and a long row of whitish snail tracks laced her ashen face.

"What you ought to try is some of the old home remedies." Sarah urged. She was an old neighboring lady who wore magic leaves round her neck sewed up in possumskin next to a dried lizard's foot. She knew how magic came about, and could do magic herself, people said.

"We going to have a us a doctor," Rannie Toomer said fiercely, walking over to shoo a fat winter fly from her child's forehead. "I don't believe in none of that swamp magic. All the old home remedies I took when I was a child come just short of killing me."

Snooks, under a pile of faded quilts, made a small gravelike mound in the bed. His head was like a ball of black putty wedged between the thin covers and the dingy yellow pillow. His little eyes were partly open, as if he were peeping out of his hard wasted skull at the chilly room, and the forceful pulse of his breathing caused a faint rustling in the sheets near his mouth like the wind pushing damp papers in a shallow ditch.

"What time you reckon that doctor'll git here?" asked Sarah, not expecting Rannie Toomer to answer her. She sat with her knees wide apart under many aprons and long dark skirts heavy with stains. From time to time she reached long cracked fingers down to sweep her damp skirts away from the live coals. It was almost spring, but the winter cold still clung to her bones and she had to almost sit in the fireplace to be warm. Her deep sharp eyes set in the rough leather of her face had aged a moist hesitant blue that gave her a quick dull stare like a hawk's. Now she gazed coolly at Rannie Toomer and rapped the hearthstones with her stick.

"White mailman, white doctor," she chanted skeptically, under her breath, as if to banish spirits.

"They gotta come see 'bout this baby," Rannie Toomer said wistfully. "Who'd go and ignore a little sick baby like my Snooks?"

"Some folks we don't know so well as we thinks we do might," the old lady replied. "What you want to give that boy of yours is one or two of the old home remedies; arrowsroot or sassyfrass and cloves, or a sugar tit soaked in cat's blood."

Rannie Toomer's face went tight.

"We don't need none of your witch's remedies," she cried, grasping her baby by his shrouded toes, trying to knead life into him as she kneaded limberness into flour dough.

"We going to git some of them shots that makes people

well, cures 'em of all they ails, cleans 'em out and makes 'em strong all at the same time."

She spoke upward from her son's feet as if he were an altar. "Doctor'll be here soon, baby," she whispered to him, then rose to look out the grimy window. "I done sent the mailman." She rubbed her face against the glass, her flat nose more flattened as she peered out into the rain.

"Howdy, Rannie Mae," the red-faced mailman had said pleasantly as he always did when she stood by the car waiting to ask him something. Usually she wanted to ask what certain circulars meant that showed pretty pictures of things she needed. Did the circulars mean that somebody was coming around later and would give her hats and suitcases and shoes and sweaters and rubbing alcohol and a heater for the house and a fur bonnet for her baby? Or, why did he always give her the pictures if she couldn't have what was in them? Or, what did the words say . . . especially the big word written in red: "S-A-L-E!"?

He would explain shortly to her that the only way she could get the goods pictured on the circulars was to buy them in town and that town stores did their advertising by sending out pictures of their goods. She would listen with her mouth hanging open until he finished. Then she would exclaim in a dull amazed way that *she* never *had* any money and he could ask anybody. *She* couldn't ever buy any of the things in the pictures—so why did the stores keep sending them to her?

He tried to explain to her that *everybody* got the circulars, whether they had any money to buy with or not. That this was one of the laws of advertising and he could do nothing about it. He was sure she never understood what he tried to teach her about advertising, for one day she asked him for any extra circulars he had and when he asked what she wanted them for—since she couldn't afford to buy any of the items advertised—she said she needed them to paper the inside of her house to keep out the wind.

Today he thought she looked more ignorant than usual as she stuck her dripping head inside his car. He recoiled from her breath and gave little attention to what she was saying about her sick baby as he mopped up the water she dripped on the plastic door handle of the car.

"Well, never *can* keep 'em dry, I mean *warm* enough, in rainy weather like this here," he mumbled absently, stuffing a wad of circulars advertising hair driers and cold creams into her hands. He wished she would stand back from his car so he could get going. But she clung to the side gabbing away about "Snooks" and "NEW-monia" and "shots" and how she wanted a "REAL doctor."

"That right?" he injected sympathetically from time to time, and from time to time he sneezed, for she was letting in wetness and damp, and he felt he was coming down with a cold. Black people as black as Rannie Mae always made him uneasy, especially when they didn't smell good, and when you could tell they didn't right away. Rannie Mae, leaning in over him out of the rain, smelt like a wet goat. Her dark dirty eyes clinging to his face with such hungry desperation made him nervous.

Why did colored folks always want you to do something for them?

Now he cleared his throat and made a motion forward as if to roll up his window. "Well, ah, *mighty* sorry to hear 'bout that little fella," he said, groping for the window crank. "We'll see what we can do!" He gave her what he hoped was a big friendly smile. God! He didn't want to hurt her feelings! She looked so pitiful hanging there in the rain. Suddenly he had an idea.

"Why'n't you try some of old Aunt Sarah's home remedies?" he suggested brightly, still smiling. He half believed with everybody else in the county that the old blue-eyed black woman possessed magic. Magic that if it didn't work on whites probably would on blacks. But Rannie Mae almost turned the car over shaking her head and body with an emphatic "NO!" She reached in a wet crusted hand to grasp his shoulder.

"We wants a doctor, a real doctor!" she screamed. She had begun to cry and drop her tears on him. "You git us a doctor from town," she bellowed, shaking the solid shoulder that bulged under his new tweed coat.

"Like I say," he drawled lamely although beginning to be furious with her, "we'll do what we can!" And he hurriedly rolled up the window and sped down the road, cringing from the thought that she had put her hands on him.

"Old home remedies! Old home remedies!" Rannie Toomer cursed the words while she licked at the hot tears that ran down her face, the only warmth about her. She turned back to the trail that led to her house, trampling the wet circulars under her feet. Under the fence she went and was in a pasture, surrounded by dozens of fat white folks' cows and an old gray horse and a mule or two. Animals lived there in the pasture all around her house, and she and Snooks lived in it.

It was less than an hour after she had talked to the mailman that she looked up expecting the doctor and saw old Sarah tramping through the grass on her walking stick. She couldn't pretend she wasn't home with the smoke climbing out the chimney, so she let her in, making her leave her bag of tricks on the front porch.

Old woman old as that ought to forgit trying to cure other people with her nigger magic . . . ought to use some of it on herself, she thought. She would not let her lay a finger on Snooks and warned her if she tried she would knock her over the head with her own cane.

"He coming all right," Rannie Toomer said firmly, looking, straining her eyes to see through the rain.

"Let me tell you, child," the old woman said almost gently,

"he ain't." She was sipping something hot from a dish. When would this one know, she wondered, that she could only depend on those who would come.

"But I *told* you," Rannie Toomer said in exasperation, as if explaining something to a backward child. "I asked the mailman to bring a doctor for my Snooks!"

Cold wind was shooting all around her from the cracks in the window framing, faded circulars blew inward from the walls. The old woman's gloomy prediction made her tremble.

"He done fetched the doctor," Sarah said, rubbing her dish with her hand. "What you reckon brung me over here in this here flood? Wasn't no desire to see no rainbows, I can tell you."

Rannie Toomer paled.

"I's the doctor, child." Sarah turned to Rannie with dull wise eyes. "That there mailman didn't git no further with that message than the road in front of my house. Lucky he got good lungs—deef as I is I had myself a time trying to make out what he was yellin'."

Rannie began to cry, moaning.

Suddenly the breathing of Snooks from the bed seemed to drown out the noise of the downpour outside. Rannie Toomer could feel his pulse making the whole house tremble.

"Here," she cried, snatching up the baby and handing him to Sarah. "Make him well. O *my lawd*, make him well!"

Sarah rose from her seat by the fire and took the tiny baby, already turning a purplish blue around the eyes and mouth.

"Let's not upset this little fella unnessarylike," she said, placing the baby back on the bed. Gently she began to examine him, all the while moaning and humming some thin pagan tune that pushed against the sound of the wind and rain with its own melancholy power. She stripped him of all his clothes, poked at his fibreless baby ribs, blew against his chest. Along his tiny flat back she ran her soft old fingers. The child hung on in deep rasping sleep, and his small glazed eyes neither opened fully nor fully closed.

Rannie Toomer swayed over the bed watching the old woman touching the baby. She thought of the time she had wasted waiting for the real doctor. Her feeling of guilt was a stone.

"I'll do anything you say do, Aunt Sarah," she cried, mopping at her nose with her dress. "Anything. Just, please God, make him git better!"

Old Sarah dressed the baby again and sat down in front of the fire. She stayed deep in thought for several moments. Rannie Toomer gazed first into her silent face and then at the baby, whose breathing seemed to have eased since Sarah picked him up.

Do something quick, she urged Sarah in her mind, wanting to believe in her powers completely. Do something that'll make him rise up and call his mama!

"The child's dying," said Sarah bluntly, staking out beforehand some limitation to her skill. "But there still might be something we can do. . . ."

"What, Aunt Sarah, what?" Rannie Toomer was on her knees before the old woman's chair, wringing her hands and crying. She fastened hungry eyes on Sarah's lips.

"What can I *do*?" she urged fiercely, hearing the faint labored breathing from the bed.

"It's going to take a strong stomach," said Sarah slowly. "A *mighty* strong stomach. And most you young peoples these days don't have 'em."

"Snooks got a strong stomach," said Rannie Toomer, looking anxiously into the old serious face.

"It ain't him that's got to have the strong stomach," Sarah said, glancing down at Rannie Toomer. "*You* the one got to have a strong stomach . . . he won't know *what* it is he's drinking."

Rannie Toomer began to tremble way down deep in her stomach. It sure was weak, she thought. Trembling like that. But what could she mean her Snooks to drink? Not cat's blood—! And not some of the messes with bat's wings she'd heard Sarah mixed for people sick in the head? . . .

"What is it?" she whispered, bringing her head close to Sarah's knee. Sarah leaned down and put her toothless mouth to her ear.

"The only thing that can save this child now is some good strong horse tea," she said, keeping her eyes on the girl's face. "The *only* thing. And if you wants him out of that bed you better make tracks to git some."

Rannie Toomer took up her wet coat and stepped across the porch into the pasture. The rain fell against her face with the force of small hailstones. She started walking in the direction of the trees where she could see the bulky lightish shapes of cows. Her thin plastic shoes were sucked at by the mud, but she pushed herself forward in search of the lone gray mare.

All the animals shifted ground and rolled big dark eyes at Rannie Toomer. She made as little noise as she could and leaned against a tree to wait.

Thunder rose from the side of the sky like tires of a big truck rumbling over rough dirt road. Then it stood a split second in the middle of the sky before it exploded like a giant firecracker, then rolled away again like an empty keg. Lightning streaked across the sky, setting the air white and charged.

Rannie Toomer stood dripping under her tree, hoping not to be struck. She kept her eyes carefully on the behind of the gray mare, who, after nearly an hour, began nonchalantly to spread her muddy knees.

At that moment Rannie Toomer realized that she had brought nothing to catch the precious tea in. Lightning struck something not far off and caused a crackling and groaning in the woods that frightened the animals away from their shelter. Rannie Toomer slipped down in the mud trying to take off one of her plastic shoes to catch the tea. And the gray mare, trickling some, broke for a clump of cedars yards away.

Rannie Toomer was close enough to catch the tea if she could keep up with the mare while she ran. So alternately holding her breath and gasping for air she started after her. Mud from her fall clung to her elbows and streaked her frizzy hair. Slipping and sliding in the mud she raced after the mare, holding out, as if for alms, her plastic shoe.

In the house Sarah sat, her shawls and sweaters tight around her, rubbing her knees and muttering under her breath. She heard the thunder, saw the lightning that lit up the dingy room and turned her waiting face to the bed. Hobbling over on stiff legs she could hear no sound; the frail breathing had stopped with the thunder, not to come again.

Across the mud-washed pasture Rannie Toomer stumbled, holding out her plastic shoe for the gray mare to fill. In spurts and splashes mixed with rainwater she gathered her tea. In parting, the old mare snorted and threw up one big leg, knocking her back into the mud. She rose, trembling and crying, holding the shoe, spilling none over the top but realizing a leak, a tiny crack at her shoe's front. Quickly she stuck her mouth there, over the crack, and ankle deep in the slippery mud of the pasture and freezing in her shabby wet coat, she ran home to give the still warm horse tea to her baby Snooks.

ENTERTAINING GOD

1

John, the son. Loving the God given him.

The boy huffed and puffed and swatted flies as he climbed the hill, pulling on the rope. He stumbled on the uneven ground, a pile of grit and gravel collected in the toe of his shoe. He could not stop to empty out his shoe, nor could he stop to rest, because he did not have the time. It was getting late in the afternoon and there was a chance the gorilla would be missed. He hoped he would not be missed until at least tomorrow, which would give him time. He jerked on the rope. He would have to reach the top of the high hill very soon or the gorilla was going to fall down and go to sleep right where he was.

"C'mon," he said encouragingly to the gorilla, who looked

at him with dreamy yellow eyes. He had been talking to him soothingly all the way but the gorilla was drowsy from the medicine the zoo keepers had given him and did not reply except to grunt sluggishly deep in his throat. He hoped to have better luck with him when he woke up tomorrow.

All around them now were trees and grass and vines and he hoped the scenery was pleasing to the gorilla. It was pleasing to him, and he was *himself* a person; who did not need trees and grass and vines. There was a faint drone from the direction of the highway as cars whizzed to and fro around the outer edges of the zoo. They sounded, he thought, like wasps or big flies, as he swatted at the gnats that were hanging around his face. Behind him he felt a tugging on the rope as the gorilla cleared the air in front of his face, too, but with a sluggish petulant swipe, and his black plastic eyelids had started to droop.

The boy leading the gorilla was young and very lean, with exceptionally black skin that seemed to curve light around his bones. The skin of his face was stretched taut by the pointed severity of his cheeks, and this flattened his nose, which was broad and rounded at the tip.

There was a wistful gentleness in his face, an effortless grace in the erect way he held his head. It was not apparent, in his stride, what he had suffered. Those first days at the zoo, when he stood crying in front of the gorilla cage, had left no lines of agony on his face. The hour of his deliverance was not stamped forever on his forehead; when he embraced the God that others—his mother—had chosen for him.

The boy tugged hard at the rope; they were going over a big lump of ground that was a half-submerged rock. The gorilla stopped abruptly, sniffed resentfully at the boy, and without further notice sat down on the ground. The boy pulled the rope once more but the gorilla didn't budge and instead stretched himself out sullenly and fell asleep. Soon he began to snore, which caused the boy to stand over him and look wonderingly into his open mouth. It was deep

rose and pink inside, trimmed in black, like a pretty cave.
His big swooping teeth were like yellowed icicles and rusty
stalagmites. There was a sturdy bush nearby to which the
boy fastened the end of the rope, looking back momentarily
at the mouth. Then he raked together leaves and grass and
branches to make the place where they would spend the
night more comfortable. Then he took from under his shirt
half a loaf of rye bread and a small bottle half full of red
wine. He laid them carefully underneath the bush around
which he had tied the rope. Then he left the gorilla sleeping
as he walked away from their camp-site to try to figure out
where they were.

They were still within the grounds of the Bronx Zoo, that
much he knew, for they had not yet come up against the
high fence that surrounded the zoo. However, it was not his
intention to get outside the zoo, so this did not bother him.
He hoped that if the zoo keepers missed the gorilla before
nightfall they would think he had been taken out of the area,
for that would keep them safe until he had got what he
wanted from the gorilla, and the gorilla would have received
the kind of homage he deserved from him.

He satisfied himself that he would be able to spot searchers
if they started up the hill toward them. There were trees and
shrubs and vines and large boulders, and if necessary—and if
he could arouse the gorilla—they could move about and lose
anyone who came after them. But for the present he was not
worried for he did not expect the gorilla to be missed until
feeding time tomorrow and by then everything would be over.

The boy walked back to the gorilla and sat down on the
grass. Dusk had begun to fall while he made his survey and
now it was quite dark. Like a drunken old man the gorilla
snorted and grumbled in his sleep. The boy supposed it was
the medicine. Each year about this time the gorillas in the
zoo got a dose of something to protect them from diseases
and it doped them up for a couple of days. That was how he

had been able to get this one out of his cage without bringing down the whole zoo; gorillas could be noisy when alert.

The boy smiled down at the black hulk of fur next to him. He looked in awe at the size of this beautiful animal. Gently he rubbed the gorilla across the back of the neck and the gorilla snorted, then sighed in complete comfort and abandonment like a huge sleepy baby. The boy stretched out next to him, laughing out loud. Soon he fell asleep and as the air got cooler toward the middle of the night he snuggled closer and closer to the clean warm fur of the big ape.

He slept dreamlessly and greeted the slow windless dawn with keen anticipation. The gorilla was still asleep, but less peacefully now. The boy thought the medicine must be just about worn off. He stood on the lump of ground over the head of the gorilla and looked in the direction of the zoo buildings and of the building from which he had taken the gorilla. All was quiet, the forest all around was still. He listened intently, waiting. Soon the birds began to chirp and the wind stirred, moving the leaves. The very air seemed alive. It was like singing or flying and the boy felt exhilarated. He stretched his hands above his head as high as they would go as he greeted the sun, which rose in slow distant majesty across a misty sky, nudging clouds gently as it made its way. The boy stared straight at the sun through the mists, delighted at the sunlike spots that stayed in his head and danced before his eyes.

The gorilla began to grunt and rake his blunt claws against the ground. The boy watched him with eyes shining with great pride. He turned away as the gorilla sat up and began picking at his coat, and proceeded to gather small twigs and moss with which to start a fire.

The gorilla sat upright, grumpily watching and picking at his hide, his bleary eyes clearing gradually like the sky. He sniffed the air, looked around him at the forest, looked in stupid bewilderment at the open sky which extended on and on in blueness the farther back he reared his head. He rolled his giant head round on his neck as if chasing away the remains of a headache. He pressed lightly against the place on his buttocks where the big hypo had gone in. He grunted loudly and impatiently. He was hungry.

The boy went about building the fire with slow ritualistic movements, his black hands caressing the wood, the leaves, his warm breath moving the fine feathery dryness of the moss. His wide bottom lip hung open in concentration. From time to time he looked up at the gorilla and smiled burstingly in suppressed jubilation.

Soon the small fire was blazing. The boy sat back from it and looked at the gorilla. He smiled. The gorilla grunted. He turned distrustingly away from the fire, then turned back to it as the boy went over to the bush, took the bag with the bread in it and walked back toward the fire. The gorilla began to fret and strain against his rope. He smelled the bread as it came from the wrapper and made a move toward it. The rope drew him up short.

"Just you wait a minute, you," the boy said softly, and gingerly held the bread over the flame. In a second he leaped up as if he had forgotten something important. He put the bread down and untied the gorilla. He led him to the shallow rise overlooking the fire and gently pushed him down. The gorilla, as if still doped and continually wringing his head on his neck, sat tamely. The boy resumed his toasting of the bread. As each piece of bread was thoroughly blackened he dropped it into the flames. Then, as the bread burned, he bowed all the way down to the ground in front of the gorilla, who sat like a hairy mystified Buddha on the shallow ledge, his greedy eyes wide in awe of the flames. Each time the boy took out a new piece of bread from the bag and the odor of rye reached him the gorilla made a move forward, slowly and hopelessly, like a turtle. The boy kept toasting the bread, then dropping it in the fire, then bowing his head to the ground. The gorilla watched. The boy mumbled all the while. When he got to the last piece of bread he halted in his prayers and reached behind him for the wine. He opened the bottle and the scent, like roses and vinegar, wafted up in the air and reached the gorilla, who became thoroughly awake for the first time. The boy bowed his dark woolly head to the ground once more, mumble, mumble, mumble, then toasted the endpiece of bread. Then, holding the bread in his hand, burned to a crisp, he poured the half-bottle of wine into the fire. The gorilla who had watched everything as if spellbound, gave a gruff howl of fierce disapproval

With his back to the sodden embers the boy bowed on his knees, still mumbling his long fervent prayer. On his knees he dragged his body up to the gorilla's feet. The gorilla's feet were black and rough like his own, with long scaly toes and straight silken hair on top that was not like his. Reverently, he lay the burnt offering at the feet of his savage idol. And the gorilla's feet, powerful and large and twitching with impatience, were the last things he saw before he was hurled out of the violent jungle of the world into nothingness and a blinding light. And the gorilla, snorting with disgust, grabbed the bread.

2

The life of John's father, another place, ending.

John's father had heard that in that last miserable second your whole life passed before your eyes. But he and the plain black girl who was his second wife moved into the moment itself with few reflections to spare. When they heard the twister coming, like twenty wild trains slamming through the houses on their block, she grabbed the baby and he the small boy and hardly noticing that the other moved each ran toward the refrigerator, frantically pulling out the meagre dishes of food, flinging a half-empty carton of milk across the room, and making a place where the vegetables and fruits should have been for the two children to crouch. With no tears, no warnings, no goodbyes, they slammed the door.

Minutes after the cyclone had leveled the street to the ground searchers would come and find the children still huddled inside the refrigerator. Almost dead, cold, the baby crying and gasping for air, the small boy numb with horror and with chill. They would peer out not into the familiar shabby kitchen but into an open field. Perhaps the church or the Red Cross or a kind neighbor would take them in, bed them down among other children similarly lost, and in twenty years the plain black girl and the man who was their father would be forgotten, recalled, if even briefly, by sudden forceful enclosures in damp and chilly places.

This, too, the future, passed before his eyes, and not one past life but two. He wondered, in that moment, only fleetingly of the God he'd sworn to serve and of the wife he held now in his arms, and thought instead of his first wife, the librarian, and of their son, John.

He had married his first wife in a gigantic two-ring ceremony, in a church, and his wife had had the wedding pictures touched up so that he did not resemble himself. In the pictures his skin was olive brown and smooth when in fact it was black and stubbly and rough. He had married his wife because she was light and loose and fun and because she had long red hair. After they were married she stopped dyeing it and let it grow out black. Then, with the black unimaginative hair and the discreet black patent-leather shoes she wore, the gray suits she seemed to love, the continual poking into books—well, she was just no longer anyone he recognized.

After he quit the post office he became a hairdresser. He liked being around women. Old women with three chins who wanted blue or purple hair, young tacky girls who adored the way platinum sparkled against black skin, even stolid reserved librarians like his wife who never seemed to want anything but a continuation of the way they were. Women like his wife intrigued him because the duller he could make them look the more respectable they felt, and the better they liked it.

But living with his wife was more difficult than straightening her hair every two weeks. He could conquer the kinks in her hair but her body and mind became rapidly harder to penetrate. He found the struggle humiliating besides.

John, unfortunately, had been too small to hold his interest. Which was not to acknowledge lack of love, simply lack of interest.

The plain black girl he married next was a sister in the Nation and would not agree to go away with him except to some forsaken place where they could preach the Word to those people who had formerly floundered without it. He too, changed his name and took an X. He was not comfortable with the X, however, because he began to feel each morning that the day before he had not existed. When his anxiety did not subside his wife claimed an inability to comprehend the persistent stubbornness of his agony. He knew what it was, of course; without a last name John would never be able to find him.

He had seen the boy once in ten years, when John was almost fifteen years old. He had been eager to talk to John, eager to please. John was eager to get away from him. Not from dislike or out of anger, that was clear. John did not blame his father for deserting him, at least that is what he said. No, John simply wanted to get up to the Bronx Zoo before it closed.

"John, I don't understand!" he had shouted, annoyed to find himself in competition with a zoo. His son watched his lips move with a curious interest, as if he could not possibly hear the words coming out. John looked at his father with impatience and pity, and with an expression faintly contemptuous, superior. It unnerved him, for it was the way John himself had been looked at when he was a baby. For John had all the physical characteristics that in the Western world are scorned. John looked like his father. An honest black. His forehead sloped backward from the bridge of his eyes. His nose was flat, his mouth too wide. John's mother was always fussing over John but hated him because he looked like his father instead of like her. She blamed her husband for what he had "done to" John. Yet he was John's father, why shouldn't the boy resemble him?

His new wife loved him fiercely, with a kind of passionate abstraction, as if he were a painting or wondrous sculpture. She wore his color and the construction of his features like a badge. She saw him as a king returning to his lands and was bitterly proud of whatever their two bodies produced.

In the South, in a hate-filled state complete with magnolias, tornadoes and broken-tongued field hands, they had settled down to raise a family of their own. The minds of their people were as harsh and flat as the land and had little time to absorb a new religion more dangerous than the old. Still, they had persisted; and in the struggle he found peace for himself. It was true that he was lost to John, but through the years his wife helped him see that John was really just a cipher, one of the millions who needed the truth their religion could bring. He had finally accepted himself, but it seemed that in the moment the beauty of this acceptance was most clear he must say good-bye to it.

A sound like twenty wild trains rushed through the street. They moved as one person will move, their children in their arms, toward the refrigerator. They threw out the food, crammed the children in. They slammed the refrigerator door and rushed, like children themselves, into each other's arms.

3

The mother of John, searching . . .

Of course John's mother was much older than the other black radical poets. She was in her forties and most of them were in their twenties or early thirties. She looked young, though, and engaged in the same kind of inflammatory rhetoric they did. She became very popular on the circuit because she said pithy, pungent, unexpected things, and because she undermined the other poets in hilarious and harmless ways. Students who heard her read almost always laughed loudly and raised their fists and stomped and yelled "Right on!" This was extremely gratifying to her, because she wanted more than anything in the world a rapport with people younger than herself. This is not to suggest she used the Black revolution to bridge the generation gap, but rather that she found it the ideal vehicle from which to vindicate herself from former ways or error.

No, she had not, as several of the poets claimed, truly believed in nonviolence or Martin Luther King (she had found his Southern accent offensive and his Christian calling ludicrous), nor had she ever worked as a token Negro in a white-owned corporation. She had never attended an interracial affair at which she was the only black, and it went without saying that all her love affairs had been correct.

On the other hand, her marriage to a lower echelon post-office functionary, who, though black indeed, was not suited for her temperamentally, foundered for many years, and shortly after the birth of a son was completely submerged. And though she was heard from coast to coast blasting the genteel Southern college she had attended for stunting her revolutionary growth and encouraging her incipient whiteness, and striking out at black preachers, teachers and leaders for being "eunuchs," "Oreos," and "fruits," it was actually the son of her unsuccessful marriage that lent fire to her poetic deliveries. He was never mentioned, of course, and none of the students to whom she lectured and read her poetry knew of his existence.

He had been dead for three or four years before she even began to think of writing poetry; before that time she had been assistant librarian at the Carver branch of the Municipal Library of New York City. Her son had died at the age of fifteen under rather peculiar circumstances—after removing a large and ferocious gorilla from its cage in the Bronx Zoo. Only his mother had been able to piece together the details of his death. She did not like to talk about it, however, and spent two months in a sanitarium afterward, tying a knot over and over in one of her nylons to make a small boy's stocking cap.

A year after she was released from the sanitarium she cut her chignoned hair, discarded her high-heel patents for sandals and boots, and bought her first pair of large hoop earrings for a dollar and fifty cents. A short time later she bought a dozen yards of African print material and made herself several bright nunnish dresses. And, in a bout of agony one day she drew small, elaborate scarification marks down her cheeks. She also tried going without a bra, but since she was well built with good-sized breasts, going braless caused back-ache, and she had to give it up. She did, however, throw away her girdle for good.

She might have been a spectacularly striking figure, with her cropped fluffy hair and her tall, statuesque body—her skin was good and surprisingly the scarification marks played up the noble severity of her cheek-bones—but her eyes were too small and tended to glint, giving her a suspicious, beady-eyed look, the look of pouncing, of grabbing hold.

The students who applauded so actively during her readings almost never stopped afterward to talk with her, and even after standing ovations she left the lecture halls un-escorted, for even the department heads who invited her found a reason, usually, to slip out and away minutes before she brought her delivery to a close. She received all payments for her readings in the mail.

And sometimes, after she'd watched the students turn and go outside, laughing and joking among themselves, puffing out their chests in the new proud blackness and identification with their beauty her poetry had given them, she leaned against the lectern and put her hands up to her eyes, feeling a weakness in her legs and an ache in her throat. And at these times she almost always saw her son sitting in one of the back rows in front of her, his hands folded in his lap, his eyes bright with enthusiasm for her teachings, his thin young back straight.

She had renamed him Jomo after his death. Softly she would call to him, "John?" "John?" "*Jomo*?" And though he never answered her he would amble down to the lectern and stand waiting while she gathered up her notes, her poems, her clippings from newspapers (her voluminous collection of the errors of others). He would wait for her to wipe her eyes. Then he would go with her as far as the door.

THE DIARY OF
AN AFRICAN NUN

Our mission school is at the foot of lovely Uganda mountains and is a resting place for travelers. Classrooms in daylight, a hotel when the sun sets.

The question is in the eyes of all who come here: Why are you—so young, so beautiful (perhaps)—a nun? The Americans cannot understand my humility. I bring them clean sheets and towels and return their too much money and candid smiles. The Germans are very different. They do not offer money but praise. The sight of a black nun strikes their sentimentality; and, as I am unalterably rooted in native ground, they consider me a work of primitive art, housed in a magical color; the incarnation of civilization, anti-heathenism, and the fruit of a triumphing idea. They are coolly passionate and smile at me lecherously with speculative crystal eyes of bright historical blue. The French find me *charm-*

ant and would like to paint a picture. The Italians, used as they are to the habit, concern themselves with the giant cockroaches in the latrines and give me hardly a glance, except in reproach for them.

I am, perhaps, as I should be. *Gloria Deum. Gloria in excelsis Deo.*

I am a wife of Christ, a wife of the Catholic church. The wife of a celibate martyr and saint. I was born in this township, a village "civilized" by American missionaries. All my life I have lived here within walking distance of the Ruwenzori mountains—mountains which show themselves only once a year under the blazing heat of spring.

2

When I was younger, in a bright blue school uniform and bare feet, I came every day to the mission school. "Good morning," I chanted to the people I met. But especially to the nuns and priests who taught at my school. I did not then know that they could not have children. They seemed so productive and full of intense, regal life. I wanted to be like them, and now I am. Shrouded in whiteness like the mountains I see from my window.

At twenty I earned the right to wear this dress, never to be without it, always to bathe myself in cold water even in winter, and to wear my mission-cropped hair well covered, my nails clean and neatly clipped. The boys I knew as a child are kind to me now and gentle, and I see them married and kiss their children, each one of them so much what our Lord wanted—did he not say, "Suffer little children to come unto me"?—but we have not yet been so lucky, and we never shall.

3

At night I sit in my room until seven, then I go, obediently to bed. Through the window I can hear the drums, smell the roasting goat's meat, feel the rhythm of the festive chants. And I sing my own chants in response to theirs: "*Pater noster, qui es in caelis, sanctificetur nomen tuum, adveniat regnum tuum, fiat voluntas tua, sicut in caelo et in terra. . . .*" My chant is less old than theirs. They do not know this—they do not even care.

Do *I* care? Must I still ask myself whether it was my husband, who came down bodiless from the sky, son of a proud father and flesh once upon the earth, who first took me and claimed the innocence of my body? Or was it the drumbeats, messengers of the sacred dance of life and death-lessness on earth? Must I still long to be within the black circle around the red, glowing fire, to feel the breath of love hot against my cheeks, the smell of love strong about my waiting thighs! Must I still tremble at the thought of the passions stifled beneath this voluminous rustling snow!

How long must I sit by my window before I lure you down from the sky? Pale lover who never knew the dance and could not do it!

I bear your colors, I am in your livery, I belong to you. Will you not come down and take me! Or are you even less passionate than your father who took but could not show his face?

4

Silence, as the dance continues—now they will be breaking out the wine, cutting the goat's meat in sinewy strips. Teeth will clutch it, wring it. Cruel, greedy, greasy lips will curl over it in an ecstasy which has never ceased wherever there were goats and men. The wine will be hot from the fire; it will cut through the obscene clutter on those lips and turn them from their goat's meat to that other.

At midnight a young girl will come to the circle, hidden in black she will not speak to anyone. She has said good morning to them all, many mornings, and has decided to be like them. She will begin the dance—every eye following the blue flashes of her oiled, slippery body, every heart pounding to the flat clacks of her dusty feet. She will dance to her lover with arms stretched upward to the sky, but her eyes are leveled at her lover, one of the crowd. He will dance with her, the tempo will increase. All the crowd can see the weakening of her knees, can feel in their own loins the loosening of her rolling thighs. Her lover makes her wait until she is in a frenzy, tearing off her clothes and scratching at the narrow cloth he wears. The eyes of the crowd are forgotten. The final taking is unbearable as they rock through the oldest dance. The red flames roar and the purple bodies crumple and are still. And the dancing begins again and the whole night is a repetition of the dance of life and the urgent fire of creation. Dawn breaks finally to the acclaiming cries of babies.

5

"Our father, which art in heaven, hallowed be thy name, thy kingdom come, thy will be done on earth—" And in heaven, would the ecstasy be quite as fierce and sweet?

"Sweet? Sister," they will say. "Have we not yet made a convert of you? Will you yet be a cannibal and eat up the life that is Christ because it eases your palate?"

What must I answer my husband? To say the truth would mean oblivion, to be forgotten for another thousand years. Still, perhaps I shall answer this to him who took me:

"Dearly Beloved, let me tell you about the mountains and the spring. The mountains that we see around us are black, it is the snow that gives them their icy whiteness. In the spring, the hot black soil melts the crust of snow on the mountains, and the water as it runs down the sheets of fiery rock burns and cleanses the naked bodies that come to wash in it. It is when the snows melt that the people here plant their crops; the soil of the mountains is rich, and its produce plentiful and good.

"What have I or my mountains to do with a childless marriage, or with eyes that can see only the snow; or with you or friends of yours who do not believe that you are really dead—pious faithful who do not yet realize that barrenness is death?

"Or perhaps I might say, 'Leave me alone; I will do your work'; or, what is more likely, I will say nothing of my melancholia at your lack of faith in the spring. . . . For what is my faith in the spring and the eternal melting of snows (you will ask) but your belief in the Resurrection? Could I convince one so wise that my belief bears more fruit?"

How to teach a barren world to dance? It is a contradiction that divides the world.

My mouth must be silent, then, though my heart jumps to the booming of the drums, as to the last strong pulse of life in a dying world.

For the drums will soon, one day, be silent. I will help muffle them forever. To assure life for my people in this world I must be among the lying ones and teach them how to die. I will turn their dances into prayers to an empty sky, and their lovers into dead men, and their babies into unsung chants that choke their throats each spring.

6

In this way will the wife of a loveless, barren, hopeless Western marriage broadcast the joys of enlightened religion to an imitative people.

THE FLOWERS

It seemed to Myop as she skipped lightly from hen house to pigpen to smokehouse that the days had never been as beautiful as these. The air held a keenness that made her nose twitch. The harvesting of the corn and cotton, peanuts and squash, made each day a golden surprise that caused excited little tremors to run up her jaws.

Myop carried a short, knobby stick. She struck out at random at chickens she liked, and worked out the beat of a song on the fence around the pigpen. She felt light and good in the warm sun. She was ten, and nothing existed for her but her song, the stick clutched in her dark brown hand, and the tat-de-ta-ta-ta of accompaniment.

Turning her back on the rusty boards of her family's share-cropper cabin, Myop walked along the fence till it ran into the stream made by the spring. Around the spring, where the *family got drinking water, silver ferns and wild-flowers grew. Along the shallow banks pigs rooted. Myop watched the tiny white bubbles disrupt the thin black scale of soil and the water that silently rose and slid away down the stream.*

She had explored the woods behind the house many times. Often, in late autumn, her mother took her to gather nuts among the fallen leaves. Today she made her own path, bouncing this way and that way, vaguely keeping an eye out for snakes. She found, in addition to various common but pretty ferns and leaves, an armful of strange blue flowers with velvety ridges and a sweetsuds bush full of the brown, fragrant buds.

By twelve o'clock, her arms were laden with sprigs of her findings, she was a mile or more from home. She had often been as far before, but the strangeness of the land made it not as pleasant as her usual haunts. It seemed gloomy in the little cove in which she found herself. The air was damp, the silence close and deep.

Myop began to circle back to the house, back to the peacefulness of the morning. It was then she stepped smack into his eyes. Her heel became lodged in the broken ridge between brow and nose, and she reached down quickly, unafraid, to free herself. It was only when she saw his naked grin that she gave a little yelp of surprise.

He had been a tall man. From feet to neck covered a long space. His head lay beside him. When she pushed back the leaves and layers of earth and debris Myop saw that he'd had large white teeth, all of them cracked or broken, long fingers, and very big bones. All his clothes had rotted away except some threads of blue denim from his overalls. The buckles of the overalls had turned green.

Myop gazed around the spot with interest. Very near where she'd stepped into the head was a wild pink rose. As she picked it to add to her bundle she noticed a raised mound, a ring, around the rose's root. It was the rotted remains of a noose, a bit of shredding plowline, now blending benignly into the soil.

Around an overhanging limb of a great spreading oak clung another piece. Frayed, rotted, bleached, and frazzled—barely there—but spinning restlessly in the breeze. Myop laid down her flowers.

And the summer was over.

WE DRINK THE WINE
IN FRANCE

(Harriet)

"Je bois, tu bois, il boit, nous buvons, vous buvez. . . ."
They are oddly like a drawing by Daumier. He, immediately perceived as Old; she, Youth with brown cheeks. His thin form—over which the double-breasted pinstripe appears to crack at the base of his spine—is bending over her. His profile is strained, flattened by its sallowness; unrelieved by quick brown eyes that twitch at one corner and heavy black eyebrows lightly frosted with white. There is a gray line of perspiration above his mouth, like an artificial moustache. His long fingers are busy arranging, pointing to the words on the paper on her desk.

She is down low, Her neck strains backward, bringing her

face up to his. She is a small, round-bosomed girl with tumbly hair pulled severely back except for bangs. Her eyes are like the lens of a camera. Now they click shut. Now they open and drink in the light. Something, a kind of light, comes from them and shines on the professor of French. He is suddenly amazed at the mixture of orange and brown that is her skin.

"*En France, nous* buvons *le vin!*" The force of his breath touches her. She draws in her own. It makes a gasping sound that shocks him. He springs upright. Something stiff, aghast, more like a Daumier than ever, about him. The girl is startled, wonders why he jumped back so fast. Thinks he does not want to mingle breaths with her. For a hot flurried moment she feels inferior.

The professor takes cover behind his desk. His eyes race over the other forms in the class. He wonders what they notice. They are even worse than adult foreigners; they are children. When they see him going to the post office underneath their windows they call their friends to come and look down on his balding head. In the classroom they watch him professionally, their brown eyes as wary as his own. The blue-eyed girl begs for, then rejects, kinship. With him. With them. Her skin is white as the ceiling. The brown and rose of the skins around her do not give her a chance to exhibit beauty. By the range of colors she is annihilated. For this he feels vaguely sorry for her. But it is a momentary pang. He is too aware of her misery ever to bring it up. Hearing the bell he turns from her. For a moment his eyes lock with those of the girl who never has her French. She is dreaming, has not heard the bell, is unaware. For a moment she drifts into his eyes, but the click comes and the eyes go blank. When she passes him at the door his heart flutters like old newspapers in a gutter disturbed by a falling gust of wind.

2

The professor goes by for his mail: it is a magazine and a letter from Mexico, where he will go as soon as summer comes. He can hardly wait to leave Mississippi for even greater sun. The surrounding beauty has crept up on him gradually since his arrival three years ago. He can no longer ignore it and it hurts him, terribly. In Mexico he will find an even slower-infecting beauty. When it becomes painful he will begin to explore countries even farther south. He has been chased across the world by the realization of beauty. He folds the letter, looks with horror at the narrow walls and low ceiling of the post office, rushes out into the bright sunshine.

3

Harriet is an ugly name. She wonders if it would sound better in French. She leans forward from the weight of six large and heavy books. She is not stupid, as the professor of French thinks. She is really rather bright. At least that is what her other teachers say. She will read every one of the thick books in her arms, and they are not books she is required to read. She is trying to feel the substance of what other people have learned. To digest it until it becomes like bread and sustains her. She is the hungriest girl in the school.

She sees the professor take out his mail; the letter, which he reads, and the magazine, which he sticks under his arm. While she scans the bulletin board noting dances to which she will not be asked the panic of his flight reaches her. She wonders if his letter was about someone who has died.

4

Later, in the car, her body is like a lump of something that only breathes. She feels her lover's hands, dry and young, rake up the impediments of her clothes. A thrust of one hand against her nipples, nearly right, then a squeeze that accomplishes nothing. She feels herself borne backward on the front seat of the car, the weight pressing her down, the movement anxious, selfish, pinning her, stabbing through. When it is over she is surprised she can sit up again, she had imagined herself impaled on the seat. Sitting up, looking out the window: "Yes, it was good"; she remembers not the movement knocking against her stomach but the completely correct account she has given the word *boire. Je bois, tu bois, il boit, nous buvons.* . . .

They move back toward the campus, she feeling outside the car, far away from the hands that manipulate the wheel. They hurry. If the gate is locked she will have to climb over the wall. For this she could be expelled. The boy sweats, worried about their safety, the future he wants. She thinks climbing walls an inconvenience but the humiliation of failure is not quite real. The knot behind her ear where a policeman struck her two weeks before begins to throb. But they are not late. She walks the two blocks to the campus gate, passes the winking guard, smells the liquor on his breath as he sniffs after her. She wonders about this injustice, her confinement, tries to construct an abstract sentence on the subject in impeccable French.

5

The professor will have cottage cheese, a soft egg, a glass of milk and cream for his meal. He has an ulcer and must take care of it. He wonders if Mademoiselle Harriet has noticed how he belches and strokes his stomach. He really must stop thinking of her. Must remember he is old. That death has had its hands on him. That his odor is of ashes while hers is of earth and sun.

As he eats his colorless meal he remembers the magazine. It opens to his own story; a story he wrote to make the new pain less than the old. It is a story about life in a concentration camp. The same camp that gobbled up his wife and daughter and made fertilizer from their bones. He recalls the Polish winter, cold and damp and in his memory always dark; the stiff movement of the long marches, bleeding feet. It is all in the story; seven years of starvation, freezing, death. The publishers have described his escape in sensational language. His survival, in their words, appears abnormal. He is a monster for not now pushing up plants in the backwoods of Poland. A criminal for crossing Europe unslaughtered; for turning up in France already knowing the language. For having had parents devoted to learning that in the end had not done them any good!

The author is now Professor of French at a school for black girls in the Deep South.

Outraged, the professor flings the acknowledgement of his existence across the room.

6

"*Mon Dieu, quelle femme!*" Harriet inspects her naked body in the glass. She imagines that the professor will climb up the fire escape outside her window, that he will creep smiling through the curtains, that she will reach out to him all naked and warm and he will bury his cold nose and lips in the hot flesh of her bare shoulder. Undressed (she imagines him first in long red underwear), he will lean over her on the bed, looking. Then into bed with her. They will lie, talking. For there is no hurry about him. He is old enough to know better. He strokes her neck below the ear and tells her of his life.

Explains the blue stenciled numbers she has seen peek from beneath his cuff—a cuff he is always adjusting. For she is ignorant of history. Her own as well as his. He must tell her why he put a tattoo there only to keep trying to hide it later. He must promise her he will not be embarrassed to remove his coat in class, especially on hot days when it is clear he is miserable. So much he must tell her . . . But now her body has completely warmed him. His body seems to melt, to flow about hers. His mouth, fuller, plays with her breasts, teasing the nipples, light as the touch of a feather. His hands find, discover, places on her back, her sides. She takes him inside herself, not wanting to make him young again, for she is already where he at old age finds himself.

A knock, harsh and resounding, announces bed check and the house mother. Harriet has time to slip into her nightgown and mumble "Yes, ma'am" before the gray-brown dream-dispelling face pokes rigidly into the room.

7

Once in bed the professor abandons himself. He thinks hungrily of his stupid pupil. He remembers her from the very first week of classes; her blurred, soft speech, which he found difficult to understand, her slow comprehension—far behind the nearly white girl with the blue eyes, who ate French sentences choppily, like a horse chopping grass—her strange brown eyes so sorrowful at her ignorance they seemed capable of moaning. She is younger than the grandchild he might have had—and more stupid, he adds. But he cannot think of her as a child. As young, yes. But not the other way. She brings the odor of Southern jails into class with her, and hundreds of aching, marching feet, and the hurtful sound of the freedom songs he has heard from the church, the wailing of souls destined for bloody eternities at the end of each completely maddened street.

Her speech, which he had thought untutored and ugly, becomes her; the sorrowful eyes have bruised him where they touched. He dreams himself into her songs. Cashes the check from the story and buys two tickets to Mexico, lies with her openly on the beaches, praises the soft roundness of her nose, the deep brown he imagines on her toes, bakes his body to bring them closer to one. All the love from his miserable life he heaps on her lap.

When he awakes from his dream sweat is on his forehead, where years ago black hair curled and fell. And he is crying, without any tears but sweat, and when he turns his face to the wall he is already planning the wording of his resignation and buying brochures for South America.

8

"*Nous* buvons *le vin*," Harriet practices before entering the class, before seeing him. But the lesson for the day has moved on. It is "*Nous ne buvons pas le vin*" that the professor forces her to repeat before hiding himself for the last time behind his desk.

TO HELL WITH DYING

"To hell with dying," my father would say. "These children want Mr. Sweet!"

Mr. Sweet was a diabetic and an alcoholic and a guitar player and lived down the road from us on a neglected cotton farm. My older brothers and sisters got the most benefit from Mr. Sweet, for when they were growing up he had quite a few years ahead of him and so was capable of being called back from the brink of death any number of times—whenever the voice of my father reached him as he lay expiring. "To hell with dying, man," my father would say, pushing the wife away from the bedside (in tears although she knew the death was not necessarily the last one unless Mr. Sweet really wanted it to be). "These children want Mr. Sweet!" And they did want him, for at a signal from Father they would come crowding around the bed and throw themselves on the covers, and whoever was the smallest at the time would kiss him all over his wrinkled brown face and begin to tickle him so that he would laugh all down in his stomach, and his moustache, which was long and sort of straggly, would shake like Spanish moss and was also that color.

Mr. Sweet had been ambitious as a boy, wanted to be a doctor or lawyer or sailor, only to find that black men fare better if they are not. Since he could become none of these things he turned to fishing as his only earnest career and playing the guitar as his only claim to doing anything extraordinarily well. His son, the only one that he and his wife, Miss Mary, had, was shiftless as the day is long and spent money as if he were trying to see the bottom of the mint, which Mr. Sweet would tell him was the clean brown palm of his hand. Miss Mary loved her "baby," however, and worked hard to get him the "Li'l necessaries" of life, which turned out mostly to be women.

Mr. Sweet was a tall, thinnish man with thick kinky hair going dead white. He was dark brown, his eyes were very squinty and sort of bluish, and he chewed Brown Mule tobacco. He was constantly on the verge of being blind drunk, for he brewed his own liquor and was not in the least a stingy sort of man, and was always very melancholy and sad, though frequently when he was "feelin' good" he'd dance around the yard with us, usually keeling over just as my mother came to see what the commotion was.

Toward all of us children he was very kind, and had the grace to be shy with us, which is unusual in grown-ups. He had great respect for my mother for she never held his drunkenness against him and would let us play with him even when he was about to fall in the fireplace from drink. Although Mr. Sweet would sometimes lose complete or nearly complete control of his head and neck so that he would loll in his chair, his mind remained strangely acute and his speech not too affected. His ability to be drunk and sober at the same time made him an ideal playmate, for he was as weak as we were and we could usually best him in wrestling, all the while keeping a fairly coherent conversation going.

We never felt anything of Mr. Sweet's age when we played with him. We loved his wrinkles and would draw some on our brows to be like him, and his white hair was my special treasure and he knew it and would never come to visit us just after he had had his hair cut off at the barbershop. Once he came to our house for something, probably to see my father about fertilizer for his crops because, although he never paid the slightest attention to his crops, he liked to know what things would be best to use on them if he ever did. Anyhow, he had not come with his hair since he had just had it shaved off at the barbershop. He wore a huge straw hat to keep off the sun and also to keep his head away from me. But as soon as I saw him I ran up and demanded that he take me up and kiss me with his funny beard which smelled so strongly of tobacco. Looking forward to burying my small fingers into his woolly hair I threw away his hat only to find he had done something to his hair, that it was no longer there! I let out a squall which made my mother think that Mr. Sweet had finally dropped me in the well or something and from that day I've been wary of men in hats. However, not long after, Mr. Sweet showed up with his hair grown out and just as white and kinky and impenetrable as it ever was.

Mr. Sweet used to call me his princess, and I believed it. He made me feel pretty at five and six, and simply outrageously devastating at the blazing age of eight and a half. When he came to our house with his guitar the whole family would stop whatever they were doing to sit around him and listen to him play. He liked to play "Sweet Georgia Brown," that was what he called me sometimes, and also he liked to play "Caldonia" and all sorts of sweet, sad, wonderful songs which he sometimes made up. It was from one of these songs that I learned that he had had to marry Miss Mary when he had in fact loved somebody else (now living in Chica-go, or De-stroy, Michigan). He was not sure that Joe Lee, her "baby," was also his baby. Sometimes he would cry and that was an indication that he was about to die again. And so we would all get prepared, for we were sure to be called upon.

I was seven the first time I remembered actually participating in one of Mr. Sweet's "revivals"—my parents told me I had participated before, I had been the one chosen to kiss him and tickle him long before I knew the rite of Mr. Sweet's rehabilitation. He had come to our house, it was a few years after his wife's death, and was very sad, and also, typically, very drunk. He sat on the floor next to me and my older brother, the rest of the children were grown up and lived elsewhere, and began to play his guitar and cry. I held his woolly head in my arms and wished I could have been old enough to have been the woman he loved so much and that I had not been lost years and years ago.

When he was leaving, my mother said to us that we'd better sleep light that night for we'd probably have to go over to Mr. Sweet's before daylight. And we did. For soon after we had gone to bed one of the neighbors knocked on our door and called my father and said that Mr. Sweet was sinking fast and if he wanted to get in a word before the crossover he'd better shake a leg and get over to Mr. Sweet's house. All the neighbors knew to come to our house if something was wrong with Mr. Sweet, but they did not know how we always managed to make him well, or at least stop him from dying, when he was often so near death. As soon as we heard the cry we got up, my brother and I and my mother and father, and put on our clothes. We hurried out of the house and down the road for we were always afraid that we might someday be too late and Mr. Sweet would get tired of dallying.

When we got to the house, a very poor shack really, we found the front room full of neighbors and relatives and someone met us at the door and said that it was all very sad that old Mr. Sweet Little (for Little was his family name, although we mostly ignored it) was about to kick the bucket. My parents were advised not to take my brother and me into the "death room," seeing we were so young and all, but we were so much more accustomed to the death room than he that we ignored him and dashed in without giving his warning a second thought. I was almost in tears, for these deaths upset me fearfully, and the thought of how much depended on me and my brother (who was such a ham most of the time) made me very nervous.

The doctor was bending over the bed and turned back to tell us for at least the tenth time in the history of my family that, alas, old Mr. Sweet Little was dying and that the children had best not see the face of implacable death (I didn't know what "implacable" was, but whatever it was, Mr. Sweet was not!). My father pushed him rather abruptly out of the way saying, as he always did and very loudly for he was saying it to Mr. Sweet, "To hell with dying, man, these children want Mr. Sweet"—which was my cue to throw myself upon the bed and kiss Mr. Sweet all around the whiskers and under the eyes and around the collar of his nightshirt where he smelled so strongly of all sorts of things, mostly liniment.

I was very good at bringing him around, for as soon as I saw that he was struggling to open his eyes I knew he was going to be all right, and so could finish my revival sure of success. As soon as his eyes were open he would begin to smile and that way I knew that I had surely won. Once, though, I got a tremendous scare, for he could not open his eyes and later I learned that he had had a stroke and that one side of his face was stiff and hard to get into motion. When he began to smile I could tickle him in earnest because I was sure that nothing would get in the way of his laughter, although once he began to cough so hard that he almost threw me off his stomach, but that was when I was very

small, little more than a baby, and my bushy hair had gotten
in his nose.

When we were sure he would listen to us we would ask
him why he was in bed and when he was coming to see us
again and could we play with his guitar, which more than
likely would be leaning against the bed. His eyes would get
all misty and he would sometimes cry out loud, but we never
let it embarrass us, for he knew that we loved him and that
we sometimes cried too for no reason. My parents would
leave the room to just the three of us; Mr. Sweet, by that
time, would be propped up in bed with a number of pillows
behind his head and with me sitting and lying on his shoulder
and along his chest. Even when he had trouble breathing he
would not ask me to get down. Looking into my eyes he would
shake his white head and run a scratchy old finger all around
my hairline, which was rather low down, nearly to my eyebrows, and made some people say I looked like a baby
monkey.

My brother was very generous in all this, he let me do all
the revivaling—he had done it for years before I was born
and so was glad to be able to pass it on to someone new.
What he would do while I talked to Mr. Sweet was pretend
to play the guitar, in fact pretend that he was a young version
of Mr. Sweet, and it always made Mr. Sweet glad to think
that someone wanted to be like him—of course, we did not
know this then, we played the thing by ear, and whatever he
seemed to like, we did. We were desperately afraid that
he was just going to take off one day and leave us.

It did not occur to us that we were doing anything special;
we had not learned that death was final when it did come.
We thought nothing of triumphing over it so many times,
and in fact became a trifle contemptuous of people who let
themselves be carried away. It did not occur to us that if our
own father had been dying we could not have stopped it,
that Mr. Sweet was the only person over whom we had power.

When Mr. Sweet was in his eighties I was studying in the

university many miles from home. I saw him whenever I went home, but he was never on the verge of dying that I could tell and I began to feel that my anxiety for his health and psychological well-being was unnecessary. By this time he not only had a moustache but a long flowing snow-white beard, which I loved and combed and braided for hours. He was very peaceful, fragile, gentle, and the only jarring note about him was his old steel guitar, which he still played in the old sad, sweet, down-home blues way.

On Mr. Sweet's ninetieth birthday I was finishing my doctorate in Massachusetts and had been making arrangements to go home for several weeks' rest. That morning I got a telegram telling me that Mr. Sweet was dying again and could I please drop everything and come home. Of course I could. My dissertation could wait and my teachers would understand when I explained to them when I got back. I ran to the phone, called the airport, and within four hours I was speeding along the dusty road to Mr. Sweet's.

The house was more dilapidated than when I was last there, barely a shack, but it was overgrown with yellow roses which my family had planted many years ago. The air was heavy and sweet and very peaceful. I felt strange walking through the gate and up the old rickety steps. But the strangeness left me as I caught sight of the long white beard I loved so well flowing down the thin body over the familiar quilt coverlet. Mr. Sweet!

His eyes were closed tight and his hands, crossed over his stomach, were thin and delicate, no longer scratchy. I remembered how always before I had run and jumped on him just anywhere; now I knew he would not be able to support my weight. I looked around at my parents, and was surprised to see that my father and mother also looked old and frail. My father, his own hair very gray, leaned over the quietly sleeping old man, who, incidentally, smelled still of wine and tobacco, and said, as he'd done so many times, "To hell with dying man! My daughter is home to see Mr. Sweet!"

My brother had not been able to come as he was in the war in Asia. I bent down and gently stroked the closed eyes and gradually they began to open. The closed, wine-stained lips twitched a little, then parted in a warm, slightly embarrassed smile. Mr. Sweet could see me and he recognized me and his eyes looked very spry and twinkly for a moment. I put my head down on the pillow next to his and we just looked at each other for a long time. Then he began to trace my peculiar hairline with his finger halted above my ear (he used to rejoice at the dirt in my ears when I was little), his hand stayed cupped around my cheek. When I opened my eyes, sure that I had reached him in time, his were closed.

Even at twenty-four how could I believe that I had failed? that Mr. Sweet was really gone? He had never gone before. But when I looked up at my parents I saw that they were holding back tears. They had loved him dearly. He was like a piece of rare and delicate china which was always being saved from breaking and which finally fell. I looked long at the old face, the wrinkled forehead, the red lips, the hands that still reached out to me. Soon I felt my father pushing something cool into my hands. It was Mr. Sweet's guitar. He had asked them months before to give it to me; he had known that even if I came next time he would not be able to respond in the old way. He did not want me to feel that my trip had been for nothing.

The old guitar! I plucked the strings, hummed "Sweet Georgia Brown." The magic of Mr. Sweet lingered still in the cool steel box. Through the window I could catch the fragrant delicate scent of tender yellow roses. The man on the high old-fashioned bed with the quilt coverlet and the flowing white beard had been my first love.

You Can't Keep a
Good Woman Down

You Can't Keep a Good Woman Down *is dedicated to my contemporaries*

I thank my sister Ruth for the stories she tells.

I thank Bessie Head, Ama Ata Aidoo, Buchi Emecheta, Wa Thiong'o Ngugi, Okos p'Bitek and Ousmane Sembene for the stories they write.

I thank Gloria Steinem, Joanne Edgar and Suzanne Braun Levine of *Ms.* magazine, who greeted each of the many stories *Ms.* published from this collection with sisterly welcome and enthusiasm.

I thank Ma Rainey, Bessie (*A Good Man Is Hard to Find*) Smith, Marnie Smith and Perry (*You Can't Keep a Good Man Down*) Bradford, among others of their generation, for insisting on the value and beauty of the authentic.

*It is harder to kill something
that is spiritually alive
than it is to bring the dead
back to life.*

—Hermann Hesse

NINETEEN FIFTY-FIVE

1955

The car is a brandnew red Thunderbird convertible, and it's passed the house more than once. It slows down real slow now, and stops at the curb. An older gentleman dressed like a Baptist deacon gets out on the side near the house, and a young fellow who looks about sixteen gets out on the driver's side. They are white, and I wonder what in the world they doing in this neighborhood.

Well, I say to J. T., put your shirt on, anyway, and let me clean these glasses offa the table.

We had been watching the ballgame on TV. I wasn't actually watching, I was sort of daydreaming, with my foots up in J. T.'s lap.

I seen 'em coming on up the walk, brisk, like they coming to sell something, and then they rung the bell, and J. T.

declined to put on a shirt but instead disappeared into the bedroom where the other television is. I turned down the one in the living room; I figured I'd be rid of these two double quick and J. T. could come back out again.

Are you Gracie Mae Still? asked the old guy, when I opened the door and put my hand on the lock inside the screen.

And I don't need to buy a thing, said I.

What makes you think we're sellin'? he asks, in that hearty Southern way that makes my eyeballs ache.

Well, one way or another and they're inside the house and the first thing the young fellow does is raise the TV a couple of decibels. He's about five feet nine, sort of womanish looking, with real dark white skin and a red pouting mouth. His hair is black and curly and he looks like a Loosianna creole.

About one of your songs, says the deacon. He is maybe sixty, with white hair and beard, white silk shirt, black linen suit, black tie and black shoes. His cold gray eyes look like they're sweating.

One of my songs?

Traynor here just *loves* your songs. Don't you, Traynor? He nudges Traynor with his elbow. Traynor blinks, says something I can't catch in a pitch I don't register.

The boy learned to sing and dance livin' round you people out in the country. Practically cut his teeth on you.

Traynor looks up at me and bites his thumbnail.

I laugh.

Well, one way or another they leave with my agreement that they can record one of my songs. The deacon writes me a check for five hundred dollars, the boy grunts his awareness of the transaction, and I am laughing all over myself by the time I rejoin J. T.

Just as I am snuggling down beside him though I hear the front door bell going off again.

Forgit his hat? asks J. T.

I hope not, I say.

The deacon stands there leaning on the door frame and once again I'm thinking of those sweaty-looking eyeballs of his. I wonder if sweat makes your eyeballs pink because his are sure pink. Pink and gray and it strikes me that nobody I'd care to know is behind them.

I forgot one little thing, he says pleasantly. I forgot to tell you Traynor and I would like to buy up all of those records you made of the song. I tell you we sure do love it.

Well, love it or not, I'm not so stupid as to let them do that without making 'em pay. So I says, Well, that's gonna cost you. Because, really, that song never did sell all that good, so I was glad they were going to buy it up. But on the other hand, them two listening to my song by themselves, and nobody else getting to hear me sing it, give me a pause.

Well, one way or another the deacon showed me where I would come out ahead on any deal he had proposed so far. Didn't I give you five hundred dollars? he asked. What white man—and don't even need to mention colored—would give you more? We buy up all your records of that particular song: first, you git royalties. Let me ask you, how much you sell that song for in the first place? Fifty dollars? A hundred, I say. And no royalties from it yet, right? Right. Well, when we buy up all of them records you gonna git royalties. And that's gonna make all them race record shops sit up and take notice of Gracie Mae Still. And they gonna push all them other records of yourn they got. And you no doubt will become one of the big name colored recording artists. And then we can offer you another five hundred dollars for letting us do all this for you. And by God you'll be sittin' pretty! You can go out and buy you the kind of outfit a star should have. Plenty sequins and yards of red satin.

I had done unlocked the screen when I saw I could get some more money out of him. Now I held it wide open while he squeezed through the opening between me and the door. He whipped out another piece of paper and I signed it.

He sort of trotted out to the car and slid in beside Traynor, whose head was back against the seat. They swung around in a u-turn in front of the house and then they was gone.

J. T. was putting his shirt on when I got back to the bedroom. Yankees beat the Orioles 10–6, he said. I believe I'll drive out to Paschal's pond and go fishing. Wanta go?

While I was putting on my pants J. T. was holding the two checks.

I'm real proud of a woman that can make cash money without leavin' home, he said. And I said *Umph*. Because we met on the road with me singing in first one little low-life jook after another, making ten dollars a night for myself if I was lucky, and sometimes bringin' home nothing but my life. And J. T. just loved them times. The way I was fast and flashy and always on the go from one town to another. He loved the way my singin' made the dirt farmers cry like babies and the womens shout Honey, hush! But that's mens. They loves any style to which you can get 'em accustomed.

1956

My little grandbaby called me one night on the phone: Little Mama, Little Mama, there's a white man on the television singing one of your songs! Turn on channel 5.

Lord, if it wasn't Traynor. Still looking half asleep from the neck up, but kind of awake in a nasty way from the waist down. He wasn't doing too bad with my song either, but it wasn't just the song the people in the audience was screeching and screaming over, it was that nasty little jerk he was doing from the waist down.

Well, Lord have mercy, I said, listening to him. If I'da closed my eyes, it could have been me. He had followed every turning of my voice, side streets, avenues, red lights, train crossings and all. It give me a chill.

Everywhere I went I heard Traynor singing my song, and all the little white girls just eating it up. I never had so many ponytails switched across my line of vision in my life. They was so *proud*. He was a *genius*.

Well, all that year I was trying to lose weight anyway and that and high blood pressure and sugar kept me pretty well occupied. Traynor had made a smash from a song of mine, I still had seven hundred dollars of the original one thousand dollars in the bank, and I felt if I could just bring my weight down, life would be sweet.

1957

I lost ten pounds in 1956. That's what I give myself for Christmas. And J. T. and me and the children and their friends and grandkids of all description had just finished dinner—over which I had put on nine and a half of my lost ten—when who should appear at the front door but Traynor. Little Mama, Little Mama! It's that white man who sings — — —. The children didn't call it my song anymore. Nobody did. It was funny how that happened. Traynor and the deacon had bought up all my records, true, but on his record he had put "written by Gracie Mae Still." But that was just another name on the label, like "produced by Apex Records."

On the TV he was inclined to dress like the deacon told him. But now he looked presentable.

Merry Christmas, said he.

And same to you, Son.

I don't why I called him Son. Well, one way or another they're all our sons. The only requirement is that they be younger than us. But then again, Traynor seemed to be aging by the minute.

You looks tired, I said. Come on in and have a glass of Christmas cheer.

J. T. ain't never in his life been able to act decent to a white man he wasn't working for, but he poured Traynor a glass of bourbon and water, then he took all the children and grandkids and friends and whatnot out to the den. After while I heard Traynor's voice singing the song, coming from the stereo console. It was just the kind of Christmas present my kids would consider cute.

I looked at Traynor, complicit. But he looked like it was the last thing in the world he wanted to hear. His head was pitched forward over his lap, his hands holding his glass and his elbows on his knees.

I done sung that song seem like a million times this year, he said. I sung it on the Grand Ole Opry, I sung it on the Ed Sullivan show. I sung it on Mike Douglas, I sung it at the Cotton Bowl, the Orange Bowl. I sung it at Festivals. I sung it at Fairs. I sung it overseas in Rome, Italy, and once in a submarine *underseas*. I've sung it and sung it, and I'm making forty thousand dollars a day offa it, and you know what, I don't have the faintest notion what that song means.

Whatchumean, what do it mean? It mean what it says. All I could think was: These suckers is making forty thousand a *day* offa my song and now they gonna come back and try to swindle me out of the original thousand.

It's just a song, I said. Cagey. When you fool around with a lot of no count mens you sing a bunch of 'em. I shrugged.

Oh, he said. Well. He started brightening up. I just come by to tell you I think you are a great singer.

He didn't blush, saying that. Just said it straight out.

And I brought you a little Christmas present too. Now you take this little box and you hold it until I drive off. Then you take it outside under that first streetlight back up the street aways in front of that green house. Then you open the box and see . . . Well, just *see*.

What had come over this boy, I wondered, holding the box. I looked out the window in time to see another white man come up and get in the car with him and then two more cars full of white mens start out behind him. They was all in long black cars that looked like a funeral procession.

Little Mama, Little Mama, what it is? One of my grandkids come running up and started pulling at the box. It was wrapped in gay Christmas paper—the thick, rich kind that it's hard to picture folks making just to throw away.

J. T. and the rest of the crowd followed me out the house, up the street to the streetlight and in front of the green house. Nothing was there but somebody's gold-grilled white Cadillac. Brandnew and most distracting. We got to looking at it so till I almost forgot the little box in my hand. While the others were busy making 'miration I carefully took off the paper and ribbon and folded them up and put them in my pants pocket. What should I see but a pair of genuine solid gold caddy keys.

Dangling the keys in front of everybody's nose, I unlocked the caddy, motioned for J. T. to git in on the other side, and us didn't come back home for two days.

1960

Well, the boy was sure nuff famous by now. He was still a mite shy of twenty but already they was calling him the Emperor of Rock and Roll.

Then what should happen but the draft.

Well, says J. T. There goes all this Emperor of Rock and Roll business.

But even in the army the womens was on him like white on rice. We watched it on the News.

Dear Gracie Mae [he wrote from Germany],

How you? Fine I hope as this leaves me doing real well. Before I come in the army I was gaining a lot of weight and gitting jittery from making all them dumb movies.

137

*But now I exercise and eat right and get plenty of rest.
I'm more awake than I been in ten years.*

I wonder if you are writing any more songs?

Sincerely,
Traynor

I wrote him back:

Dear Son,

*We is all fine in the Lord's good grace and hope this
finds you the same. J. T. and me be out all times of the
day and night in that car you give me—which you know
you didn't have to do. Oh, and I do appreciate the mink
and the new self-cleaning oven. But if you send anymore
stuff to eat from Germany I'm going to have to open up
a store in the neighborhood just to get rid of it. Really,
we have more than enough of everything. The Lord is
good to us and we don't know Want.*

*Glad to here you is well and gitting your right rest.
There ain't nothing like exercising to help that along. J.
T. and me work some part of every day that we don't go
fishing in the garden.*

Well, so long Soldier.

Sincerely,
Gracie Mae

He wrote:

Dear Gracie Mae,

*I hope you and J. T. like that automatic power tiller I
had one of the stores back home send you. I went through
a mountain of catalogs looking for it—I wanted something that even a woman could use.*

*I've been thinking about writing some songs of my own
but every time I finish one it don't seem to be about
nothing I've actually lived myself. My agent keeps sending*

*me other people's songs but they just sound mooney. I can
hardly git through 'em without gagging.*

*Everybody still loves that song of yours. They ask me
all the time what do I think it means, really. I mean, they
want to know just what I want to know. Where out of
your life did it come from?*

*Sincerely,
Traynor*

1968

I didn't see the boy for seven years. No. Eight. Because just
about everybody was dead when I saw him again. Malcolm
X, King, the president and his brother, and even J. T. J. T.
died of a head cold. It just settled in his head like a block of
ice, he said, and nothing we did moved it until one day he
just leaned out the bed and died.

His good friend Horace helped me put him away, and then
about a year later Horace and me started going together. We
was sitting out on the front porch swing one summer night,
dusk-dark, and I saw this great procession of lights winding
to a stop.

Holy Toledo! said Horace. (He's got a real sexy voice like
Ray Charles.) Look *at* it. He meant the long line of flashy
cars and the white men in white summer suits jumping out
on the drivers' sides and standing at attention. With wings
they could pass for angels, with hoods they could be the
Klan.

Traynor comes waddling up the walk.

And suddenly I know what it is he could pass for. An Arab
like the ones you see in storybooks. Plump and soft and with
never a care about weight. Because with so much money,
who cares? Traynor is almost dressed like someone from a
storybook too. He has on, I swear, about ten necklaces. Two

sets of bracelets on his arms, at least one ring on every finger, and some kind of shining buckles on his shoes, so that when he walks you get quite a few twinkling lights.

Gracie Mae, he says, coming up to give me a hug. J. T.

I explain that J. T. passed. That this is Horace.

Horace, he says, puzzled but polite, sort of rocking back on his heels, Horace.

That's it for Horace. He goes in the house and don't come back.

Looks like you and me is gained a few, I say.

He laughs. The first time I ever heard him laugh. It don't sound much like a laugh and I can't swear that it's better than no laugh a'tall.

He's gitting fat for sure, but he's still slim compared to me. I'll never see three hundred pounds again and I've just about said (excuse me) fuck it. I got to thinking about it one day an' I thought: aside from the fact that they say it's unhealthy, my fat ain't never been no trouble. Mens always have loved me. My kids ain't never complained. Plus they's fat. And fat like I is I looks distinguished. You see me coming and know somebody's *there*.

Gracie Mae, he says, I've come with a personal invitation to you to my house tomorrow for dinner. He laughed. What did it sound like? I couldn't place it. See them men out there? he asked me. I'm sick and tired of eating with them. They don't never have nothing to talk about. That's why I eat so much. But if you come to dinner tomorrow we can talk about the old days. You can tell me about that farm I bought you.

I sold it, I said.

You did?

Yeah, I said, I did. Just cause I said I liked to exercise by working in a garden didn't mean I wanted five hundred acres! Anyhow, I'm a city girl now. Raised in the country it's true. Dirt poor—the whole bit—but that's all behind me now.

Oh well, he said, I didn't mean to offend you.

We sat a few minutes listening to the crickets.

Then he said: You wrote that song while you was still on the farm, didn't you, or was it right after you left?

You had somebody spying on me? I asked.

You and Bessie Smith got into a fight over it once, he said.

You *is* been spying on me!

But I don't know what the fight was about, he said. Just like I don't know what happened to your second husband. Your first one died in the Texas electric chair. Did you know that? Your third one beat you up, stole your touring costumes and your car and retired with a chorine to Tuskegee. He laughed. He's still there.

I had been mad, but suddenly I calmed down. Traynor was talking very dreamily. It was dark but seems like I could tell his eyes weren't right. It was like some*thing* was sitting there talking to me but not necessarily with a person behind it.

You gave up on marrying and seem happier for it. He laughed again. I married but it never went like it was supposed to. I never could squeeze any of my own life either into it or out of it. It was like singing somebody else's record. I copied the way it was sposed to be *exactly* but I never had a clue what marriage meant.

I bought her a diamond ring big as your fist. I bought her clothes. I built her a mansion. But right away she didn't want the boys to stay there. Said they smoked up the bottom floor. Hell, there were *five* floors.

No need to grieve, I said. No need to. Plenty more where she come from.

He perked up. That's part of what that song means, ain't it? No need to grieve. Whatever it is, there's plenty more down the line.

I never really believed that way back when I wrote that song, I said. It was all bluffing then. The trick is to live long enough to put your young bluffs to use. Now if I was to sing that song today I'd tear it up. 'Cause I done lived long enough to know it's *true*. Them words could hold me up.

I ain't lived that long, he said.

Look like you on your way, I said. I don't know why, but the boy seemed to need some encouraging. And I don't know, seem like one way or another you talk to rich white folks and you end up reassuring *them*. But what the hell, by now I feel something for the boy. I wouldn't be in his bed all alone in the middle of the night for nothing. Couldn't be nothing worse than being famous the world over for something you don't even understand. That's what I tried to tell Bessie. She wanted that same song. Overheard me practicing it one day, said, with her hands on her hips: Gracie Mae, I'ma sing your song tonight. I *likes* it.

Your lips be too swole to sing, I said. She was mean and she was strong, but I trounced her.

Ain't you famous enough with your own stuff? I said. Leave mine alone. Later on, she thanked me. By then she was Miss Bessie Smith to the World, and I was still Miss Gracie Mae Nobody from Notasulga.

The next day all these limousines arrived to pick me up. Five cars and twelve bodyguards. Horace picked that morning to start painting the kitchen.

Don't paint the kitchen, fool, I said. The only reason that dumb boy of ours is going to show me his mansion is because he intends to present us with a new house.

What you gonna do with it? he asked me, standing there in his shirtsleeves stirring the paint.

Sell it. Give it to the children. Live in it on weekends. It don't matter what I do. He sure don't care.

Horace just stood there shaking his head. Mama you sure looks *good*, he says. Wake me up when you git back.

Fool, I say, and pat my wig in front of the mirror.

The boy's house is something else. First you come to this mountain, and then you commence to drive and drive up this road that's lined with magnolias. Do magnolias grow on mountains? I was wondering. And you come to lakes and you come to ponds and you come to deer and you come up on some sheep. And I figure these two is sposed to represent England and Wales. Or something out of Europe. And you just keep on coming to stuff. And it's all pretty. Only the man driving my car don't look at nothing but the road. Fool. And then *finally*, after all this time, you begin to go up the driveway. And there's more magnolias—only they're not in such good shape. It's sort of cool up this high and I don't think they're gonna make it. And then I see this building that looks like if it had a name it would be The Tara Hotel. Columns and steps and outdoor chandeliers and rocking chairs. Rocking chairs? Well, and there's the boy on the steps dressed in a dark green satin jacket like you see folks wearing on TV late at night, and he looks sort of like a fat dracula with all that house rising behind him, and standing beside him there's this little white vision of loveliness that he introduces as his wife.

He's nervous when he introduces us and he says to her: This is Gracie Mae Still, I want you to know me. I mean . . . and she gives him a look that would fry meat.

Won't you come in, Gracie Mae, she says, and that's the last I see of her.

He fishes around for something to say or do and decides to escort me to the kitchen. We go through the entry and the parlor and the breakfast room and the dining room and the servants' passage and finally get there. The first thing I notice is that, altogether, there are five stoves. He looks about to introduce me to one.

Wait a minute, I say. Kitchens don't do nothing for me. Let's go sit on the front porch.

Well, we hike back and we sit in the rocking chairs rocking until dinner.

Gracie Mae, he says down the table, taking a piece of fried

chicken from the woman standing over him, I got a little surprise for you.

It's a house, ain't it? I ask, spearing a chitlin.

You're getting *spoiled*, he says. And the way he says *spoiled* sounds funny. He slurs it. It sounds like his tongue is too thick for his mouth. Just that quick he's finished the chicken and is now eating chitlins *and* a pork chop. *Me* spoiled, I'm thinking.

I already got a house. Horace is right this minute painting the kitchen. I bought that house. My kids feel comfortable in that house.

But this one I bought you is just like mine. Only a little smaller.

I still don't need no house. And anyway who would clean it?

He looks surprised.

Really, I think, some peoples advance *so* slowly.

I hadn't thought of that. But what the hell, I'll get you somebody to live in.

I don't want other folks living 'round me. Makes me nervous.

You *don't*? It *do*?

What I want to wake up and see folks I don't even know for?

He just sits there downtable staring at me. Some of that feeling is in the song, ain't it? Not the words, the *feeling*. What I want to wake up and see folks I don't even know for? But I see twenty folks a day I don't even know, including my wife.

This food wouldn't be bad to wake up to though, I said. The boy had found the genius of corn bread.

He looked at me real hard. He laughed. Short. They want what you got but they don't want you. They want what I got only it ain't mine. That's what makes 'em so hungry for me when I sing. They getting the flavor of something but they ain't getting the thing itself. They like a pack of hound dogs trying to gobble up a scent.

You talking 'bout your fans?

Right. Right. He says.

Don't worry 'bout your fans, I say. They don't know their asses from a hole in the ground. I doubt there's a honest one in the bunch.

That's the point. Dammit, that's the point! He hits the table with his fist. It's so solid it don't even quiver. You need a honest audience! You can't have folks that's just gonna lie right back to you.

Yeah, I say, it was small compared to yours, but I had one. It would have been worth my life to try to sing 'em somebody else's stuff that I didn't know nothing about.

He must have pressed a buzzer under the table. One of his flunkies zombies up.

Git Johnny Carson, he says.

On the phone? asks the zombie.

On the phone, says Traynor, what you think I mean, git him offa the front porch? Move your ass.

So two weeks later we's on the Johnny Carson show.

Traynor is all corseted down nice and looks a little bit fat but mostly good. And all the woman that grew up on him and my song squeal and squeal. Traynor says: The lady who wrote my first hit record is here with us tonight, and she's agreed to sing it for all of us, just like she sung it forty-five years ago. Ladies and Gentlemen, the great Gracie Mae Still!

Well, I had tried to lose a couple of pounds my own self, but failing that I had me a very big dress made. So I sort of rolls over next to Traynor, who is dwarfted by me, so that when he puts his arm around back of me to try to hug me it looks funny to the audience and they laugh.

I can see this pisses him off. But I smile out there at 'em. Imagine squealing for twenty years and not knowing why you're squealing? No more sense of endings and beginnings than hogs.

It don't matter, Son, I say. Don't fret none over me.

I commence to sing. And I sound—wonderful. Being able to sing good ain't all about having a good singing voice a'tall. A good singing voice helps. But when you come up in the Hard Shell Baptist church like I did you understand early that the fellow that sings is the singer. Them that waits for programs and arrangements and letters from home is just good voices occupying body space.

So there I am singing my own song, my own way. And I give it all I got and enjoy every minute of it. When I finish Traynor is standing up clapping and clapping and beaming at first me and then the audience like I'm his mama for true. The audience claps politely for about two seconds.

Traynor looks disgusted.

He comes over and tries to hug me again. The audience laughs.

Johnny Carson looks at us like we both weird.

Traynor is mad as hell. He's supposed to sing something called a love ballad. But instead he takes the mike, turns to me and says: Now see if my imitation still holds up. He goes into the same song, *our* song, I think, looking out at his flaky audience. And he sings it just the way he always did. My voice, my tone, my inflection, everything. But he forgets a couple of lines. Even before he's finished the matronly squeals begin.

He sits down next to me looking whipped.

It don't matter, Son, I say, patting his hand. You don't even know those people. Try to make the people you know happy.

Is that in the song? he asks.

Maybe. I say.

1977

For a few years I hear from him, then nothing. But trying to lose weight takes all the attention I got to spare. I finally faced up to the fact that my fat is the hurt I don't admit, not even to myself, and that I been trying to bury it from the day I was born. But also when you git real old, to tell the truth, it ain't as pleasant. It gits lumpy and slack. Yuck. So one day I said to Horace, I'ma git this shit offa me.

And he fell in with the program like he always try to do and Lord such a procession of salads and cottage cheese and fruit juice!

One night I dreamed Traynor had split up with his fifteenth wife. He said: *You meet 'em for no reason. You date 'em for no reason. You marry 'em for no reason. I do it all but I swear it's just like somebody else doing it. I feel like I can't remember Life.*

The boy's in trouble, I said to Horace.

You've always said that, he said.

I have?

Yeah. You always said he looked asleep. You can't sleep through life if you wants to live it.

You not such a fool after all, I said, pushing myself up with my cane and hobbling over to where he was. Let me sit down on your lap, I said, while this salad I ate takes effect.

In the morning we heard Traynor was dead. Some said fat, some said heart, some said alcohol, some said drugs. One of the children called from Detroit. Them dumb fans of his is on a crying rampage, she said. You just ought to turn on the TV.

But I didn't want to see 'em. They was crying and crying and didn't even know what they was crying for. One day this is going to be a pitiful country, I thought.

How Did I Get Away with Killing One of the Biggest Lawyers in the State? It Was Easy.

"My mother and father were not married. I never knew him. My mother must have loved him, though; she never talked against him when I was little. It was like he never existed. We lived on Poultry Street. Why it was called Poultry Street I never knew. I guess at one time there must have been a chicken factory somewhere along there. It was right near the center of town. I could walk to the state capitol in less than ten minutes. I could see the top—it was gold—of the capitol building from the front yard. When I was a little girl I used to think it was real gold, shining up there, and then they bought an eagle and put him on top, and when I used to walk up there I couldn't see the top of the building from the ground, it was so high, and I used to reach down and run my hand over the grass. It was like a rug, that grass was, so springy and silky and deep. They had these big old trees, too. Oaks and magnolias; and I thought the magnolia trees were beautiful and one night I climbed up in one of them and got a bloom and took it home. But the air in our house blighted it; it turned brown the minute I took it inside and the petals dropped off.

"Mama worked in private homes. That's how she described her job, to make it sound nicer. 'I work in private homes,' she would say, and that sounded nicer, she thought, than saying 'I'm a maid.'

"Sometimes she made six dollars a day, working in two private homes. Most of the time she didn't make that much. By the time she paid the rent and bought milk and bananas there wasn't anything left.

"She used to leave me alone sometimes because there was no one to keep me—and then there was an old woman up the street who looked after me for a while—and by the time she died she was more like a mother to me than Mama was. Mama was so tired every night when she came home I never hardly got the chance to talk to her. And then sometimes she would go out at night, or bring men home—but they never thought of marrying her. And they sure didn't want to be bothered with me. I guess most of them were like my own father; had children somewhere of their own that they'd left. And then they came to my Mama, who fell for them every time. And I think she may have had a couple of abortions, like some of the women did, who couldn't feed any more mouths. But she tried.

"Anyway, she was a nervous kind of woman. I think she had spells or something because she was so tired. But I didn't understand anything then about exhaustion, worry, lack of a proper diet; I just thought she wanted to work, to be away from the house. I didn't blame her. Where we lived people sometimes just threw pieces of furniture they didn't want over the railing. And there was broken glass and rags everywhere. The place stunk, especially in the summer. And children were always screaming and men were always cussing and women were always yelling about something. . . . It was nothing for a girl or woman to be raped. I was raped myself, when I was twelve, and my Mama never knew and I never told anybody. For, what could they do? It was just a boy, passing through. Somebody's cousin from the North.

"One time my Mama was doing day's work at a private home and took me with her. It was like being in fairyland. Everything was spotless and new, even before Mama started cleaning. I met the woman in the house and played with her children. I didn't even see the man, but he was in there somewhere, while I was out in the yard with the children. I was fourteen, but I guess I looked like a grown woman. Or maybe I looked fourteen. Anyway, the next day, he picked me up when I was coming from school and he said my Mama had asked him to do it. I got in the car with him . . . he took me to his law office, a big office in the middle of town, and he started asking me questions about 'how do you all live?' and 'what grade are you in?' and stuff like that. And then he began to touch me, and I pulled away. But he kept touching me and I was scared . . . he raped me. But afterward he told me he hadn't forced me, that I felt something for him, and he gave me some money. I was crying, going down the stairs. I wanted to kill him.

"I never told Mama. I thought that would be the end of it. But about two days later, on my way from school, he stopped his car again, and I got in. This time we went to his house; nobody was there. And he made me get into his wife's bed. After we'd been doing this for about three weeks, he told me he loved me. I didn't love him, but he had begun to look a little better to me. Really, I think, because he was so clean. He bathed a lot and never smelled even alive, to tell the truth. Or maybe it was the money he gave me, or the presents he bought. I told Mama I had a job after school baby-sitting. And she was glad that I could buy things I needed for school. But it was all from him.

"This went on for two years. He wouldn't let me get pregnant, he said, and I didn't. I would just lay up there in his wife's bed and work out algebra problems or think about what new thing I was going to buy. But one day, when I got home, Mama was there ahead of me, and she saw me get out of his car. I knew when he was driving off that I was going to get it.

"Mama asked me didn't I know he was a white man? Didn't I know he was a married man with two children? Didn't I have good sense? And do you know what I told her? *I told her he loved me.* Mama was crying and praying at the same time by then. The neighbors heard both of us screaming and crying, because Mama beat me almost to death with the cord from the electric iron. She just hacked it off the iron, still on the ironing board. She beat me till she couldn't raise her arm. And then she had one of her fits, just twitching and sweating and trying to claw herself into the floor. This scared me more than the beating. That night she told me something I hadn't paid much attention to before. She said: 'On top of everything else, that man's daddy goes on the TV every night and says folks like us ain't even human.' It was his daddy who had stood in the schoolhouse door saying it would be over his dead body before any black children would come into a white school.

"But do you think that stopped me? No. I would look at his daddy on TV ranting and raving about how integration was a communist plot, and I would just think of how different his son Bubba was from his daddy! Do you understand what I'm saying. I thought he *loved* me. That *meant* something to me. What did I know about 'equal rights'? What did I care about 'integration'? I was sixteen! I wanted somebody to tell me I was pretty, and he was telling me that all the time. I even thought it was *brave* of him to go with me. History? What did I know about History?

"I began to hate Mama. We argued about Bubba all the time, for months. And I still slipped out to meet him, because Mama had to work. I told him how she beat me, and about how much she despised him—he was really pissed off that any black person could despise him—and about how she had these spells. . . . Well, the day I became seventeen, the *day* of my seventeenth birthday, I signed papers in his law office, and I had my mother committed to an insane asylum.

"After Mama had been in Carthage Insane Asylum for three months, she managed somehow to get a lawyer. An old slick-headed man who smoked great big black cigars. People laughed at him because he didn't even have a law office, but he was the only lawyer that would touch the case, because Bubba's daddy was such a big deal. And we all gathered in the judge's chambers—because he wasn't about to let this case get out. Can you imagine, if it had? And Mama's old lawyer told the judge how Bubba's daddy had tried to buy him off. And Bubba got up and swore he'd never touched me. And then I got up and said Mama was insane. And do you know what? By that time it was true. Mama *was* insane. She had no mind left at all. They had given her shock treatments or something. . . . God knows what else they gave her. But she was as vacant as an empty eye socket. She just sat sort of hunched over, and her hair was white.

"And after all this, Bubba wanted us to keep going together. Mama was just an obstacle that he felt he had removed. But I just suddenly—in a way I don't even pretend to understand—woke up. It was like everything up to then had been some kind of dream. And I told him I wanted to get Mama out. But he wouldn't do it; he just kept trying to make me go with him. And sometimes—out of habit, I guess—I did. My body did what it was being paid to do. And Mama died. And I killed Bubba.

"How did I get away with killing one of the biggest lawyers in the state? It was easy. He kept a gun in his desk drawer at the office and one night I took it out and shot him. I shot him while he was wearing his thick winter overcoat, so I wouldn't have to see him bleed. But I don't think I took the time to wipe off my fingerprints, because, to tell the truth, I couldn't stand it another minute in that place. No one came after me, and I read in the paper the next day that he'd been killed by burglars. I guess they thought 'burglars' had stolen all that money Bubba kept in his safe—but I had it. One of the carrots Bubba always dangled before me was that he was going to send me to college: I didn't see why he shouldn't do it.

"The strangest thing was, Bubba's wife came over to the house and asked me if I'd mind looking after the children while she went to Bubba's funeral. I did it, of course, because I was afraid she'd suspect something if I didn't. So on the day he was buried I was in his house, sitting on his wife's bed with his children, and eating fried chicken his wife, Julie, had cooked."

ELETHIA

A certain perverse experience shaped Elethia's life, and made it possible for it to be true that she carried with her at all times a small apothecary jar of ashes.

There was in the town where she was born a man whose ancestors had owned a large plantation on which everything under the sun was made or grown. There had been many slaves, and though slavery no longer existed, this grandson of former slaveowners held a quaint proprietary point of view where colored people were concerned. He adored them, of course. Not in the present—it went without saying—but at that time, stopped, just on the outskirts of his memory: his grandfather's time.

This man, whom Elethia never saw, opened a locally famous restaurant on a busy street near the center of town. He called it "Old Uncle Albert's." In the window of the restaurant was a stuffed likeness of Uncle Albert himself, a small brown dummy of waxen skin and glittery black eyes. His lips were intensely smiling and his false teeth shone. He carried a covered tray in one hand, raised level with his shoulder, and over his other arm was draped a white napkin.

Black people could not eat at Uncle Albert's, though they worked, of course, in the kitchen. But on Saturday afternoons a crowd of them would gather to look at "Uncle Albert" and discuss how near to the real person the dummy looked. Only the very old people remembered Albert Porter, and their eyesight was no better than their memory. Still there was a comfort somehow in knowing that Albert's likeness was here before them daily and that if he smiled as a dummy in a fashion he was not known to do as a man, well, perhaps both memory and eyesight were wrong.

The old people appeared grateful to the rich man who owned the restaurant for giving them a taste of vicarious fame. They could pass by the gleaming window where Uncle Albert stood, seemingly in the act of sprinting forward with his tray, and know that though niggers were not allowed in the front door, ole Albert was already inside, and looking mighty pleased about it, too.

For Elethia the fascination was in Uncle Albert's fingernails. She wondered how his creator had got them on. She wondered also about the white hair that shone so brightly under the lights. One summer she worked as a salad girl in the restaurant's kitchen, and it was she who discovered the truth about Uncle Albert. He was not a dummy; he was stuffed. Like a bird, like a moose's head, like a giant bass. He was stuffed.

One night after the restaurant was closed someone broke in and stole nothing but Uncle Albert. It was Elethia and her friends, boys who were in her class and who called her "Thia." Boys who bought Thunderbird and shared it with her. Boys who laughed at her jokes so much they hardly remembered she was also cute. Her tight buddies. They carefully burned Uncle Albert to ashes in the incinerator of their high school, and each of them kept a bottle of his ashes. And for each of them

what they knew and their reaction to what they knew was
profound.

The experience undercut whatever solid foundation Elethia
had assumed she had. She became secretive, wary, looking over
her shoulder at the slightest noise. She haunted the museums
of any city in which she found herself, looking, usually, at the
remains of Indians, for they were plentiful everywhere she
went. She discovered some of the Indian warriors and maidens
in the museums were also real, stuffed people, painted and
wigged and robed, like figures in the Rue Morgue. There were
so many, in fact, that she could not possibly steal and burn
them all. Besides, she did not know if these figures—with their
valiant glass eyes—would wish to be burned.

About Uncle Albert she felt she knew.

What kind of man was Uncle Albert?

Well, the old folks said, he wasn't nobody's uncle and
wouldn't sit still for nobody to call him that, either.

Why, said another old-timer, I recalls the time they hung a
boy's privates on a post at the end of the street where all the
black folks shopped, just to scare us all, you understand, and
Albert Porter was the one took 'em down and buried 'em. Us
never did find the rest of the boy though. It was just like
always—they would throw you in the river with a big old green
log tied to you, and down to the bottom you sunk.

He continued:

Albert was born in slavery and he remembered that his
mama and daddy didn't know nothing about slavery'd done
ended for near 'bout ten years, the boss man kept them so
ignorant of the law, you understand. So he was a mad so-an'-
so when he found out. They used to beat him severe trying to
make him forget the past and grin and act like a nigger.
(Whenever you saw somebody acting like a nigger, Albert said,
you could be sure he seriously disremembered his past.) But
he never would. Never would work in the big house as head
servant, neither—always broke up stuff. The master at that

time was always going around pinching him too. Looks like he hated Albert more than anything—but he never would let him get a job anywhere else. And Albert never would leave home. Too stubborn.

Stubborn, yes. My land, another one said. That's why it do seem strange to see that dummy that sposed to be ole Albert with his mouth open. All them teeth. Hell, all Albert's teeth was knocked out before he was grown.

Elethia went away to college and her friends went into the army because they were poor and that was the way things were. They discovered Uncle Alberts all over the world. Elethia was especially disheartened to find Uncle Alberts in her textbooks, in the newspapers and on TV.

Everywhere she looked there was an Uncle Albert (and many Aunt Albertas, it goes without saying).

But she had her jar of ashes, the old-timers' memories written down, and her friends who wrote that in the army they were learning skills that would get them through more than a plate glass window.

And she was careful that, no matter how compelling the hype, Uncle Alberts, in her own mind, were not permitted to exist.

THE LOVER

For Joanne

Her husband had wanted a child and so she gave him one as a gift, because she liked her husband and admired him greatly. Still, it had taken a lot out of her, especially in the area of sexual response. She had never been particularly passionate with him, not even during the early years of their marriage; it was more a matter of being sexually comfortable. After the birth of the child she simply never thought of him sexually at all. She supposed their marriage was better than most, even so. He was a teacher at a University near their home in the Midwest and cared about his students—which endeared him to her, who had had so many uncaring teachers; and toward her own work, which was poetry (that she set very successfully to jazz), he showed the utmost understanding and respect.

She was away for two months at an artists' colony in New England and that is where she met Ellis, whom she immediately dubbed, once she had got over thinking he resembled (with his top lip slightly raised over his right eye-tooth when he smiled) a wolf, "The Lover." They met one evening before dinner as she was busy ignoring the pompous bullshit of a fellow black poet, a man many years older than she who had no concept of other people's impatience. He had been rambling on about himself for over an hour and she had at first respectfully listened because she was the kind of person whose adult behavior—in a situation like this—reflected her childhood instruction; and she was instructed as a child, to be polite.

She was always getting herself stuck in one-sided conversations of this sort because she was—the people who talked to her seemed to think—an excellent listener. She was, up to a point. She was genuinely interested in older artists in particular and would sit, entranced, as they spun out their tales of art and lust (the gossip, though old, was delicious!) of forty years ago.

But there had been only a few of these artists whose tales she had listened to until the end. For as soon as a note of bragging entered into the conversation—a famous name dropped here, an expensive Paris restaurant's menu dropped there, and especially the names of the old artist's neglected books and on what occasion the wretched creature had insulted this or that weasel of a white person—her mind began to turn about upon itself until it rolled out some of her own thoughts to take the place of the trash that was coming in.

And so it was on that evening before dinner. The old poet—whose work was exceedingly mediocre, and whose only attractions, as far as she was concerned, were his age and his rather bitter wit—fastened his black, bloodshot eyes upon her (in which she read desperation and a prayer of unstrenuous seduction) and held her to a close attention to his words.

Except that she had perfected the trick—as had many of her contemporaries who hated to be rude and who, also, had a strong sense of self-preservation (because the old poet, though, she thought, approaching senility, was yet a powerful figure in black literary circles and thought nothing of using his considerable influence to thwart the careers of younger talents)—of keeping her face quite animated and turned full onto the speaker, while inside her head she could be trying out the shades of paint with which to improve the lighting of her house. In fact, so intense did her concentration appear, it seemed she read the speaker's lips.

Ellis, who would be her lover, had come into the room and sat down on a chair by the fire. For although it was the middle of summer, a fire was needed against the chilly New England evenings.

"Have you been waiting long?" he asked.

And it suddenly occurred to her that indeed she had.

"But of course," she answered absently, noting the crooked smile that reminded her of a snarling, though not disagreeable, wolf—and turned back just as the old poet jealously reached out his hand to draw her attention to the, for him, hilarious ending of his story. She laughed and slapped her knee, a gesture of such fraudulent folksiness that she was soon laughing in earnest. Catching Ellis's eye as she thus amused herself she noticed therein a particular gleam that she instantly recognized.

"My lover," she thought, noticing for the first time his head of blue-black curls, his eyes as brown as the Mississippi, his skin that was not as successfully tanned as it might have been but which would definitely do. He was thin and tall, with practically no hips in the beige twill jeans he wore.

At dinner they sat together, looking out at the blue New England mountains in the distance, as the sun left tracings of orange and pink against the pale blue sky. He had heard she'd won some sort of prize—a prestigious one—for her "jazzed-up" poetry, and the way he said it made her glance critically at his long fingers wrapped around his wine glass. She wondered if they would be as sensitive on her skin as they looked. She had never heard of him, though she did not say so, probably because he had already said it for her. He talked a good deal—easily and early—about himself, and she was quite relaxed—even entertained—in her listener's role.

He wondered what, *if anything*, younger poets like herself had to say, since he was of the opinion that not much was learned about life until the middle years. He was in his forties. Of course he didn't look it, but he was much older than she, he said, and the reason that he was not better known was because he could not find a publisher for his two novels (still, by the way, unpublished—in case she knew publishers) or for his poetry, which an acquaintance of his had compared to something or other by Montaigne.

"You're lovely," he said into the brief silence.

"And you seem bright," she automatically replied.

She had blocked him out since his mention of the two unpublished novels. By the time he began complaining about the preferential treatment publishers now gave minorities and women she was on the point of yawning or gazing idly about the room. But she did not do either for a very simple reason: when she had first seen him she had thought—after the wolf thing—"my lover," and had liked, deep down inside, the illicit sound of it. She had never had a lover; he would be her first. Afterwards, she would be truly a woman of her time. She also responded to his curly hair and slim, almost nonexistent hips, in a surprisingly passionate way.

She was a woman who, after many tribulations in her life, few of which she ever discussed even with close friends, had reached the point of being generally pleased with herself. This self-acceptance was expressed in her eyes, which were large, dark and clear and which, more often than not, seemed predisposed to smile. Though not tall, her carriage gave the illusion of height, as did her carefully selected tall sandals and her naturally tall hair, which stood in an elegant black afro with exactly seven strands of silver hair—of which she was very proud (she was just thirty-one)—shining across the top. She wore long richly colored skirts that—when she walked—parted without warning along the side, and exposed a flash of her creamy brown thigh, and legs that were curvaceous and strong. If she came late to the dining room and stood in the doorway a moment longer than necessary—looking about for a place to sit after she had her tray—for that moment the noise from the cutlery already in use was still.

What others minded at the Colony—whether too many frogs in the frog pond (which was used for swimming) or not enough wine with the veal (there was talk of cutting out wine with meals altogether, and thereby ending a fine old Colony tradition!)—she did not seem to mind. She seemed open, bright, occasionally preoccupied, but always ready with an appreciative ear, or at times a humorous, if outdated joke of her own (which she nevertheless told with gusto and found funny herself, because she would laugh and laugh at it, regardless of what her listeners did). She seemed never to strain over her work, and literally never complained about its progress—or lack thereof. It was as if she worked only for herself, for her own enjoyment (or salvation) and was—whether working or simply thinking of working—calm about it.

Even the distraction caused by the birth of her child was a price she was, ultimately, prepared to pay. She did not intend to have a second one, after all—that would be too stupid—and this one would, before she knew it, be grown up enough for boarding school.

Relishing her short freedom during the summer as much as she contemplated enjoyment of her longer future one, she threw herself headlong into the interim relationship with Ellis, a professional lover of mainly older women artists who came to the Colony every year to work and play.

A New York Jew of considerable charm, intellectual petti-

ness, and so vast and uncritical a love of all things European
it struck one as an illness (and who hated Brooklyn—where
he had grown up—his parents, Jewish culture, and all he
had observed of black behavior in New York City), Ellis found
the listening silence of "the dark woman," as he euphemistic-
ally called her, restorative—after his endless evenings with
talkative women who wrote for *Esquire* and the *New York
Times*. Such women made it possible for him to be included
in the proper tennis sets and swimming parties at the
Colony—in which he hoped to meet contacts who would
help his career along—but they were also driven to examine
each and every one of their own thoughts aloud. His must
be the attentive ear, since they had already "made it" and
were comfortable exposing their own charming foibles to
him, while he, not having made it yet, could afford to expose
nothing that might discourage their assistance in his behalf.

It amused and thrilled him to almost hear the "click" when
his eyes met those of the jazz poet. "Sex," he thought. And,
"rest."

Of course he mistook her intensity.

After sitting before her piano for hours, setting one of her
poems to music, she would fling open her cabin door and
wave to him as he walked by on his way to or from the lake.
He was writing a novella about his former wife and composed
it in longhand down at the lake ("So if I get fed up with it I
can toss myself in," he joked) and then took it back to his
studio with him to type. She would call to him, her hair
and clothing very loose, and entice him into her cabin with
promises of sympathy and half her lunch.

When they made love she was disappointed. He did not
appear to believe in unhurried pleasure, and thought the
things she suggested he might do to please her very awkward
at the least. But it hardly mattered, since what mattered was
the fact of having a lover. She liked snuggling up to him,
liked kissing him along the sides of his face—his cheeks were
just beginning to be a trifle flabby but would still be good

for several years—and loved to write him silly letters—scorching with passion and promises of abandon—that made her seem head over heels in love. She enjoyed writing the letters because she enjoyed feeling to her full capacity and for as long as possible the excitement having a lover brought. It was the kind of excitement she'd felt years ago, in high school and perhaps twice in college (once when she'd fallen for a student and once when she was seduced—with her help and consent—by a teacher), and she recognized it as a feeling to be enjoyed for all it was worth. Her body felt on fire, her heart jumped in her breast, her pulse raced—she was aware, for the first time in years, of actually *needing* to make love.

He began to think he must fight her off, at least a little bit. She was too intense, he said. He did not have time for intense relationships, that's why he had finally accepted a divorce from his wife. He was also writing a great poem which he had begun in 1950 and which—now that he was at the Colony—he hoped to finish. She should concentrate on her own work if she expected to win any more prizes. She *wanted* to win more, didn't she?

She laughed at him, but would not tell him why. Instead she tried, very gently (while sitting on his lap with her bosom maternally opposite his face), to tell him he misunderstood. That she wanted nothing from him beyond the sensation of being in love itself. (His stare was at first blank, then cynical, at this.) As for her work, she did not do hers the way he apparently did his. Hers did not mean to her what he seemed to think it meant. It did not get in the way of her living, for example, and if it ever did, she felt sure she would remove it. Prizes were nice—especially if they brought one money (which one might then use to explore Barbados! China! Mozambique!)—but they were not rewards she could count on. Her life, on the other hand, *was* a reward she could count on. (He became impatient with this explanation and a little angry.)

It was their first quarrel.

When he saw her again she had spent the weekend (which had been coming up) in nearby Boston. She looked cheerful, happy and relaxed. From her letters to him—which he had thought embarrassingly self-revealing and erotic, though flattering, of course, to him—he had assumed she was on the point of declaring her undying love and of wanting to run away with him. Instead, she had gone off for two days, without mentioning it to him. And she had gone, so she said, by herself!

She soothed him as best she could. Lied, which she hated more than anything, about her work. "It was going so *poorly*," she complained (and the words rang metallic in her mouth); "I just couldn't bear staying here doing nothing where working conditions are so *idyllic*!" He appeared somewhat mollified. Actually, her work was going fine and she had sent off to her publishers a completed book of poems and jazz arrangements—which was what she had come to the Colony to do. "Your work was going swimmingly down at the lake," she giggled. "I didn't wish to disturb you."

And yet it was clear he was disturbed.

So she did not tell him she had flown all the way home.

He was always questioning her now about her town, her house, her child, her husband. She found herself describing her husband as if to a prospective bride. She lingered over the wiry bronze of his hair, the evenness of his teeth, his black, black eyes, the thrilling timbre of his deep voice. It *was* an exceptionally fine voice, it seemed to her now, listening to Ellis's rather whining one. Though, on second thought, it was perhaps nothing special.

At night, after a rousing but unsatisfactory evening with Ellis, she dreamed of her husband making love to her on the kitchen floor at home, where the sunlight collected in a pool beneath the window, and lay in bed next day dreaming of all the faraway countries, daring adventures, passionate lovers still to be found.

PETUNIAS

*This is what they read on the next to the last page of the diary
they found after her death in the explosion:*

As soon as my son got off the bus from Vietnam I could tell
he was different. He said, Mama, I'm going to show you how
to make bombs. He went with me to the house, me thinking
it was all a big joke. He had all of the stuff in a footlocker
and in his duffel bag among his clothes. So it wouldn't jar,
he said.

Son, I said, I don't think I want that stuff in my house.

But he just laughed. Let's make a big noise in Tranquil,
Mississippi, he said.

We have always lived in Tranquil. My daddy's grandmama
was a slave on the Tearslee Plantation. They dug up her grave
when I started agitating in the Movement. One morning I
found her dust dumped over my verbena bed, a splintery leg
bone had fell among my petunias.

167

COMING APART

BY WAY OF INTRODUCTION TO LORDE, TEISH AND GARDNER

*In 1979 I was invited by Laura Lederer to write an introduc-
tion to the Third World Women's chapter of a book she was
then editing about pornography called* Take Back the Night.
*When I agreed to write it, she sent me three essays, by Audre
Lorde, Luisah Teish and Tracy A. Gardner. I was moved by
the essays and the following "introduction"—published
in* Ms. *before book publication simply as "A Fable"—was the
result.*

*The "fable" works, I think, as a story, and in fact it appears
as one, rather than as an introduction, in* Take Back the
Night. *However, if I had written it as a story originally, making
up all the parts myself, or choosing my informants, my analysis
of the roots of vicious white male pornographic treatment of*

*white women would have been somewhat different, with a
longer historical perspective.*

    *While not denying the obvious connections between the
lynching of black men and women (which, as Gardner states,
became prevalent only after the Civil War), and the pornographic abuse of white women, I would have argued that the
more ancient roots of modern pornography are to be found in
the almost always pornographic treatment of black women,
who, from the moment they entered slavery, even in their own
homelands, were subjected to rape as the "logical" convergence
of sex and violence. Conquest, in short.*

    *For centuries the black woman has served as the primary
pornographic "outlet" for white men in Europe and America.
We need only think of the black women used as breeders, raped
for the pleasure and profit of their owners. We need only think
of the license the "master" of the slave woman enjoyed. But,
most telling of all, we need only study the old slave societies of
the South to note the sadistic treatment—at the hands of white
"gentlemen"—of "beautiful, young quadroons and octoroons"
who became increasingly (and were deliberately bred to
become) indistinguishable from white women, and were the
more highly prized as slave mistresses because of this.*

    *Although this "fable," "story," "introduction" was itself lab-
eled pornographic and banned temporarily by at least one
school district in the United States, I believe it is only by
writing stories in which pornography is confronted openly and
explicitly that writers can make a contribution, in their own
medium, to a necessary fight.*

A middle-aged husband comes home after a long day at the
office. His wife greets him at the door with the news that
dinner is ready. He is grateful. First, however, he must use
the bathroom. In the bathroom, sitting on the commode, he
opens up the *Jiveboy* magazine he has brought home in his
briefcase. There are a couple of jivemate poses that particularly arouse him. He studies the young women—blonde, per-

haps (the national craze), with elastic waists and inviting eyes—and strokes his penis. At the same time, his bowels stir with the desire to defecate. He is in the bathroom a luxurious ten minutes. He emerges spent, relaxed—hungry for dinner.

His wife, using the bathroom later, comes upon the slightly damp magazine. She picks it up with mixed emotions. She is a brownskin woman with black hair and eyes. She looks at the white blondes and brunettes. Will he be thinking of them, she wonders, when he is making love to me?

"Why do you need these?" she asks.

"They mean nothing," he says.

"But they hurt me somehow," she says.

"You are being a.) silly, b.) a prude, and c.) ridiculous," he says. "You know I love you."

She cannot say to him: But they are not me, those women. She cannot say she is jealous of pictures on a page. That she feels invisible. Rejected. Overlooked. She says instead, to herself: He is right. I will grow up. Adjust. Swim with the tide.

He thinks he understands her, what she has been trying to say. It is *Jiveboy*, he thinks. The white women.

Next day he brings home *Jivers*, a black magazine, filled with bronze and honey-colored women. He is in the bathroom another luxurious ten minutes.

She stands, holding the magazine: on the cover are the legs and shoes of a well-dressed black man, carrying a briefcase and a rolled *Wall Street Journal* in one hand. At his feet—she turns the magazine cover around and around to figure out how exactly the pose is accomplished—there is a woman, a brownskin woman like herself, twisted and contorted in such a way that her head is not even visible. Only her glistening body—her back and derriere—so that she looks like a human turd at the man's feet.

He is on a business trip to New York. He has brought his wife along. He is eagerly sharing 42nd Street with her. "Look!" he says. "How *free* everything is! A far cry from Bolton!" (The small town they are from.) He is elated to see the blonde, spaced-out hookers, with their black pimps, trooping down the street. Elated at the shortness of the black hookers' dresses, their long hair, inevitably false and blond. She walks somehow behind him, so that he will encounter these wonders first. He does not notice until he turns a corner that she has stopped in front of a window that has caught her eye. While she is standing alone, looking, two separate pimps ask her what stable she is in or if in fact she is in one. Or simply "You workin'?"

He struts back and takes her elbow. Looks hard for the compliment implied in these questions, then shares it with his wife. "*You* know you're foxy!"

She is immovable. Her face suffering and wondering. "But look," she says, pointing. Four large plastic dolls—one a skinny Farrah Fawcett (or so the doll looks to her) posed for anal inspection; one, an oriental, with her eyes, strangely, closed, but her mouth, a pouting red suction cup, open; an enormous eskimo woman, with fur around her neck and ankles, and vagina; and a black woman dressed entirely in a leopard skin, complete with tail. The dolls are all life-size, and the efficiency of their rubber genitals is explained in detail on a card visible through the plate glass.

For her this is the stuff of nightmares—possibly because all the dolls are smiling. She will see them for the rest of her life. For him the sight is also shocking, but arouses a prurient curiosity. He will return, another time, alone. Meanwhile, he must prevent her from seeing such things, he resolves, whisking her briskly off the street.

Later, in their hotel room, she watches TV as two black women sing their latest hits: the first woman, dressed in a gold dress (because her song is now "solid gold!") is nonetheless wearing a chain around her ankle—the wife imagines she sees a chain—because the woman is singing: "Free me from my freedom, chain me to a tree!"

"What do you think of that?" she asks her husband.

"She's a fool," says he.

But when the second woman sings: "Ready, aim, fire, my name is desire," with guns and rockets going off all around her, he thinks the line "Shoot me with your love!" explains everything.

She is despondent.

She looks in a mirror at her plump brown and black body, crinkly hair and black eyes and decides, foolishly, that she is not beautiful. And that she is not hip, either. Among her other problems is the fact that she does not like the word "nigger" used by anyone at all, and is afraid of marijuana. These restraints, she feels, make her old, too much like her own mother, who loves sex (she has lately learned) but is highly religious and, for example, thinks cardplaying wicked and alcohol deadly. Her husband would not consider her mother sexy, she thinks. Since she herself is aging, this thought frightens her. But, surprisingly, while watching herself become her mother in the mirror, she discovers that *she* considers her mother—who carefully braids her average-length, average-grade, graying hair every night before going to bed; the braids her father still manages to fray during the night—*very* sexy.

At once she feels restored.

Resolves to fight.

"You're the only black woman in the world that worries about any of this stuff," he tells her, unaware of her resolve, and moody at her months of silent studiousness.

She says, "Here, Colored Person, read this essay by Audre Lorde."

He hedges. She insists.

He comes to the line about Lorde "moving into sunlight against the body of a woman I love," and bridles. "Wait a minute," he says, "what kind of a name is 'Audre' for a man? They must have meant 'André.'"

"It *is* the name of a woman," she says. "Read the rest of that page."

"No dyke can tell me anything," he says, flinging down the pages.

She has been calmly waiting for this. She brings in *Jiveboy* and *Jivers*. In both, there are women eating women they don't even know. She takes up the essay and reads:

> *This brings me to the last consideration of the erotic. To share the power of each other's feelings is different from using another's feelings as we would use Kleenex. And when we look the other way from our experience, erotic or otherwise, we use rather than share the feelings of those others who participate in the experience with us. And use without consent of the used is abuse.*

He looks at her with resentment, because she is reading this passage over again, silently, absorbedly, to herself, holding the pictures of the phony lesbians (a favorite, though unexamined, turn-on) absent-mindedly on her lap. He realizes he can never have her again sexually the way he has had her since their second year of marriage, as though her body belonged to someone else. He sees, down the road, the dissolution of the marriage, a constant search for more perfect bodies, or dumber wives. He feels oppressed by her incipient struggle, and feels somehow as if her struggle to change the pleasure he has enjoyed is a violation of his rights.

Now she is busy pasting Audre Lorde's words on the cabinet over the kitchen sink.

When they make love she tries to look him in the eye, but he refuses to return her gaze.

For the first time he acknowledges the awareness that the

pleasure of coming without her is bitter and lonely. He thinks of eating stolen candy alone, behind the barn. And yet, he thinks greedily, it is better than nothing, which he considers her struggle's benefit to him.

The next day, she is reading another essay when he comes home from work. It is called "A Quiet Subversion," and is by Luisah Teish. "Another dyke?" he asks.

"Another one of your sisters," she replies, and begins to read, even before he's had dinner:

> During the "Black Power Movement" much cultural education was focused on the black physique. One of the accomplishments of that period was the popularization of African hairstyles and the Natural. Along with this new hair-do came a new self-image and way of relating. Then the movie industry put out "Superfly", and the Lord Jesus Look, the Konked head, and an accompanying attitude, ran rampant in the black community. Films like "Shaft" and "Lady Sings the Blues" portray black "heroes" as cocaine-snorting, fast-life fools. In these movies a black woman is always caught in a web of violence. . . .
>
> A popular Berkeley theatre featured a porno movie titled "Slaves of Love." Its advertisement portrayed two black women, naked, in chains, and a white man standing over them with a whip! How such racist pornographic material escaped the eye of black activists presents a problem. . . .

Typically, he doesn't even hear the statement about the women. "What does the bitch know about the Black Power Movement?" he fumes. He is angry at his wife for knowing him so long and so well. She knows, for instance, that because of the Black Power Movement (and really because of the Civil Rights Movement before it), and not because he was at all active in it, he holds the bourgeois job he has. She remembers when his own hair was afroed. Now it is loosely curled. It occurs to him that, because she knows him as he was, he cannot make love to her as she is. Cannot, in fact, *love* her as she is. There is a way in which, in some firmly repressed corner of his mind, he considers his wife to be *still* black, whereas he feels himself to have moved to some other plane.

(This insight, a glimmer of which occurs to him, frightens him so much that he will resist it for several years. Should he accept it at once, however unsettling, it would help him understand the illogic of his acceptance of pornography used against black women: that he has detached himself from his own blackness in attempting to identify black women only by their sex.)

The wife has never considered herself a feminist—though she is, of course, a "womanist."* A womanist is a feminist, only more common. (The author of this piece is a womanist.) So she is surprised when her husband attacks her as a "women's libber," a "white women's lackey," a "pawn" in the hands of Gloria Steinem, an incipient bra-burner! What possible connection could there by, he wants to know, between her and white women—those overprivileged hags now (he's recently read in *Newsweek*) marching and preaching their puritanical horseshit up and down Times Square!

(He remembers only the freedom he felt there, not her long standing before the window of the plastic doll shop.) And if she is going to make a lot of new connections with dykes and whites, where will that leave him, the black man, the most brutalized and oppressed human being on the face of the earth? (*Is it because he can now ogle white women in freedom and she has no similar outlet of expression that the thinks of her as still black and himself as something else?* This thought underlines what he is actually saying, and his wife

* "Womanist" approximates "black feminist."

175

is unaware of it.) Didn't she know it is over these very same white bodies he has been lynched in the past, and is lynched still, by the police and the U.S. prison system, dozens of times a year *even now!?*

The wife has cunningly saved Tracy A. Gardner's essay for just this moment. Because Tracy A. Gardner has thought about it *all*, not just presently, but historically, and she is clear about all the abuse being done to herself as a black person and as a woman, and she is bold and she is cold— she is furious. The wife, given more to depression and self-abnegation than to fury, basks in the fire of Gardner's high-spirited anger.

She begins to read:

> *Because from my point of view, racism is everywhere, including in the women's movement, and the only time I really need to say anything about it is when I do not see it . . . and the first time that happens, I will tell you about it.*

The husband, surprised, thinks this very funny, not to say pertinent. He slaps his knee and sits up. He is dying to make some sort of positive dyke comment, but nothing comes to mind.

> *American slavery relied on the denial of the humanity of Black folks, and the undermining of our sense of nationhood and family, on the stripping away of the Black man's role as protector and provider, and on the structuring of Black women into the American system of white male domination. . . .*

"In other words," she says, "white men think they have to be on top. Other men have been known to savor life from other positions."

> *The end of the Civil War brought the end of a certain*

176

"form" of slavery for Black folks. It also brought the end of any "job security" and the loss of the protection of their white enslaver. Blacks were now free game, and the terrorization and humiliation of Black people, especially Black men, began anew. Now the Black man could have his family and prove his worth, but he had no way to support or protect them, or himself. . . .

As she reads, he feels ashamed and senses his wife's wounded embarrassment, for him and for herself. For their history together. But doggedly, she continues to read:

After the Civil War, popular justice, which meant there usually was no trial and no proof needed, began its reign in the form of the castration, burning at the stake, beheading, and lynching of Black men. As many as 5,000 white people would turn out to witness these events, as though going to a celebration. [She pauses, sighs: *beheading?*] *Over 2,000 Black men were lynched in a 10 year period from 1889–99. There were also a number of Black women lynched.* [She reads this sentence quickly and forgets it.] *Over 50% of the lynched Black males were charged with rape or attempted rape.*

He cannot imagine a woman being lynched. He has never even considered the possibility. Perhaps this is why the image of a black woman chained and bruised excites rather than horrifies him? It is the fact that the lynching of her body has never stopped that forces the wife, for the time being, to blot out the historical record. She is not prepared to connect her own husband with the continuation of that past.

She reads:

If a Black man had sex with a consenting white woman, it was rape. [Why am I always reading about, thinking about, worrying about, my man having sex with white women? she thinks, despairingly, underneath the read-*

ing.] *If he insulted a white woman by looking at her, it was attempted rape.*

"Yes," he says softly, as if in support of her dogged reading, "I've read Ida B.—what's her last name?"

"By their lynchings, the white man was showing that he hated the Black man carnally, biologically; he hated his color, his features, his genitals. Thus he attacked the Black man's body, and like a lover gone mad, maimed his flesh, violated him in the most intimate, pornographic fashion. . . ."

I believe that this obscene, inhuman treatment of Black men by white men, has a direct correlation to white men's increasingly obscene and inhuman treatment of women, particularly white women, in pornography and real life. White women, working towards their own strength and identity, their own sexuality, have in a sense become uppity niggers. As the Black man threatens the white man's masculinity and power, so now do women.

"That girl's onto something," says the husband, but thinks, for the first time in his life, that when he is not thinking of fucking white women—fantasizing over *Jiveboy* or clucking at them on the street—he is very often thinking of ways to humiliate them. Then he thinks that, given his history as a black man in America, it is not surprising that he has himself confused fucking them *with* humiliating them. But what does that say about how he sees himself? This thought smothers his inward applause for Gardner, and instead he casts a bewildered, disconcerted look at his wife. He knows that to make love to his wife as she really is, as who she really is— indeed, to make love to any other human being as they really are—will require a soul-rending look into himself, and the thought of this virtually straightens his hair.

His wife continues:

Some Black men, full of the white man's perspective and

values, see the white woman or Blond Goddess as part of the American winning image. Sometimes when he is with the Black woman, he is ashamed of how she has been treated and how he has been powerless, and that they have always had to work together and protect each other. [Yes, she thinks, we were always all we had, until now. He thinks: We are all we have still, only now we can live without permitting ourselves to know this.] *Frantz Fanon said about white women, "By loving me she proves that I am worthy of white love. I am loved like a white man. I am a white man. I marry the culture, white beauty, white whiteness. When my restless hands caress those white breasts, they grasp white civilization and dignity and make them mine."* [She cannot believe he meant to write "white dignity."]

She pauses, looks at her husband: "So how does a black woman feel when her black man leaves *Playboy* on the coffee table?"

For the first time he understands fully a line his wife read the day before: "The pornography industry's exploitation of the black woman's body is *qualitatively* different from that of the white woman," because she is holding the cover of *Jivers* out to him and asking: "What does this woman look like?"

What he has refused to see—because to see it would reveal yet another area in which he is unable to protect or defend black women—is that where white women are depicted in pornography as "objects," black women are depicted as animals. Where white women are depicted at least as human bodies if not beings, black women are depicted as shit.

He begins to feel sick. For he realizes that he has bought some if not all of the advertisements about women, black and white. And further, inevitably, he has bought the advertisements about himself. In pornography the black man is portrayed as being capable of fucking anything . . . even a piece of shit. He is defined solely by the size, readiness and unselectivity of his cock.

Still, he does not know how to make love without the fantasies fed to him by movies and magazines. Those movies and magazines (whose characters' pursuits are irrelevant or antithetical to his concerns) that have insinuated themselves between him and his wife, so that the totality of her body, her entire corporeal reality is alien to him. Even to clutch her in lust is automatically to shut his eyes. Shut his eyes, and . . . he chuckles bitterly . . . dream of England.

For years he has been fucking himself.

At first, reading Lorde together, they reject celibacy. Then they discover they need time apart to clear their heads, to search out damage, to heal. In any case, she is unable to fake response; he is unwilling for her to do so. She goes away for a while. Left alone, he soon falls hungrily on the magazines he had thrown out. Strokes himself raw over the beautiful women, spread like so much melon (he begins to see how stereotypes transmute) before him. But he cannot refuse what he knows—or what he knows his wife knows, walking along a beach in some black country where all the women are bleached and straightened and the men never look at themselves; and are ugly, in any case, in their imitation of white men.

Long before she returns he is reading her books and thinking of her—and of her struggles alone and his fear of sharing them—and when she returns, it is sixty percent *her* body that he moves against in the sun, her own black skin affirmed in the brightness of his eyes.

FAME

"In order to *see* anything, and therefore to create," Andrea Clement White was saying to the young woman seated across from her and listening very attentively, "one must not be famous."

"But *you* are famous," said the young woman, in mock perplexity, for the television cameras.

"Am I?" asked Andrea Clement White, and then added, "I suppose I am. But not *really* famous, you know, like . . . like . . ." But she could not bring herself to utter a rival's name, because this would increase the rival's fame, she felt, while diminishing her own.

"Your books have sold millions of copies," the young interviewer was saying. "They've been translated into a dozen languages. Into German and Dutch and Portuguese . . ."

"Into Spanish and French and Japanese and Italian and Swahili," Andrea Clement White completed the list for her, omitting, because they never came to mind, Russian, Greek, Polish and Lithuanian.

"And you've made from your work, how much? Hundreds of thousands of dollars. Isn't that true?"

"Yes, yes," said Andrea Clement White, in a little girl's voice that mixed pride with peevishness. "I can't complain, as to sales."

And so the interview continued. A gentle interrogation with no embarrassing questions, because Andrea Clement White was now old and had become an institution and there was never anyone in her presence who did not evince respect.

"Let me put it this way," she said. "It is more important that they are *people*, from the novelist's point of view. A botanist might say of a flower, it is a *red* flower. He is really studying flowers."

(Her mind had switched to automatic. No one had asked an interesting question in years.)

If she was famous, she wondered fretfully behind the alert face she raised for television, why didn't she *feel* famous? She had made money, as the young woman—lamentably informed in other respects—had said. Lots of money. Thousands upon thousands of dollars. She had seen her work accepted around the world, welcomed even, which was more than she'd ever dreamed possible for it. And yet—there remained an emptiness, no, an ache, which told her she had not achieved what she had set out to achieve. And instead must live out her life always in the shadow of those who had accomplished more than she, or had, in any case, received a wider and more fervid recognition. But, on closer scrutiny, those "others" she immediately thought of—the talk show guests, the much reviewed, the oft quoted—had *not* received more acclaim or been more praised than she; why then did she feel they had?

(She knew she would not be satisfied with the interview when it was aired. She would come across as a fatuous, smug know-everything, or as an irritable, spacy old fool. Her chronic dissatisfaction was always captured by television, no matter how cleverly she tried to disguise it as, oh, fatigue, too much to think about, doddering old age, or whatever.)

She left the studio thinking of the luncheon for her that same afternoon. It was at the college where she'd taught English literature (how she'd *struggled* to prove Charles Chesnutt wrote in English!) for over a decade. The president would be there and all her colleagues, with whom she'd battled, sometimes successfully, sometimes not (for five years they'd resisted Chesnutt, for example) over the years. They would fulsomely praise her—obliterating from memory the times they'd wished her dead; she would graciously acquiesce. She thought of Cooke, the dean, now retired of course, but unthinkable that he would not show up; how he had always been the first to kiss her whenever she returned from even the slightest triumph, and how she had detested that kiss—his lips rough, cluttered and gluey—and how she had told him, explicitly, her feelings. "But ladies are *meant* to be kissed!" he replied. She had thrown up her hands—and endured. Or had avoided him, which, because they shared an office, was not easy.

Then there was Mrs. Hyde, her secretary, also retired from the college though still working for Andrea Clement White in her office at home, who was the closest thing she had to someone to lean on. Any time of the day or night she was able to call on Mrs. Hyde—and Mrs. Hyde seemed to have nothing better to do than serve her. She understood she represented to Mrs. Hyde a glamour utterly missing from her own life, and Andrea Clement White had, over the thirty years of *their* acquaintanceship, ridiculed *Mr.* Hyde unmercifully. Because, in truth, she grew used to being served by Mrs. Hyde, had come to expect her service as her due, and was jealous and contemptuous of Mr. Hyde—a dull little man with the flat, sour cheeks of a snake—who provided his wife little of the excitement Andrea Clement White felt was generated spontaneously in her own atmosphere.

Mrs. Hyde was, in fact, driving the car, Mrs. Clement White seated beside her. And one could tell from the restful silence in the car that they shared a very real life together. If Andrea Clement White sat in the same car with her husband it was clear *they* shared a life. He was a man who cared little for Literature, having—as he said—married it and seen how crazy it was. But the quality of the silence was quite different. In her husband's silence there was tension, criticism of her, impatience. He held his tongue the better to make her know what he thought. Mrs. Hyde held hers as a comfort; she knew Mrs. Clement White needed the silence— after an encounter with other people—to settle into herself again.

"Imagine thinking that black people write only about being black and not about being people." Andrea Clement White fumed, rummaging through her purse for a tissue. "Disgusting make-up," she said, running a tissue around her collar and bringing it down a very dark brown. "Can you imagine, as many shades of brown as there are, they have only one jar to cover everything? And one jar, of course, for *them*, but then *they* only need one jar." Mrs. Hyde did not say anything. She drove expertly, smoothly. Enjoying the luxury of the car, a silver Mercedes 350SL. Her foot barely touched the pedal and the car *slid* along, effortlessly.

I walked into the studio, Andrea Clement White replayed herself, as she did all the time (someone called this the curse—or was it the blessing?—of the artist; she thought everyone did it), and right away, as usual, I knew it was going to be awful. That the questions would be boring and the interviewer ill read, ahistorical and poorly educated. It was enough when white liberals told you they considered what you said or wrote to be new in the world (and one was expected to fall for this flattery); one never expected them to know one's history well enough to recognize an evolution, a variation, when they saw it; they meant *new* to *them*. But how cutely ignorant the young black woman interviewer had been! "You are the first!" she had boomed—strangely unbleached black voice as yet, but TV would whiten it out—and when Andrea Clement White said, "But there's no such thing as a first, an absolute first in the area of human relations, only perhaps in Science," the woman had though her coy, and had grinned, indulgently. (Andrea Clement White hated to be indulged when she was not seeking indulgence. It was at that point that she switched her mind to automatic.)

And now the lilacs along the road rushed as if drawn against the silver of the car; and lilacs and television interviewer mixed: there was an image of the interviewer with a sprig of lilacs in her hair. But why so many so far south? Had they been creeping south with the harsher winters? Or had they been here always? Andrea Clement White could not remember. She saw herself among the lilacs on her college campus in upstate New York. I stood *drenched* in the smell of lilacs. It was my perfume for twenty years, with one year out for an experiment with patchouli. . . .

Mrs. Hyde had stopped the car and reached into the back seat and fetched up the cane that made walking a somewhat more steady affair for Mrs. Clement White. It was a lovely oak cane, hand carved by a famous eighteenth-century carver who fell into the hands of a mistress who demanded twenty such carved canes a week; these she sold in the marketplace in Charleston, and thus, after her husband lost his money gambling and ran off with a woman who supplied him with more, she had supported herself. The carver, sick of carving and unbelieving that the Civil War would free the slaves, and too much of a gentleman to rebel or run away from a helpless white woman who needed him, cut off three fingers from his left hand, "accidentally," while "branching" a tree. But he had not reckoned on the Scarlett O'Hara persistence of his mistress. She limited the number of canes she expected weekly to fifteen.

I was standing watching Ben make the canes, thought

Andrea Clement White, because I was his daughter. Was I pretty? She thought probably she was. And she had been his other hand until freedom came. Freedom had come and everyone had had ideas about what it was for, even Ben. He had simply died. I was at the burying, of course. It was I, in fact, who dug the grave, along with . . . then she wondered if she would have had to be a boy to help dig the grave. She saw herself as one. Handsome, was he? She thought probably yes. But then she thought she would not have had to be a boy to do it because she had been doing every kind of work on the plantation *as a girl*, and no one thought anything of it, so she'd stay a girl. She sighed with relief.

Rudolph Miller opened the car door on her side and she looked out and up into his lapel. He had the unctuous, shit-eating grin she'd despised for—thirty years. How had she stood it without throwing up? It seemed to be made of wet papier-mâché. Took his hand: dry, plump, *old* hand, horny nails. *Yuck.* (Her grandchildren's expressions came in handy at times like this.) Mrs. Hyde trotted around the car with the cane. So fat, Mrs. Hyde, and given to hyperventilation. But oh, the lilacs! Even here. "When lilacs last in the dooryard bloomed . . ." Abe Lincoln had probably never dreamed there would be colleges like this, for blacks, in the South. What *had* he dreamed? To be better looking, she didn't doubt.

Now she had liver spots on her cheeks and her hair was slowly receding, but that wasn't so bad. She could look infinitely worse and there'd still be a luncheon for her, a banquet later tonight and book parties and telegrams and people *beaming* at her well into the future. Success was the best bone structure. Or the best cosmetic. But was she a success? she asked herself. And herself answered, in a chorus, *exasperated*, Of *Course* You Are! Only a small voice near the back faltered. She stifled it.

There was, oh, McGeorge Grundy. Bundy. Ford Foundation. Going up the stairs. (They had really scrounged for dignitaries for this affair.) It would turn into a fund raiser, as everything did. And did she mind? She was making a speech as McGeorge: I give you all the money in one lump. You'll never have to worry about money again. Or beg. Period. Good-bye. Cheering. Throwing of hats in the air. People actually used to do that. But few people wore hats today. Of course Nigerians, she heard, threw people, but that was depressing.

"This little lady has done . . ." Would he have said "This little man . . ."? But of course not. No man wanted to be called little. He thought it referred to his penis. But to say "little lady" made men think of virgins. Tight, tiny pussies, and moments of rape.

But this was fame, thought Andrea Clement White, poking at her Rock Cornish hen, which slid gracefully if speedily into Mrs. Hyde's lap. There are the multitudes. *Is* the multitude? Anyhow, every bored, numbskull student I ever taught, every mediocre professor I've ever wanted to axe. And the president doing what he does best—"This little lady" . . .

It was probably with the patchouli that she had caught William Litz White, her husband. He'd never smelled anything like it—successful doctor, intense billiards player that he was—and had never intended to. Bohemian. Bohemian Belle, he had called her. She had wanted to *be* bohemian: to write on a kitchen table perhaps; but *not* among her children's unwashed cereal bowls. Patchouli was as close as she got.

The hen was still nesting on Mrs. Hyde's lap. Like most people who are not famous a small thing like getting a Rock Cornish hen out of her lap and back on the table paralyzed her. How could she be so indecorous as to plop the bird back into Andrea Clement White's plate? That famous and fastidious lady (she had read interviews to the effect that she *was* fastidious; this was not necessarily her own opinion). She began to sweat.

"He's a bore," said Andrea Clement White, audibly and

viciously (she had discovered viciousness amused)—but then, she was forgiven everything because of her fame, her use as a fund raiser, and age—and began to feel around Mrs. Hyde's broad knees for the tiny chicken. Dragging it up stuck to Mrs. Hyde's dress—Mrs. Hyde meanwhile going gray with embarrassment—Mrs. Clement White raised it to her lips— and took a bite.

Five hundred in the audience did the same.

Was there a point, she wondered, chewing, in thinking about what one ate at functions like this? The rocklike hen, the red ring of spicy, soggy apple. The broccoli that no one in the South had learned to cook, only to boil? She thought not, and ate it all without thinking beyond the fact that she was hungry, had to pee, was bored to tears, and her bra strap was biting into the radical edges of her latest mastectomy.

A slow, aged string of tipsy wasps (he who owned the newspaper that said Negroes had no use for higher education, though perhaps the trades; she who told far and wide the remarkable insights of her grandmother's enslaved cook; he who . . .) now rose to drone her praises. She munched her chicken and five hundred others munched along with her, their chewing a noisy, incessant and exuberant ignoring. She was suddenly back at the plantation. But where? Mississippi? Too hot, and already a cliché. Ditto Alabama, Georgia and Louisiana. She picked Virginia, where there were cool mountains and where it was not too severe a stretch of the imagination to match five hundred and one chickens to that many hungry slaves. *Crunch*. She was smiling and chewing but without any intention of listening. She nodded—still grinning and chewing as each person sat down. "In *spite* of you I'm sitting here," she thought, and reached over for the apple ring from Mrs. Hyde's plate. This second apple ring was always saved for her to eat at the end of the meal. It was her mouthwash.

She projected herself ahead a few minutes to being presented to the audience by Tedious Taylor, the president: she was battling him with her eyes. DON'T YOU *DARE* KISS ME! But he closed his froglike eyes, descended his head, his pendulous lips, and kissed the most prominent of her liver spots. *Yuck*. So *many* Yucks. Because then there would creep up behind her Dean Cooke (whom she would have kept tabs on until now), who would glue his mouth to her neck in an attitude of falling.

She saw herself hit him in the groin with her award, a sharp-beaked silver goose. But was it a silver goose? It would be duck, swan or goose. (Bird awards were lately "in.") Perhaps all three, and it would be not silver but silver plate, and there would be eggs. (She was a woman, after all!) Golden.

She felt briefly terrific, imagining Cooke's piglike squeal, and gnawed her chicken savagely, her eyes quite glazed over, in abstracted glee.

But now there came in front of the audience—with a slight bow to Mrs. Clement White—a small girl the color of chocolate. But *really* the color of chocolate. Hack writers always said black people were chocolate colored; this saved them the work of looking. Andrea Clement White was amused that this child really was the exact shade of brown of a chocolate drop.

She opened her mouth and began to sing with assurance an old, emphatically familiar song.

A slave song. Authorless.

Picked drumsticks fell onto plates like hail. Profound silence at last prevailed.

And it was this child's confident memory, *that* old anonymous song, that gave Andrea Clement White the energy to stand up and endure with dignity (the audience surreptitiously nibbling at dessert as she began to speak) the presentation of her one hundred and eleventh major award.

THE ABORTION

They had discussed it, but not deeply, whether they wanted the baby she was now carrying. "I don't *know* if I want it," she said, eyes filling with tears. She cried at anything now, and was often nauseous. That pregnant women cried easily and were nauseous seemed banal to her, and she resented banality.

"Well, think about it," he said, with his smooth reassuring voice (but with an edge of impatience she now felt) that used to soothe her.

It was all she *did* think about, all she apparently *could*; that he could dream otherwise enraged her. But she always lost, when they argued. Her temper would flare up, he would become instantly reasonable, mature, responsible, if not responsive precisely, to her mood, and she would swallow down her tears and hate herself. It was because she believed him "good." The best human being she had ever met.

"It isn't as if we don't already have a child," she said in a calmer tone, carelessly wiping at the tear that slid from one eye.

"We have a perfect child," he said with relish, "thank the Good Lord!"

Had she ever dreamed she'd marry someone humble enough to go around thanking the Good Lord? She had not.

Now they left the bedroom, where she had been lying down on their massive king-size bed with the forbidding ridge in the middle, and went down the hall—hung with bright prints—to the cheerful, spotlessly clean kitchen. He put water on for tea in a bright yellow pot.

She wanted him to want the baby so much he would try to save its life. On the other hand, she did not permit such presumptuousness. As he praised the child they already had, a daughter of sunny disposition and winning smile, Imani sensed subterfuge, and hardened her heart.

"What am I talking about," she said, as if she'd been talking about it. "Another child would kill me. I can't imagine life with two children. Having a child is a good experience *to have had*, like graduate school. But if you've had one, you've had the experience and that's enough."

He placed the tea before her and rested a heavy hand on her hair. She felt the heat and pressure of his hand as she touched the cup and felt the odor and steam rise up from it. Her throat contracted.

"I can't drink that," she said through gritted teeth. "Take it away."

There were days of this.

Clarice, their daughter, was barely two years old. A miscarriage brought on by grief (Imani had lost her fervidly environmentalist mother to lung cancer shortly after Clarice's birth; the asbestos ceiling in the classroom where she taught first graders had leaked for twenty years) separated Clarice's birth from the new pregnancy. Imani felt her body had been assaulted by these events and was, in fact, considerably weakened, and was also, in any case, chronically anaemic and run down. Still, if she had wanted the baby more than she did not want it, she would not have planned to abort it.

They lived in a small town in the South. Her husband, Clarence, was, among other things, legal adviser and defender of the new black mayor of the town. The mayor was much in their lives because of the difficulties being the first black mayor of a small town assured, and because, next to the major leaders of black struggles in the South, Clarence respected and admired him most.

Imani reserved absolute judgment, but she did point out that Mayor Carswell would never look at her directly when she made a comment or posed a question, even sitting at her own dinner table, and would instead talk to Clarence as if she were not there. He assumed that as a woman she would not be interested in, or even understand, politics. (He would comment occasionally on her cooking or her clothes. He noticed when she cut her hair.) But Imani understood every shade and variation of politics: she understood, for example, why she fed the mouth that did not speak to her; because for the present she must believe in Mayor Carswell, even as he could not believe in her. Even understanding this, however, she found dinners with Carswell hard to swallow.

But Clarence was dedicated to the mayor, and believed his success would ultimately mean security and advancement for them all.

On the morning she left to have the abortion, the mayor and Clarence were to have a working lunch, and they drove her to the airport deep in conversation about municipal funds, racist cops, and the facilities for teaching at the chaotic, newly integrated schools. Clarence had time for the briefest kiss and hug at the airport ramp.

"Take care of yourself," he whispered lovingly as she walked away. He was needed, while she was gone, to draft the city's new charter. She had agreed this was important; the mayor was already being called incompetent by local businessmen and the chamber of commerce, and one inferred from television that no black person alive even knew what a city charter was.

"Take care of myself." Yes, she thought. I see that is what I have to do. But she thought this self-pityingly, which invalidated it. She had expected *him* to take care of her, and she blamed him for not doing so now.

Well, she was a fraud, anyway. She had known after a year of marriage that it bored her. "The Experience of Having a Child" was to distract her from this fact. Still, she expected him to "take care of her." She was lucky he didn't pack up and leave. But he seemed to know, as she did, that if anyone packed and left, it would be her. Precisely *because* she was a fraud and because in the end he would settle for fraud and she could not.

On the plane to New York her teeth ached and she vomited bile—bitter, yellowish stuff she hadn't even been aware her body produced. She resented and appreciated the crisp help of the stewardess, who asked if she needed anything, then stood chatting with the cigarette-smoking white man next to her, whose fat hairy wrist, like a large worm, was all Imani could bear to see out of the corner of her eye.

Her first abortion, when she was still in college, she frequently remembered as wonderful, bearing as it had all the marks of a supreme coming of age and a seizing of the direction of her own life, as well as a comprehension of existence that never left her: that life—what one saw about one and called Life—was not a facade. There was nothing behind it which used "Life" as its manifestation. Life was itself. Period. At the time, and afterwards, and even now, this seemed a marvelous thing to know.

The abortionist had been a delightful Italian doctor on the Upper East Side in New York, and before he put her under he told her about his own daughter who was just her age, and a junior at Vassar. He babbled on and on until she was out, but not before Imani had thought how her thousand dollars, for which she would be in debt for years, would go to keep her there.

When she woke up it was all over. She lay on a brown Naugahyde sofa in the doctor's outer office. And she heard, over her somewhere in the air, the sound of a woman's voice. It was a Saturday, no nurses in attendance, and she presumed it was the doctor's wife. She was pulled gently to her feet by this voice and encouraged to walk.

"And when you leave, be sure to walk as if nothing is wrong," the voice said.

Imani did not feel any pain. This surprised her. Perhaps he didn't do anything, she thought. Perhaps he took my thousand dollars and put me to sleep with two dollars' worth of ether. Perhaps this is a racket.

But he was so kind, and he was smiling benignly, almost fatherly, at her (and Imani realized how desperately she needed this "fatherly" look, this "fatherly" smile). "Thank you," she murmured sincerely: she was thanking him for her life.

Some of Italy was still in his voice. "It's nothing, nothing," he said. "A nice, pretty girl like you; in school like my own daughter, you didn't need this trouble."

"He's nice," she said to herself, walking to the subway on her way back to school. She lay down gingerly across a vacant seat, and passed out.

She hemorrhaged steadily for six weeks, and was not well again for a year.

But this was seven years later. An abortion law now made it possible to make an appointment at a clinic, and for seventy-five dollars a safe, quick, painless abortion was yours.

Imani had once lived in New York, in the Village, not five blocks from where the abortion clinic was. It was also near the Margaret Sanger clinic, where she had received her very first diaphragm, with utter gratitude and amazement that someone apparently understood and actually cared about young women as alone and ignorant as she. In fact, as she walked up the block, with its modern office buildings side by side with older, more elegant brownstones, she felt how close she was still to that earlier self. Still not in control of her sensuality, and only through violence and with money (for the flight, for the operation itself) in control of her body.

She found that abortion had entered the age of the assembly line. Grateful for the lack of distinction between herself and the other women—all colors, ages, states of misery or nervousness—she was less happy to notice, once the doctor started to insert the catheter, that the anesthesia she had been given was insufficient. But assembly lines don't stop because the product on them has a complaint. Her doctor whistled, and assured her she was all right, and carried the procedure through to the horrific end. Imani fainted some seconds before that.

They laid her out in a peaceful room full of cheerful colors. Primary colors: yellow, red, blue. When she revived she had the feeling of being in a nursery. She had a pressing need to urinate.

A nurse, kindly, white-haired and with firm hands, helped her to the toilet. Imani saw herself in the mirror over the sink and was alarmed. She was literally gray, as if all her blood had leaked out.

"Don't worry about how you look," said the nurse. "Rest a bit here and take it easy when you get back home. You'll be fine in a week or so."

She could not imagine being fine again. Somewhere her child—she never dodged into the language of "fetuses" and "amorphous growths"—was being flushed down a sewer. Gone all her or his chances to see the sunlight, savor a fig.

"Well," she said to this child, "it was you or me, Kiddo, and I chose me."

There were people who thought she had no right to choose herself, but Imani knew better than to think of those people now.

It was a bright, hot Saturday when she returned.

Clarence and Clarice picked her up at the airport. They had brought flowers from Imani's garden, and Clarice presented them with a stout-hearted hug. Once in her mother's lap she rested content all the way home, sucking her thumb, stroking her nose with the forefinger of the same hand, and kneading a corner of her blanket with the three fingers that were left.

"How did it go?" asked Clarence.

"It went," said Imani.

There was no way to explain abortion to a man. She thought castration might be an apt analogy, but most men, perhaps all, would insist this could not possibly be true.

"The anesthesia failed," she said. "I thought I'd never faint in time to keep from screaming and leaping off the table."

Clarence paled. He hated the thought of pain, any kind of violence. He could not endure it; it made him physically ill. This was one of the reasons he was a pacifist, another reason she admired him.

She knew he wanted her to stop talking. But she continued in a flat, deliberate voice.

"All the blood seemed to run out of me. The tendons in my legs felt cut. I was gray."

He reached for her hand. Held it. Squeezed.

"But," she said, "at least I know what I don't want. And I intend never to go through any of this again."

They were in the living room of their peaceful, quiet and colorful house. Imani was in her rocker, Clarice dozing on her lap. Clarence sank to the floor and rested his head against her knees. She felt he was asking for nurture when she needed it herself. She felt the two of them, Clarence and Clarice, clinging to her, using her. And that the only way she could claim herself, feel herself distinct from them, was by doing something painful, self-defining but self-destructive.

She suffered the pressure of his head as long as she could. "Have a vasectomy," she said, "or stay in the guest room. Nothing is going to touch me anymore that isn't harmless."

He smoothed her thick hair with his hand. "We'll talk about it," he said, as if that was not what they were doing. "We'll see. Don't worry. We'll take care of things."

She had forgotten that the third Sunday in June, the following day, was the fifth memorial observance for Holly Monroe, who had been shot down on her way home from her high-school graduation ceremony five years before. Imani *always* went to these memorials. She liked the reassurance that her people had long memories, and that those people who fell in struggle or innocence were not forgotten. She was, of course, too weak to go. She was dizzy and still losing blood. The white lawgivers attempted to get around assassination—which Imani considered extreme abortion—by saying the victim provoked it (there had been some difficulty saying this about Holly Monroe, but they had tried) but were antiabortionist to a man. Imani thought of this as she resolutely showered and washed her hair.

Clarence had installed central air conditioning their second year in the house. Imani had at first objected. "I want to smell the trees, the flowers, the natural air!" she cried. But the first summer of 110-degree heat had cured her of giving a damn about any of that. Now she wanted to be cool. As much as she loved trees, on a hot day she would have sawed through a forest to get to an air conditioner.

In fairness to him, she had to admit he asked her if she thought she was well enough to go. But even to be asked annoyed her. She was not one to let her own troubles prevent her from showing proper respect and remembrance toward the dead, although she understood perfectly well that once dead, the dead do not exist. So respect, remembrance was for herself, and today herself needed rest. There was something mad about her refusal to rest, and she felt it as she tottered about getting Clarice dressed. But she did not stop. She ran a bath, plopped the child in it, scrubbed her plump body on her knees, arms straining over the tub awkwardly in a way that made her stomach hurt—but not yet her uterus—dried her hair, lifted her out and dried the rest of her on the kitchen table.

"You are going to remember as long as you live what kind of people they are," she said to the child, who, gurgling and cooing, looked into her mother's stern face with light-hearted fixation.

"You are going to hear the music," Imani said. "The music, they've tried to kill. The music they try to steal." She felt feverish and was aware she was muttering. She didn't care.

"They think they can kill a continent—people, trees, buffalo—and then fly off to the moon and just forget about it. But you and me we're going to remember the people, the trees and the fucking buffalo. Goddammit."

"Buffwoe," said the child, hitting at her mother's face with a spoon.

She placed the baby on a blanket in the living room and turned to see her husband's eyes, full of pity, on her. She wore pert green velvet slippers and a lovely sea green robe. Her body was bent within it. A reluctant tear formed beneath his gaze.

"Sometimes I look at you and I wonder 'What is this man doing in my house?'"

This had started as a joke between them. Her aim had been never to marry, but to take in lovers who could be sent home at dawn, freeing her to work and ramble.

"I'm here because you love me," was the traditional answer. But Clarence faltered, meeting her eyes, and Imani turned away.

It was a hundred degrees by ten o'clock. By eleven, when the memorial service began, it would be ten degrees hotter. Imani staggered from the heat. When she sat in the car she had to clench her teeth against the dizziness until the motor prodded the air conditioning to envelop them in coolness. A dull ache started in her uterus.

The church was not of course air conditioned. It was authentic Primitive Baptist in every sense.

Like the four previous memorials this one was designed by Holly Monroe's classmates. All twenty-five of whom—fat and thin—managed to look like the dead girl. Imani had never seen Holly Monroe, though there were always photographs of her dominating the pulpit of this church where she had been baptized and where she had sung in the choir— and to her, every black girl of a certain vulnerable age *was* Holly Monroe. And an even deeper truth was that Holly Monroe was herself. Herself shot down, aborted on the eve of becoming herself.

She was prepared to cry and to do so with abandon. But she did not. She clenched her teeth against the steadily increasing pain and her tears were instantly blotted by the heat.

Mayor Carswell had been waiting for Clarence in the vestibule of the church, mopping his plumply jowled face with a voluminous handkerchief and holding court among half a dozen young men and women who listened to him with awe. Imani exchanged greetings with the mayor, he ritualistically kissed her on the cheek, and kissed Clarice on the cheek, but his rather heat-glazed eye was already fastened on her husband. The two men huddled in a corner away from the awed young group. Away from Imani and Clarice, who passed hesitantly, waiting to be joined or to be called back, into the church.

There was a quarter hour's worth of music.

"Holly Monroe was five feet, three inches tall, and weighed one hundred and eleven pounds," her best friend said, not reading from notes, but talking to each person in the audience. "She was a stubborn, loyal Aries, the best kind of friend to have. She had black kinky hair that she experimented with

199

a lot. She was exactly the color of this oak church pew in the summer; in the winter she was the color [pointing up] of this heart pine ceiling. She loved green. She did not like lavender because she said she also didn't like pink. She had brown eyes and wore glasses, except when she was meeting someone for the first time. She had a sort of rounded nose. She had beautiful large teeth, but her lips were always chapped so she didn't smile as much as she might have if she'd ever gotten used to carrying Chap Stick. She had elegant feet.

"Her favorite church song was 'Leaning on the Everlasting Arms.' Her favorite other kind of song was 'I Can't Help Myself—I Love You and Nobody Else.' She was often late for choir rehearsal though she loved to sing. She made the dress she wore to her graduation in Home Ec. She *hated* Home Ec. . . ."

Imani was aware that the sound of low, murmurous voice had been the background for this statement all along. Everything was quiet around her, even Clarice sat up straight, absorbed by the simple friendliness of the young woman's voice. All of Holly Monroe's classmates and friends in the choir wore vivid green. Imani imagined Clarice entranced by the brilliant, swaying color as by a field of swaying corn.

Lifting the child, her uterus burning, and perspiration already a stream down her back, Imani tiptoed to the door. Clarence and the mayor were still deep in conversation. She heard "board meeting . . . aldermen . . . city council." She beckoned to Clarence.

"Your voices are carrying!" she hissed.

She meant: How dare you not come inside.

They did not. Clarence raised his head, looked at her, and shrugged his shoulders helplessly. Then, turning, with the abstracted air of priests, the two men moved slowly toward the outer door, and into the churchyard, coming to stand some distance from the church beneath a large oak tree. There they remained throughout the service.

Two years later, Clarence was furious with her: What is the matter with you? he asked. You never want me to touch you. You told me to sleep in the guest room and I did. You told me to have a vasectomy I didn't want and *I did*. (Here, there was a sob of hatred for her somewhere in the anger, the humiliation: he thought of himself as a eunuch, and blamed her.)

She was not merely frigid, she was remote.

She had been amazed after they left the church that the anger she'd felt watching Clarence and the mayor turn away from the Holly Monroe memorial did not prevent her accepting a ride home with him. A month later it did not prevent her smiling on him fondly. Did not prevent a trip to Bermuda, a few blissful days of very good sex on a deserted beach screened by trees. Did not prevent her listening to his mother's stories of Clarence's youth as though she would treasure them forever.

And yet. From that moment in the heat at the church door, she had uncoupled herself from him, in a separation that made him, except occasionally, little more than a stranger.

And he had not felt it, had not known.

"What have I done?" he asked, all the tenderness in his voice breaking over her. She smiled a nervous smile at him, which he interpreted as derision—so far apart had they drifted.

They had discussed the episode at the church many times. Mayor Carswell—whom they never saw anymore—was now a model mayor, with wide biracial support in his campaign for the legislature. Neither could easily recall him, though television frequently brought him into the house.

"It was so important that I help the mayor!" said Clarence. "He was our *first*!"

Imani understood this perfectly well, but it sounded humorous to her. When she smiled, he was offended.

She had known the moment she left the marriage, the

exact second. But apparently that moment had left no perceptible mark.

They argued, she smiled, they scowled, blamed and cried—as she packed.

Each of them almost recalled out loud that about this time of the year their aborted child would have been a troublesome, "terrible" two-year-old, a great burden on its mother, whose health was by now in excellent shape, each wanted to think aloud that the marriage would have deteriorated anyway, because of that.

PORN

Like many thoughtful women of the seventies, she had decided women were far more interesting than men. But, again like most thoughtful women, she rarely admitted this aloud. Besides, again like her contemporaries, she maintained a close connection with a man.

It was a sexual connection.

They had met in Tanzania when it was still Tanganyika; she was with an international group of students interested in health care in socialist African countries; he with an American group intent upon building schools. They met. Liked each other. Wrote five or six letters over the next seven years. Married other people. Had children. Lived in different cities. Divorced. Met again to discover they now·shared a city and lived barely three miles apart.

A strong bond between them was that they respected their former spouses and supported their children. They had each arranged a joint custody settlement and many of their favorite outings were amid a clash of children. Still, her primary interest in him was sexual. It was not that she did not respect his mind; she did. It was a fine mind. More scientific than hers, more given to abstractions. But also a mind curious about nature and the hidden workings of things (it was probably this, she thought, that made him such a good lover) and she enjoyed following his thoughts about the distances of stars and whole galaxies from the earth, the difference between low clouds and high fog, and the complex survival mechanisms of the snail.

But sex together was incredibly good: like conversation with her women friends, who were never abstract, rarely distant enough from nature to be critical in their appraisal of it, and whose own mechanisms for survival were hauled out in discussion for all to see. The touch of his fingers— sensitive, wise, exploring the furthest reaches of sensation— were like the tongues of women, talking, questing, searching for the *true* place, the place which, when touched, has no choice but to respond.

She was aflame with desire for him.

On those evenings when all the children were with their other parents, he would arrive at the apartment at seven. They would walk hand in hand to a Chinese restaurant a mile away. They would laugh and drink and eat and touch hands and knees over and under the table. They would come home. Smoke a joint. He would put music on. She would run water in the tub with lots of bubbles. In the bath they would lick and suck each other, in blissful delight. They would admire the rich candle glow on their wet, delectably earth-toned skins. Sniff the incense—the odor of sandal and redwood. He would carry her in to bed.

> *Music. Emotion. Sensation. Presence.*
> *Satisfaction like rivers*
> *flowing and silver.*

On the basis of their sexual passion they built the friendship that sustained them through the outings with their collective children, through his loss of a job (temporarily),
through her writer's block (she worked as a freelance
journalist), through her bouts of frustration and boredom
when she perceived that, in conversation, he could only *be*
scientific, only *be* abstract, and she was, because of her
intrepid, garrulous women friends—whom she continued frequently, and often in desperation, to see—used to so much
more.

In short, they had devised an almost perfect arrangement.

One morning at six o'clock they were making "morning love."
"Morning love" was relaxed, clearheaded. Fresh. No music
but the birds and cars starting. No dope.

They came within seconds of each other.

This inspired him. He thought they could come together.

She was sated, indifferent, didn't wish to think about the
strain.

But then he said: "Did I ever show you [he knew he hadn't]
my porn collection?"

"What could it be?' she inevitably wondered. Hooked.

His hands are cupping her ass. His fingers like warm grass
or warm and supple vines. One thumb—she fancies she feels
the whorled print—makes a circle in the wetness of her anus.
She shivers. His tongue gently laps her vulva as it enters her,
his top lip caressing the clitoris. For five minutes she is
moving along as usual. Blissed *out*, she thinks to herself.
Then she stops.

"What have you got?" she has asked him.

"This," he replied. "And this."

*A gorgeous black woman who looks like her friend Fannie has
a good friend (white boy from her hometown down South) who
is basically gay. Though—. "Fannie" and let us call him "Fred"*

pick up a hick tourist in a bar. They both dig him, the caption says. He is not gorgeous. He is short, pasty, dirty blond. Slightly cross-eyed. In fact, looks retarded. Fred looks very much the same. "Fannie" invites them to her place where without holding hands or eating or bathing or putting on music, they strip and begin to fondle each other. "Fannie" looks amused as they take turns licking and sucking her. She smiles benignly as they do the same things to each other. . . .

"And this."

A young blonde girl from Minnesota [probably kidnapped, she thinks, reading] *is far from home in New York, lonely and very horny. She is befriended by two of the blackest men on the East Coast. (They had been fighting outside a bar and she had stopped them by flinging her naive white self into the fray.) In their gratitude for her peacemaking they take her to their place and do everything they can think of to her. She grinning liberally the whole time. Finally they make a sandwich of her: one filling the anus and the other the vagina, so that all that is visible of her body between them is a sliver of white thighs.* [And we see that these two pugilists have finally come together on something.]

She is sitting with her back against the headboard of the bed so that her breasts hang down. This increases sensation in her already very aroused nipples. He crawls up to her on all fours like a gentle but ravenous bear and begins to nuzzle her. He nuzzles and nuzzles until her nipples virtually aim themselves at him. He takes one into his mouth. She begins to flow.

But the flow stops.

Once he said to her: "I could be turned on by bondage." No, he said "by 'a little *light* bondage.' " She had told him of a fantasy in which she lay helpless, bound, waiting for the pleasure worse than death.

PORN

There is no plot this time. No story of an improbable friendship down South, no goldilocks from the Midwestern plains. Just page after page of women: yellow, red, white, brown, black [she had let him tie her up very loosely once; it was not like her fantasy at all. She had wanted to hold him, caress him, snuggle and cuddle] *bound, often gagged. Their legs open. Forced to their knees.*

He is massaging the back of her neck, her shoulders. Her buttocks. The backs of her thighs. She has bent over a hot typewriter all day and is tired. She sinks into the feeling of being desired and pampered. Valued. Loved. Soon she is completely restored. Alert. She decides to make love to him. She turns over. She cradles his head in her arms. Kisses his forehead. His eyes. Massages his scalp with her fingers. Buries her nose in his neck. Kisses his neck. Caresses his chest. Flicks his nipples, back and forth, with her tongue. Slowly she moves down his body. His penis (which he thinks should not be called "penis"—"a white boy's word"; he prefers "cock") is standing. She takes it—she is on her knees—into her mouth.

She gags.

The long-term accommodation that protects marriage and other such relationships is, she knows, forgetfulness. She will forget what turns him on.

"No, no," he says, very sorry he has shown her his collection: in fact, vowing passionately to throw it away. "The point is for *you* to be turned on by it *too!*"

She thinks of the lovely black girl—whom she actually thinks of as her friend Fannie—and is horrified. What is Fannie doing in such company? she wonders. She panics as he is entering her. Wait! she says, and races to the phone.

The phone rings and rings.

Her friend Fannie is an out-of-work saleswoman. She is

also a lesbian. She proceeds to write in her head a real story about Fannie based on what she knows. Her lover at work on her body the whole time.

Fannie and Laura share a tiny loft apartment. They almost never make love. Not because they are not loving—they do a lot of caressing and soothing—but they are so guilty about what they feel that sexuality has more or less dried up. [She feels her own juices drying up at this thought.]

They have both been out of work for a long time. Laura's mother is sick. Fannie's young brother has entered Howard University. There is only Fannie to send him money for books, clothes and entertainment. Fannie is very pretty but basically unskilled in anything but selling, and salespersons by the thousands have been laid off in the recession. Unemployment is not enough.

But Fannie is really very beautiful. Men stop her on the street all the time to tell her so. It is the way they chose to tell her so, when she was barely pubescent, that makes her return curses for "compliments" even today.

But these men would still stop her on the street, offer her money "for a few hours' work." . . .

By now she has faked all kinds of things, and exhausted her lover. He is sound asleep. She races to Fannie and Laura's apartment. Sits waiting for them on the stoop. Finally they come home from seeing a Woody Allen movie. They are in high spirits, and besides, because she shares part of her life with a man, care much less for her than she does for them. They yawn loudly, kiss her matronizingly on both cheeks, and send her home again.

Now, when he makes love to her, she tries to fit herself into the white-woman, two-black-men story. But who will she be? The men look like her brothers, Bobo and Charlie. She is disgusted, and worse, bored, by Bobo and Charlie. The white woman is like the young girl who, according to the *Times*, *was* seduced off a farm in Minnesota by a black pimp and turned out on 42nd Street. She cannot stop herself from thinking: *Poor: Ignorant: Sleazy: Depressing.* This does not excite or stimulate.

He watches her face as he makes expert love to her. He knows his technique is virtually flawless, but he thinks perhaps it can be improved. Is she moving less rhythmically under him? Does she seem distracted? There seems to be a separate activity in her body, to which she is attentive, and which is not connected to the current he is sending through his fingertips. He notices the fluttering at the corners of her eyelids. Her eyes could fly open at any moment, he thinks, and look objectively at him. He shudders. Holds her tight.

He thinks frantically of what she might be thinking of him. Realizes he is moving in her *desperately*, as if he is climbing the walls of a closed building. As if she reads his mind, she moans encouragingly. But it is a distracted moan—that offends him.

He bites the pillow over her head: Where *is* she? he thinks. Is she into fantasy or not?

He must be.

He slips her into the role of "Fannie" with some hope. But nothing develops. As "Fannie" she refuses even to leave her Southern town. Won't speak to, much less go down on, either of the two gays.

He races back and forth between an image of her bound and on her knees, to two black men and a white woman becoming acquainted outside a bar.

This does not help.

Besides, she is involved in the activity inside herself and holding him—nostalgically.

He feels himself sliding down the wall that is her body, and expelled from inside her.

ADVANCING LUNA—AND
IDA B. WELLS

I met Luna the summer of 1965 in Atlanta where we both attended a political conference and rally. It was designed to give us the courage, as temporary civil rights workers, to penetrate the small hamlets farther south. I had taken a bus from Sarah Lawrence in New York and gone back to Georgia, my home state, to try my hand at registering voters. It had become obvious from the high spirits and sense of almost divine purpose exhibited by black people that a revolution was going on, and I did not intend to miss it. Especially not this summery, student-studded version of it. And I thought it would be fun to spend some time on my own in the South.

Luna was sitting on the back of a pickup truck, waiting for someone to take her from Faith Baptist, where the rally was held, to whatever gracious black Negro home awaited her. I remember because someone who assumed I would also be traveling by pickup introduced us. I remember her face when I said, "No, no more back of pickup trucks for me. I know Atlanta well enough, I'll walk." She assumed of course (I guess) that I did not wish to ride beside her because she was white, and I was not curious enough about what she might have thought to explain it to her. And yet I was struck by her passivity, her *patience* as she sat on the truck alone and ignored, because someone had told her to wait there quietly until it was time to go.

This look of passively waiting for something changed very little over the years I knew her. It was only four or five years in all that I did. It seems longer, perhaps because we met at such an optimistic time in our lives. John Kennedy and Malcolm X had already been assassinated, but King had not been and Bobby Kennedy had not been. Then too, the lethal, bizarre elimination by death of this militant or that, exiles, flights to Cuba, shoot-outs between former Movement friends sundered forever by lies planted by the FBI, the gunning down of Mrs. Martin Luther King, Sr., as she played the Lord's Prayer on the piano in her church (was her name Alberta?), were still in the happily unfathomable future.

We believed we could change America because we were young and bright and held ourselves *responsible* for changing it. We did not believe we would fail. This is what lent fervor (revivalist fervor, in fact; we would *revive* America!) to our songs, and lent sweetness to our friendships (in the beginning almost all interracial), and gave a wonderful fillip to our sex (which, too, in the beginning, was almost always interracial).

What first struck me about Luna when we later lived together was that she did not own a bra. This was curious to me, I suppose, because she also did not need one. Her chest was practically flat, her breasts like those of a child. Her face was round, and she suffered from acne. She carried with her always a tube of that "skin-colored" (if one's skin is pink or eggshell) medication designed to dry up pimples. At the oddest times—waiting for a light to change, listening to

211

voter registration instructions, talking about her father's new girlfriend, she would apply the stuff, holding in her other hand a small brass mirror the size of her thumb, which she also carried for just this purpose.

We were assigned to work together in a small, rigidly segregated South Georgia town that the city fathers, incongruously and years ago, had named Freehold. Luna was slightly asthmatic and when overheated or nervous she breathed through her mouth. She wore her shoulder-length black hair with bangs to her eyebrows and the rest brushed behind her ears. Her eyes were brown and rather small. She was attractive, but just barely and with effort. Had she been the slightest bit overweight, for instance, she would have gone completely unnoticed, and would have faded into the background where, even in a revolution, fat people seem destined to go. I have a photograph of her sitting on the steps of a house in South Georgia. She is wearing tiny pearl earrings, a dark sleeveless shirt with Peter Pan collar, Bermuda shorts, and a pair of those East Indian sandals that seem to adhere to nothing but a big toe.

The summer of '65 was as hot as any other in that part of the South. There was an abundance of flies and mosquitoes. Everyone complained about the heat and the flies and the hard work, but Luna complained less than the rest of us. She walked ten miles a day with me up and down those straight Georgia highways, stopping at every house that looked black (one could always tell in 1965) and asking whether anyone needed help with learning how to vote. The simple mechanics: writing one's name, or making one's "X" in the proper column. And then, though we were required to walk, everywhere, we were empowered to offer prospective registrants a car in which they might safely ride down to the county courthouse. And later to the polling places. Luna, almost overcome by the heat, breathing through her mouth like a dog, her hair plastered with sweat to her head, kept looking straight ahead, and walking as if the walking itself was her reward.

I don't know if we accomplished much that summer. In retrospect, it seems not only minor, but irrelevant. A bunch of us, black and white, lived together. The black people who took us in were unfailingly hospitable and kind. I took them for granted in a way that now amazes me. I realize that at each and every house we visited I *assumed* hospitality, I *assumed* kindness. Luna was often startled by my "boldness." If we walked up to a secluded farmhouse and half a dozen dogs ran up barking around our heels and a large black man with a shotgun could be seen whistling to himself under a tree, she would become nervous. I, on the other hand, felt free to yell at this stranger's dogs, slap a couple of them on the nose, and call over to him about his hunting.

That month with Luna of approaching new black people every day taught me something about myself I had always suspected: I thought black people superior people. Not simply superior to white people, because even without thinking about it much, I assumed almost everyone was superior to them; but to everyone. Only white people, after all, would blow up a Sunday-school class and grin for television over their "victory," *i.e.,* the death of four small black girls. Any atrocity, at any time, was expected from them. On the other hand, it never occurred to me that black people *could* treat Luna and me with anything but warmth and concern. Even their curiosity about the sudden influx into their midst of rather ignorant white and black Northerners was restrained and courteous. I was treated as a relative, Luna as a much welcomed guest.

Luna and I were taken in by a middle-aged couple and their young school-age daughter. The mother worked outside the house in a local canning factory, the father worked in the paper plant in nearby Augusta. Never did they speak of the danger they were in of losing their jobs over keeping us, and never did their small daughter show any fear that her house might be attacked by racists because we were there. Again, I did not expect this family to complain, no matter what happened to them because of us. Having understood the danger, they had assumed the risk. I did not think them particularly brave, merely typical.

I think Luna liked the smallness—only four rooms—of the house. It was in this house that she ridiculed her mother's lack of taste. Her yellow-and-mauve house in Cleveland, the eleven rooms, the heated garage, the new car every year, her father's inability to remain faithful to her mother, their divorce, the fight over the property, even more bitter than over the children. Her mother kept the house and the children. Her father kept the car and his new girlfriend, whom he wanted Luna to meet and "approve." I could hardly imagine anyone disliking her mother so much. Everything Luna hated in her she summed up in three words: *"yellow and mauve."*

I have a second photograph of Luna and a group of us being bullied by a Georgia state trooper. This member of Georgia's finest had followed us out into the deserted countryside to lecture us on how misplaced—in the South— was our energy, when "the Lord knew" the North (where he thought all of us lived, expressing disbelief that most of us were Georgians) was just as bad. (He had a point that I recognized even then, but it did not seem the point where we were.) Luna is looking up at him, her mouth slightly open as always, a somewhat dazed look on her face. I cannot detect fear on any of our faces, though we were all afraid. After all, 1965 was only a year after 1964 when three civil rights workers had been taken deep into a Mississippi forest by local officials and sadistically tortured and murdered. Luna almost always carried a flat black shoulder bag. She is standing with it against her side, her thumb in the strap.

At night we slept in the same bed. We talked about our schools, lovers, girlfriends we didn't understand or missed. She dreamed, she said, of going to Goa. I dreamed of going to Africa. My dream came true earlier than hers: an offer of a grant from an unsuspected source reached me one day as I was writing poems under a tree. I left Freehold, Georgia, in the middle of summer, without regrets, and flew from New York to London, to Cairo, to Kenya, and, finally, to Uganda, where I settled among black people with the same assumptions of welcome and kindness I had taken for granted in Georgia. I was taken on rides down the Nile as a matter of course, and accepted all invitations to dinner, where the best local dishes were superbly prepared in my honor. I became, in fact, a lost relative of the people, whose ancestors had foolishly strayed, long ago, to America.

I wrote to Luna at once.

But I did not see her again for almost a year. I had graduated from college, moved into a borrowed apartment in Brooklyn Heights, and was being evicted after a month. Luna, living then in a tenement on East 9th Street, invited me to share her two-bedroom apartment. If I had seen the apartment before the day I moved in I might never have agreed to do so. Her building was between Avenues B and C and did not have a front door. Junkies, winos, and others often wandered in during the night (and occasionally during the day) to sleep underneath the stairs or to relieve themselves at the back of the first-floor hall.

Luna's apartment was on the third floor. Everything in it was painted white. The contrast between her three rooms and kitchen (with its red bathtub) and the grungy stairway was stunning. Her furniture consisted of two large brass beds inherited from a previous tenant and stripped of paint by Luna, and a long, high-backed church pew which she had managed somehow to bring up from the South. There was a simplicity about the small apartment that I liked. I also liked the notion of extreme contrast, and I do to this day. Outside our front window was the decaying neighborhood, as ugly and ill-lit as a battleground. (And allegedly as hostile, though somehow we were never threatened with bodily harm by the

Hispanics who were our neighbors, and who seemed, more than anything, *bewildered* by the darkness and filth of their surroundings.) Inside was the church pew, as straight and spare as Abe Lincoln lying down, the white walls as spotless as a monastery's, and a small, unutterably pure patch of blue sky through the window of the back bedroom. (Luna did not believe in curtains, or couldn't afford them, and so we always undressed and bathed with the lights off and the rooms lit with candles, causing rather nun-shaped shadows to be cast on the walls by the long-sleeved high-necked nightgowns we both wore to bed.)

Over a period of weeks, our relationship, always marked by mutual respect, evolved into a warm and comfortable friendship which provided a stability and comfort we both needed at that time. I had taken a job at the Welfare Department during the day, and set up my typewriter permanently in the tiny living room for work after I got home. Luna worked in a kindergarten, and in the evenings taught herself Portuguese.

It was while we lived on East 9th Street that she told me she had been raped during her summer in the South. It is hard for me, even now, to relate my feeling of horror and incredulity. This was some time before Eldridge Cleaver wrote of being a rapist/revolutionary; of "practicing" on black women before moving on to white. It was also, unless I'm mistaken, before LeRoi Jones (as he was then known; now of course Imamu Baraka, which has an even more presumptuous meaning than "the King") wrote his advice to young black male insurrectionaries (women were not told what to do with *their* rebelliousness): "Rape the white girls. Rape their fathers." It was clear that he meant this literally and also as: to rape a white girl *is* to rape her father. It was the misogynous cruelty of this latter meaning that was habitually lost on black men (on men in general, actually), but nearly always perceived and rejected by women of whatever color.

"Details?" I asked.

She shrugged. Gave his name. A name recently in the news, though in very small print.

He was not a Movement star or anyone you would know. We had met once, briefly. I had not liked him because he was coarse and spoke of black women as "our" women. (In the early Movement, it was pleasant to think of black men wanting to own us as a group; later it became clear that owning us meant exactly *that* to them.) He was physically unattractive, I had thought, with something of the hoodlum about him: a swaggering, unnecessarily mobile walk, small eyes, rough skin, a mouthful of wandering or absent teeth. He was, ironically, among the first persons to shout the slogan everyone later attributed solely to Stokeley Carmichael—Black Power! Stokeley was chosen as the originator of this idea by the media, because he was physically beautiful and photogenic and articulate. Even the name—Freddie Pye—was diminutive, I thought, in an age of giants.

"What did you do?"

"Nothing that required making a noise."

"Why didn't you scream?" I felt I would have screamed my head off.

"You know why."

I did. I had seen a photograph of Emmett Till's body just after it was pulled from the river. I had seen photographs of white folks standing in a circle roasting something that had talked to them in their own language before they tore out its tongue. I knew why, all right.

"What was he trying to prove?"

"I don't know. Do you?"

"Maybe you filled him with unendurable lust," I said.

"I don't think so," she said.

Suddenly I was embarrassed. Then angry. Very, very angry. *How dare she tell me this!* I thought.

Who knows what the black woman thinks of rape? Who has

217

asked her? Who *cares*? Who has even properly acknowledged that *she* and not the white woman in this story is the most likely victim of rape? Whenever interracial rape is mentioned, a black woman's first thought is to protect the lives of her brothers, her father, her sons, her lover. A history of lynching has bred this reflex in her. I feel it as strongly as anyone. While writing a fictional account of such a rape in a novel, I read Ida B. Wells's autobiography three times, as a means of praying to her spirit to forgive me.

My prayer, as I turned the pages, went like this: *"Please forgive me. I am a writer."* (This self-revealing statement alone often seems to me sufficient reason to require perpetual forgiveness; since the writer is guilty not only of always wanting to know—like Eve—but also of trying—again like Eve—to find out.) *"I cannot write contrary to what life reveals to me. I wish to malign no one. But I must struggle to understand at least my own tangled emotions about interracial rape. I know, Ida B. Wells, you spent your whole life protecting, and trying to protect, black men accused of raping white women, who were lynched by white mobs, or threatened with it. You know, better than I ever will, what it means for a whole people to live under the terror of lynching. Under the slander that their men, where white women are concerned, are creatures of uncontrollable sexual lust. You made it so clear that the black men accused of rape in the past were innocent victims of white criminals that I grew up believing black men literally did not rape white women. At all. Ever. Now it would appear that some of them, the very twisted, the terribly ill, do. What would you have me write about them?"*

Her answer was: *"Write nothing. Nothing at all. It will be used against black men and therefore against all of us. Eldridge Cleaver and LeRoi Jones don't know who they're dealing with. But you remember. You are dealing with people who brought their children to witness the murder of black human beings, falsely accused of rape. People who handed out, as trophies, black fingers and toes. Deny! Deny! Deny!"*

And yet, I have pursued it: "*Some black men themselves do not seem to know what the meaning of raping someone is. Some have admitted rape in order to denounce it, but others have accepted rape as a part of rebellion, of 'paying whitey back.' They have gloried in it.*"

"*They know nothing of America,*" she says. "*And neither, apparently, do you. No matter what you think you know, no matter what you feel about it, say nothing. And to your dying breath!*"

Which, to my mind, is virtually useless advice to give to a writer.

Freddie Pye was the kind of man I would not have looked at then, not even once. (Throughout that year I was more or less into exotica: white ethnics who knew languages were a peculiar weakness; a half-white hippie singer; also a large Chinese mathematician who was a marvelous dancer and who taught me to waltz.) There was no question of belief.

But, in retrospect, there was a momentary *suspension* of belief, a kind of *hope* that perhaps it had not really happened; that Luna had made up the rape, "as white women have been wont to do." I soon realized this was unlikely. I was the only person she had told.

She looked at me as if to say: "I'm glad *that* part of my life is over." We continued our usual routine. We saw every interminable, foreign, depressing, and poorly illuminated film ever made. We learned to eat brown rice and yogurt and to tolerate kasha and odd-tasting teas. My half-black hippie singer friend (now a well-known reggae singer who says he is from "de I-lands" and not Sheepshead Bay) was "into" tea and kasha and Chinese vegetables.

And yet the rape, the knowledge of the rape, out in the open, admitted, pondered over, was now between us. (And I began to think that perhaps—whether Luna had been raped or not—it had always been so; that her power over my life was exactly the power *her word on rape* had over the lives of black men, over *all* black men, whether they were guilty or not, and therefore over my whole people.)

Before she told me about the rape, I think we had assumed a lifelong friendship. The kind of friendship one dreams of having with a person one has known in adversity; under heat and mosquitoes and immaturity and the threat of death. We would each travel, we would write to each other from the three edges of the world.

We would continue to have an "international list" of lovers whose amorous talents or lack of talents we would continue (giggling into our dotage) to compare. Our friendship would survive everything, be truer than everything, endure even our respective marriages, children, husbands—assuming we *did*, out of desperation and boredom someday, marry, which did not seem a probability, exactly, but more in the area of an amusing idea.

But now there was a cooling off of our affection for each other. Luna was becoming mildly interested in drugs, because everyone we knew was. I was envious of the open-endedness of her life. The financial backing to it. When she left her job at the kindergarten because she was tired of working, her errant father immediately materialized. He took her to dine on scampi in an expensive restaurant, scolded her for living on East 9th Street, and looked at me as if to say: "Living in a slum of this magnitude must surely have been your idea." As a cullud, of course.

For me there was the welfare department every day, attempting to get the necessary food and shelter to people who would always live amid the dirty streets I knew I must soon leave. I was, after all, a Sarah Lawrence girl "with talent." It would be absurd to rot away in a building that had no front door.

I slept late one Sunday morning with a painter I had met at the Welfare Department. A man who looked for all the world like Gene Autry, the singing cowboy, but who painted wonderful surrealist pictures of birds and ghouls and fruit with *teeth*. The night before, three of us—me, the painter, and "an old Navy buddy" who looked like his twin and who had just arrived in town—had got high on wine and grass.

That morning the Navy buddy snored outside the bedrooms like a puppy waiting for its master. Luna got up early, made an immense racket getting breakfast, scowled at me as I emerged from my room, and left the apartment, slamming the door so hard she damaged the lock. (Luna had made it a rule to date black men almost exclusively. My insistence on dating, as she termed it, "anyone" was incomprehensible to her, since in a politically diseased society to "sleep with the enemy" was to become "infected" with the enemy's "political germs." There is more than a grain of truth in this, of course, but I was having too much fun to stare at it for long. Still, coming from Luna it was amusing, since she never took into account the risk her own black lovers ran by sleeping with "the white woman," and she had apparently been convinced that a summer of relatively innocuous political work in the South had cured her of any racial, economic, or sexual political disease.)

Luna never told me what irked her so that Sunday morning, yet I remember it as the end of our relationship. It was not, as I at first feared, that she thought my bringing the two men to the apartment was inconsiderate. The way we lived allowed us to *be* inconsiderate from time to time. Our friends were varied, vital, and often strange. Her friends especially were deeper than they should have been into drugs.

The distance between us continued to grow. She talked more of going to Goa. My guilt over my dissolute if pleasurable existence coupled with my mounting hatred of welfare work, propelled me in two directions: south and to West Africa. When the time came to choose, I discovered that *my* summer in the South had infected me with the need to return, to try to understand, and write about, the people I'd merely lived with before.

We never discussed the rape again. We never discussed, really, Freddie Pye or Luna's remaining feelings about what had happened. One night, the last month we lived together, I noticed a man's blue denim jacket thrown across the church pew. The next morning, out of Luna's bedroom walked Freddie Pye. He barely spoke to me—possibly because as a black woman I was expected to be hostile toward his presence in a white woman's bedroom. I was too surprised to exhibit hostility, however, which was only a part of what I felt, after all. He left.

Luna and I did not discuss this. It is odd, I think now, that we didn't. It was as if he was never there, as if he and Luna had not shared the bedroom that night. A month later, Luna went alone to Goa, in her solitary way. She lived on an island and slept, she wrote, on the beach. She mentioned she'd found a lover there who protected her from the local beachcombers and pests.

Several years later, she came to visit me in the South and brought a lovely piece of pottery which my daughter much later dropped and broke, but which I glued back together in such a way that the flaw improves the beauty and fragility of the design.

AFTERWORDS, AFTERWARDS
SECOND THOUGHTS

That is the "story." It has an "unresolved" ending. That is because Freddie Pye and Luna are still alive, as am I. However, one evening while talking to a friend, I heard myself say that I had, in fact, written *two* endings. One, which follows, I considered appropriate for such a story published in a country truly committed to justice, and the one above, which is the best I can afford to offer a society in which lynching is still reserved, at least subconsciously, as a means of racial control.

I said that if we in fact lived in a society committed to the establishment of justice for everyone ("justice" in this case encompassing equal housing, education, access to work, adequate dental care, et cetera), thereby placing Luna and Freddie Pye in their correct relationship to each other, *i.e.*, that of brother and sister, *compañeros*, then the two of them would be required to struggle together over what his rape of her had meant.

Since my friend is a black man whom I love and who loves me, we spent a considerable amount of time discussing what this particular rape meant to us. Morally wrong, we said, and not to be excused. Shameful; politically corrupt. Yet, as we thought of what might have happened to an indiscriminate number of innocent young black men in Freehold, Georgia, had Luna screamed, it became clear that more than a little of Ida B. Wells's fear of probing the rape issue was running through us, too. The implications of this fear would not let me rest, so that months and years went by with most of the story written but with me incapable, or at least unwilling, to finish or to publish it.

In thinking about it over a period of years, there occurred a number of small changes, refinements, puzzles, in angle. Would these shed a wider light on the continuing subject? I do not know. In any case, I returned to my notes, hereto appended for the use of the reader.

LUNA: IDA B. WELLS—DISCARDED NOTES

Additional characteristics of Luna: At a time when many in and out of the Movement considered "nigger" and "black" synonymous, and indulged in a sincere attempt to fake Southern "hip" speech, Luna resisted. She was the kind of WASP who could not easily imitate another's ethnic style, nor could she even exaggerate her own. She was what she was. A very straight, clear-eyed, coolly observant young woman with no talent for existing outside her own skin.

IMAGINARY KNOWLEDGE

Luna explained the visit from Freddie Pye in this way:

"He called that evening, said he was in town, and did I know the Movement was coming north? I replied that I did know that."

When could he see her? he wanted to know.

"Never," she replied.

He had burst into tears, or something that sounded like tears, over the phone. He was stranded at wherever the evening's fund-raising event had been held. Not in the place itself, but outside, in the street. The "stars" had left, everyone had left. He was alone. He knew no one else in the city. Had found her number in the phone book. And had no money, no place to stay.

Could he, he asked, crash? He was tired, hungry, broke— and even in the South had had no job, other than the Movement, for months. Et cetera.

When he arrived, she had placed our only steak knife in the waistband of her jeans.

He had asked for a drink of water. She gave him orange juice, some cheese, and a couple of slices of bread. She had told him he might sleep on the church pew and he had lain down with his head on his rolled-up denim jacket. She had retired to her room, locked the door, and tried to sleep. She was amazed to discover herself worrying that the church pew was both too narrow and too hard.

At first he muttered, groaned, and cursed in his sleep. Then he fell off the narrow church pew. He kept rolling off. At two in the morning she unlocked her door, showed him her knife, and invited him to share her bed.

Nothing whatever happened except they talked. At first, only he talked. Not about the rape, but about his life.

"He was a small person physically, remember?" Luna asked me. (She was right. Over the years he had grown big and, yes, burly, in my imagination, and I'm sure in hers.) "That night he seemed tiny. A child. He was still fully dressed, except for the jacket and he, literally, hugged his side of the bed. I hugged mine. The whole bed, in fact, was between us. We were merely hanging to its edges."

At the fund-raiser—on Fifth Avenue and 71st Street, as it turned out—his leaders had introduced him as the unskilled, barely literate, former Southern fieldworker that he was. They had pushed him at the rich people gathered there as an example of what "the system" did to "the little people" in the South. They asked him to tell about the thirty-seven times he had been jailed. The thirty-five times he had been beaten. The one time he had lost consciousness in the "hot" box. They told him not to worry about his grammar. "Which, as you may recall," said Luna, "was horrible." Even so, he had tried to censor his "ain'ts" and his "us'es." He had been painfully aware that he was on exhibit, like Frederick Douglass had been for the Abolitionists. But unlike Douglass he had no oratorical gift, no passionate language, no silver tongue. He knew the rich people and his own leaders perceived he was nothing: a broken man, unschooled, unskilled at anything. . . .

Yet he had spoken, trembling before so large a crowd of rich, white Northerners—who clearly thought their section of the country would never have the South's racial problems—begging, with the painful stories of his wretched life, for their money.

At the end, all of them—the black leaders, too—had gone. They left him watching the taillights of their cars, recalling the faces of the friends come to pick them up: the women dressed in African print that shone, with elaborately arranged hair, their jewelry sparkling, their perfume exotic. They were so beautiful, yet so strange. He could not imagine that one of *them could comprehend his life. He did not ask for a ride, because of that, but also because he had no place to go. Then he had remembered Luna.*

Soon Luna would be required to talk. She would mention her confusion over whether, in a black community surrounded by whites with a history of lynching blacks, she had a right to scream as Freddie Pye was raping her. For her, this was the crux of the matter.

And so they would continue talking through the night.

This is another ending, created from whole cloth. If I believed Luna's story about the rape, and I did (had she told anyone else I might have dismissed it), then this reconstruction of what might have happened is as probable an accounting as any is liable to be. Two people have now become "characters."

I have forced them to talk until they reached the stumbling block of the rape, *which they must remove themselves*, before proceeding to a place from which it will be possible to insist on a society in which Luna's word alone on rape can never be used to intimidate an entire people, and in which an innocent black man's protestation of innocence of rape is unprejudicially heard. Until such a society is created, relationships of affection between black men and white women will always be poisoned—from within as from without—by historical fear and the threat of violence, and solidarity among black and white women is only rarely likely to exist.

POSTSCRIPT: HAVANA, CUBA, NOVEMBER 1976

I am in Havana with a group of other black American artists. We have spent the morning apart from our Cuban hosts bringing each other up to date on the kind of work (there are no apolitical artists among us) we are doing in the United States. I have read "Luna."

High above the beautiful city of Havana I sit in the Havana Libre pavilion with the muralist/photographer in our group. He is in his mid-thirties, a handsome, brown, erect individual whom I have know casually for a number of years. During the sixties he designed and painted street murals for both SNCC and the Black Panthers, and in an earlier discussion with Cuban artists he showed impatience with their explanation of why we had seen no murals covering some of the city's rather dingy walls: Cuba, they had said, unlike Mexico, has no mural tradition. "But the point of a revolution," insisted Our Muralist, "is to make new traditions!" And he had pressed his argument with such passion for the *usefulness*, for revolutionary communication, of his craft, that the Cubans were both exasperated and impressed. They drove us around the city for a tour of their huge billboards, all advancing socialist thought and the heroism of men like Lenin, Camilo, and Che Guevara, and said, "These, *these* are our 'murals'!"

While we ate lunch, I asked Our Muralist what he'd thought of "Luna." Especially the appended section.

"Not much," was his reply. "Your view of human weakness is too biblical," he said. "You are unable to conceive of the man without conscience. The man who cares nothing about the state of his soul because he's long since sold it. In short," he said, "you do not understand that some people are simply evil, a disease on the lives of other people, and that to remove the disease altogether is preferable to trying to interpret, contain, or forgive it. Your 'Freddie Pye,' " and he laughed, "was probably raping white women on the instructions of his government."

Oh ho, I thought. Because, of course, for a second, during which I stalled my verbal reply, this comment made both very little and very much sense.

"I *am* sometimes naive and sentimental," I offered. I am sometimes both, though frequently by design. Admission in this way is tactical, a stimulant to conversation.

227

"And shocked at what I've said," he said, and laughed again. "Even though," he continued, "you know by now that blacks could be hired to blow up other blacks, and could be hired *by someone* to shoot down Brother Malcolm, and hired *by someone* to provide a diagram of Fred Hampton's bedroom so the pigs could shoot him easily while he slept, you find it hard to believe a black man could be hired *by someone* to rape white women. But think a minute, and you will see why it is the perfect disruptive act. Enough blacks raping or accused of raping enough white women and any political movement that cuts across racial lines is doomed.

"Larger forces are at work than your story would indicate," he continued. "You're still thinking of lust and rage, moving slowly into aggression and purely racial hatred. But you should be considering money—which the rapist would get, probably from your very own tax dollars, in fact—and a maintaining of the status quo; which those hiring the rapist would achieve. I know all this," he said, "because when I was broke and hungry and selling my blood to buy the food and the paint that allowed me to work, I was offered such 'other work.'"

"But you did not take it."

He frowned. "There you go again. How do you know I didn't take it? It paid, and I was starving."

"You didn't take it," I repeated.

"No," he said. "A black and white 'team' made the offer. I had enough energy left to threaten to throw them out of the room."

"But even if Freddie Pye *had been* hired *by someone* to rape Luna, that still would not explain his second visit."

"Probably nothing will explain that," said Our Muralist. "But assuming Freddie Pye *was* paid to disrupt—by raping a white woman—the black struggle in the South, he may have wised up enough later to comprehend the significance of Luna's decision not to scream."

"So you are saying he *did have* a conscience?" I asked.

"Maybe," he said, but his look clearly implied I would never understand anything about evil, power, or corrupted human beings in the modern world.

But of course he is wrong.

LAUREL

It was during that summer in the mid-sixties that I met Laurel.

There was a new radical Southern newspaper starting up . . . it was only six months old at the time, and was called *First Rebel*. The title referred, of course, to the black slave who was rebelling all over the South long before the white rebels fought the Civil War. Laurel was in Atlanta to confer with the young people on its staff, and, since he wished to work on a radical, racially mixed newspaper himself, to see if perhaps *First Rebel* might be it.

I was never interested in working on a newspaper, however radical. I agree with Leonard Woolf that to write against a weekly deadline deforms the brain. Still, I attended several of the editorial meetings of *First Rebel* because while wandering out of the first one, fleeing it, in fact, I'd bumped into Laurel, who, squinting at me through cheap, fingerprint-smudged blue-and-gray-framed bifocals, asked if I knew where the meeting was.

He seemed a parody of the country hick; he was tall, slightly stooped, with blackish hair cut exactly as if someone had put a bowl over his head. Even his ears stuck out, and were large and pink.

Really, I thought.

Though he was no more than twenty-two, two years older than me, he seemed older. No doubt his bifocals added to this impression, as did his nonchalant gait and slouchy posture. His eyes were clear and brown and filled with an appropriate country slyness. It was his voice that held me. It had a charming lilt to it.

"Would you say that again?" I asked.

"Sure," he said, making it two syllables, the last syllable a higher pitch than the first. "I'm looking for where *First Rebel,* the newspaper, is meeting. What are *you* doing?"

The country slyness was clumsily replaced by a look of country seduction.

Have mercy! I thought. And burst into laughter.

Laurel grinned, his ears reddening.

And so we became involved in planning a newspaper that was committed to combating racism and other violence in the South . . . (until it ran out of funds and folded three years and many pieces of invaluable investigative journalism later).

Laurel's was not a variation of a Southern accent, as I'd at first thought. His ancestors had immigrated to the United States in the early 1800s. They had settled in California because there they found the two things they liked best: wine grapes and apples.

I'd never heard anything like Laurel's speech. He could ask a question like "How d'you happen t' be here?" and it sounded as if two happy but languid children were slowly jumping rope under apple trees in the sun. And on Laurel himself, while he spoke, I seemed to smell apples and the faint woodruffy bouquet of May wine.

He was also effortlessly complimentary. He would say, as we went through the cafeteria line "You're beaut-ti-ful, reel-i," and it was like hearing it and caring about hearing it for the first time. Laurel, who loved working among the grapes, and had done so up to the moment of leaving the orchards for Atlanta, had dirt, lots of it, under his nails.

That's it, I thought. I can safely play here. No one brings such dirty nails home to dinner. That was Monday. By Tuesday I thought that dirty nails were just the right nonbourgeois attribute and indicated a lack of personal concern for appearances that included the smudged bifocals and the frazzled but beautifully fitting jeans; in a back pocket of which was invariably a half-rolled, impressively battered paperback book. It occurred to me that I could not look at Laurel without wanting to make love with him.

He was the same.

For a while, I blamed it on Atlanta in the spring . . . the cherry trees that blossomed around the campus buildings, the wonderful honeysuckle smells of our South, the excitement of being far away from New York City and its never-to-be-gotten-used-to dirt. But it was more: if we both walked into a room from separate doors, even if we didn't see each other, a current dragged us together. At breakfast neither of us could eat, except chokingly, so intense was our longing to be together. Minus people, table, food.

A veritable movie.

Throughout the rest of the week we racked our brains trying to think of a place to make love. But the hotels were still segregated, and once, after a Movement party at somebody's house, we were severely reprimanded for walking out into the Southern night, blissfully hand in hand.

"*Don't you know this is outrageous?*" a young black man asked us, pulling us into his car, where I sat on Laurel's lap in a kind of sensual stupor—hearing his words, agreeing with them, knowing the bloody History behind them . . . but not caring in the least.

In short, there was no place for us to make love, as that term is popularly understood. We were housed in dormitories. Men in one. Women in another. Interracial couples were under surveillance wherever the poor things raised their heads anywhere in the city, We were reduced to a kind of sexual acrobatics on a bench close beside one of the dormitories. And, as lovers know, acrobatics of a sexual sort puts a strain on one's powers of physical ingenuity while making one's lust all the more a resident of the brain, where it quickly becomes all-pervading, insatiable, and profound.

The state of lust itself is not a happy one if there is no relief in sight. Though I am happy enough to enter that state whenever it occurs, I have learned to acknowledge its many and often devastating limitations. For example, the most monumental issues fade from one's consciousness as if erased by a swift wind. Movements of great social and political significance seem but backdrops to one's daily exchanges—be they ever so muted and circumscribed—with the Object of One's Desire. (I at least was not yet able to articulate how the personal is the political, as was certainly true in Laurel's and my case. Viz., nobody wanted us to go to bed with each other, except us, and they had made laws to that effect. And of course whether we slept together or not was nobody's business, except ours.)

The more it became impossible to be with Laurel, to make love fully and naturally, the more I wanted nothing but that. If the South had risen again during one of our stolen kisses— his hands on my breasts, my hands on his (his breasts were sensitive, we discovered quite by acrobatic invention and accident)—we would have been hard pressed to notice. This is "criminal" to write, of course, given the myths that supposedly make multiracial living so much easier to bear, but it is quite true. And yet, after our week together—passionate, beautiful, haunting, and never, never to be approximated between us again, our desire to make love never to be fulfilled (though we did not know this then), we went our separate ways. Because in fact, while we kissed and said Everything Else Be Damned! the South *was* rising again. *Was* murdering people. Was imprisoning our colleagues and friends. Was keeping us from strolling off to a clean, cheap hotel.

It was during our last night together that he told me about his wife. We were dancing in a local Movement-oriented nightclub. What would today be called a disco. He had an endearing way of dancing, even to slow tunes (during which we clung together shamelessly); he did a sort of hop, fast or slow depending on the music, from one foot to the other, almost in time with the music—and that was dance to him. It didn't bother me at all. Our bodies easily found their own rhythms anyway, and touching alone was our reason for being on the floor. *There* we could make a sort of love, in a dark enough corner, that was not exactly grace but was not, was definitely not, acrobatics.

He peered at me through the gray-and-blue-framed glasses. "I've got a wife back home."

What I've most resented as "the other woman" is being made responsible for the continued contentment and happiness of the wife. On our last night together, our lust undiminished and apparently not to be extinguished, given our surroundings, what was I supposed to do with this information?

All I could think was: She's not *my* wife.

She was, from what little he said, someone admirable. She was away from home for the summer, studying for an advanced degree. He seemed perplexed by this need of hers to continue her education instead of settling down to have his children, but lonely rather than bitter.

So it was *just sex* between us, after all, I thought.

(To be fair, I was engaged to a young man in the Peace Corps. I didn't mind if it *was* just sex, since by that time our mutual lust had reached a state, almost, of mysticism.)

Laurel, however, was tormented.

(I never told him about my engagement. As far as I was

concerned, it remained to be seen whether my engagement was relevant to my relationships with others. I thought not, but realized I was still quite young.)

That night, Laurel wrung his hands, pulled his strangely cut hair and cried, as we brazenly walked out along Atlanta's dangerous, cracker-infested streets.

I cried because he did, and because in some odd way it relieved my lust. Besides, I enjoyed watching myself pretend to suffer... Such moments of emotional dishonesty are always paid for, however, and that I did not know this at the time attests to my willingness to believe our relationship would not live past the moment itself.

And yet.

There was one letter from him to me after I'd settled in a small Georgia town (a) to picket the jailhouse where a local schoolteacher was under arrest for picketing the jailhouse where a local parent was under arrest for picketing the jailhouse where a local child was under arrest for picketing... and (b) to register voters.

He wrote that he missed me.

I missed him. He was the principal other actor in all my fantasies. I wrote him that I was off to Africa, but would continue to write. I gave him the address of my school, to which he could send letters.

Once in Africa, my fiancé (who was conveniently in the next country from mine and free to visit) and I completed a breakup that had been coming for our entire two-year period of engagement. He told me, among other things, that it was not uncommon for Peace Corps men to sleep with ten-year-old African girls. *At that age, you see, they were still attractive.* I wrote about that aspect of the Peace Corps' activities to Laurel, as if I'd heard about it from a stranger.

Laurel, I felt, would never take advantage of a ten-year-old child. And I loved him for it.

Loving him, I was not prepared for the absence of letters from him, back at my school. Three months after my return

I still had heard nothing. Out of depression over this and the distraction schoolwork provided, I was a practicing celibate. Only rarely did I feel lustful, and then of course I always thought of Laurel, as of a great opportunity, much missed. I thought of his musical speech and his scent of apples and May wine with varying degrees of regret and tenderness. However, our week of passion—magical, memorable, but far too brief—gradually assumed a less than central place even in my most sanguine recollections.

In late November, six months after Laurel and I met, I received a letter from his wife.

My first thought, when I saw the envelope, was: She has the same last name as his. It was the first time their marriage was real for me. I was also frightened that she wrote to accuse me of disturbing her peace. Why else would a wife write?

She wrote that on July fourth of the previous summer (six weeks after Laurel and I met) Laurel had had an automobile accident. He was driving his van, delivering copies of *First Rebel*. He had either fallen asleep at the wheel or been run off the road by local rebels of the other kind. He had sustained a broken leg, a fractured back, and a severely damaged brain. He had been in a coma for the past four months. Nothing could rouse him. She had found my letter in his pocket. Perhaps I would come see him?

(I was never to meet Laurel's wife, but I admired this gesture then, and I admire it now.)

It was a small Catholic hospital in Laurel's hometown. In the entryway a bloody, gruesome, ugly Christ the color of a rutabaga, stood larger than life. Nuns dressed in black and white habits reminded one of giant flies. Floating moonlike above their "wings," their pink, cherubic faces were kind and comical.

Laurel's father looked very much like Laurel. The same bifocals, the same plain clothing, the same open-seeming face—but on closer look, wide rather than open. The same lilt to his voice. Laurel's sister was also there. She, unaccountably, embraced me.

"We're so glad you came," she said.

She was like Laurel too. Smaller, pretty, with short blond hair and apple cheeks.

She reached down and took Laurel's hand.

Laurel alone did not look like Laurel. He who had been healthy, firm-fleshed, virile, lay now on his hospital bed a skeleton with eyes. Tubes entered his body everywhere. His head was shaved, a bandage covering the hole that had been drilled in the top. His breathing was hardly a whistle through a hole punched in his throat.

I took the hands that had given such pleasure to my breasts, and they were bones, unmoving, cold, in mine. I touched the face I'd dreamed about for months as I would the face of someone already in a coffin.

His sister said, "Annie is here," her voice carrying the lilt.

Laurel's eyes were open, jerking, twitching, in his head. His mouth was open. But he was not there. Only his husk, his shell. His father looked at me—as he would look at any other treatment. Speculatively. Will it work? Will it revive my son?

I did not work. I did not revive his son. Laurel lay, wheezing through the hole in his throat, helpless, insensate. I was eager to leave.

Two years later, the letters began to arrive. Exactly as if he thought I still waited for them at my school.

"My darling," he wrote, "I am loving you. Missing you and out of coma after a year and everybody given up on me. My brain damaged. Can you come to me? I am still bedridden."

But I was not in school. I was married, living in the South.

"Tell him you're married now," my husband advised. "He should know not to hurt himself with dreaming."

I wrote that I was not only married but "happily."

My marital status meant nothing to Laurel.

"Please come," he wrote. "There are few black people here. You would be lonesome but I will be here loving you."

I wrote again. This time I reported I was married, pregnant, and had a dog for protection.

"I dream of your body so luscious and fertile. I want so much to make love to you as we never could do. I hope you know how I lost part of my brain working for your people in the South. I miss you. Come soon."

I wrote: "Dear Laurel, I am so glad you are better. I'm sorry you were hurt. So sorry. I cannot come to you because I am married. I love my husband. I cannot bear to come. I am pregnant—nauseous all the time and anxious because of the life I/We lead." Etc., etc.

To which he replied: "You married a jew. [I had published a novel and apparently reviewers had focused on my marriage instead of my work as they often did.] There are no jews here either. I guess you have a taste for the exotic though I was not exotic. I am a cripple now with part of my brain in somebody's wastepaper basket. We could have children if you will take the responsibility for bringing them up. I cannot be counted on. Ha. Ha."

I asked my husband to intercept the letters that came to our house. I asked the president of my college to collect and destroy those sent to me there. I dreaded seeing them.

"I dream of your body, so warm and brown, whereas mine is white and cold to me now. I could take you as my wife here the people are prejudiced against blacks they were happy martin luther king was killed. I want you here. We can be happy and black and beautiful and crippled and missing part of my brain together. I want you but I guess you are tied up with that jew husband of yours. I mean no disrespect to him but we belong together you know that."

"Dear Laurel, I am a mother. [I hoped this would save me. It didn't.] I have a baby daughter. I hope you are well. My husband sends his regards."

Most of Laurel's letters I was not shown. Assuming that my

husband confiscated his letters without my consent, Laurel telegraphed: ANNIE, I AM COMING BY GREYHOUND BUS DON'T LET YOUR DOG BITE ME, LAUREL.

My husband said: "Fine, let him come. Let him see that you are not the woman he remembers. His memory is frozen on your passion for each other. Let him see how happy you and I are."

I waited, trembling.

It was a cold, clear evening. Laurel hobbled out of the taxi on crutches, one leg shorter than the other. He had regained his weight and, though pale, was almost handsome. He glanced at my completely handsome husband once and dismissed him. He kept his eyes on me. He smiled on me happily, pleased with me.

I knew only one dish then, chicken tarragon; I served it.

I was frightened. Not of Laurel, exactly, but of feeling all the things I felt.

(My husband's conviction notwithstanding, I suspected marriage could not keep me from being, in some ways, exactly the woman Laurel remembered.)

I woke up my infant daughter and held her, disgruntled, flushed and ludicrously alert, in front of me.

While we ate, Laurel urged me to recall our acrobatic nights on the dormitory bench, our intimate dancing. Before my courteous husband, my cheeks flamed. Those nights that seemed so far away to me seemed all he clearly remembered; he recalled less well how his accident occurred. Everything before and after that week had been swept away. The moment was real to him. I was real to him. Our week together long ago was very real to him. But that was all. His speech was as beautifully lilting as ever, with a zaniness that came from a lack of connective knowledge. But he was hard to listen to: he was both overconfident of his success with me—based on what he recalled of our mutual passion—and so intense that his gaze had me on the verge of tears.

Now that he was here and almost well, I must drop everything, including the baby on my lap—whom he barely seemed to see—and come away with him. Had I not flown off to Africa, though it meant leaving the very country in which he lived?

Finally, after the riddles within riddles that his words became (and not so much riddles as poems, and disturbing ones), my husband drove Laurel back to the bus station. He had come over a thousand miles for a two-hour visit.

My husband's face was drawn when he returned. He loved me, I was sure of that. He was glad to help me out. Still, he wondered.

"*It lasted a week!*" I said. "Long before I met you!"

"I know," he said. "Sha, sha, baby," he comforted me. I had crept into his arms, trembling from head to foot. "It's all right. We're safe."

But *were we*?

And Laurel? Zooming through the night back to his home? The letters continued. Sometimes I asked to read one that came to the house.

"I am on welfare now. I hate being alive. Why didn't my father let me die? The people are prejudiced here. If you came they would be cruel to us but maybe it would help them see something. You are more beautiful than ever. You are so sexy you make me ache—it is not only because you are black that would be racism but because when you are in the same room with me the room is full of color and scents and I am all alive."

He offered to adopt my daughter, shortly after he received a divorce from his wife.

After my husband and I were divorced (some seven years after Laurel's visit and thirteen years after Laurel and I met), we sat one evening discussing Laurel. He recalled him perfectly, with characteristic empathy and concern.

"If I hadn't been married to you, I would have gone off with him," I said, "Maybe."

"Really?" He seemed surprised.

Out of habit I touched his arm. "I loved him, in a way."

"I know," he said, and smiled.

"A lot of the love was lust. That threw me off for years until I realized lust can be a kind of love."

He nodded.

"I felt guilty about Laurel. When he wrote me, I became anxious. When he came to visit us, I was afraid."

"He was not the man you knew."

"I don't think I knew him well enough to tell. Even so, I was afraid the love and lust would come flying back, along with the pity. And that even if they didn't come back, I would run off with him anyway, because of the pity—*and for the adventure*."

It was the word "adventure" and the different meaning it had for each of us that finally separated us. We had come to understand that, and to accept it without bitterness.

"I wanted to ask you to let me go away with him, for just a couple of months," I said. "*To let me go* . . ."

"He grew steadily worse, you know. His last letters were brutal. He blamed you for everything, even the accident, accusing you of awful, nasty things. He became a bitter, vindictive man."

He knew me well enough to know I heard this and I did not hear it.

He sighed. "It would have been tough for me," he said. "Tough for our daughter. Tough for you. Toughest of all for Laurel."

("*Tell me it's all right that I didn't go!*" I wanted to plead, but didn't.)

"Right," I said instead, shrugging, and turning our talk to something else.

A LETTER OF THE TIMES, OR SHOULD THIS SADO-MASOCHISM BE SAVED?

Dear Lucy,

You ask why I snubbed you at the Women for Elected Officials Ball. I don't blame you for feeling surprised and hurt. After all, we planned the ball together, expecting to raise our usual pisspot full of money for a good cause. Such a fine idea, our ball: Come as the feminist you most admire! But I did not know you most admired Scarlett O'Hara and so I was, for a moment, taken aback.

I don't know; maybe I should see that picture again. Sometimes when I see movies that hurt me as a child, the pain is minor; I can laugh at the things that made me sad. My trouble with Scarlett was always the forced buffoonery of

242

Prissy, whose strained, slavish voice, as Miz Scarlett pushed her so masterfully up the stairs, I could never get out of my head.

But there is another reason I could not speak to you at the ball that had nothing to do with what is happening just now between us: this heavy bruised silence, this anger and distrust. The day of the ball was my last class day at the University, and it was a very heavy and discouraging day.

Do you remember the things I told you about the class? Its subject was God. That is, the inner spirit, the inner voice; the human compulsion when deeply distressed to seek healing counsel within ourselves, and the capacity within ourselves both to create this counsel and to receive it.

(It had always amused me that the God who spoke to Harriet Tubman and Sojourner Truth told them exactly what they needed to hear, no less than the God of the Old Testament constantly reassured the ancient Jews.)

Indeed, as I read the narratives of black people who were captured and set to slaving away their lives in America, I saw that this inner spirit, this inner capacity for self-comforting, this ability to locate God within that they expressed, demonstrated something marvelous about human beings. Nature has created us with the capacity to know God, to experience God, just as it has created us with the capacity to know speech. The experience of God, or in any case the possibility of experiencing God, *is innate*!

I suppose this has all been thought before; but it came to me as a revelation after reading how the fifth or sixth black woman, finding herself captured, enslaved, sexually abused, starved, whipped, the mother of children she could not want, lover of children she could not have, crept into the corners of the fields, among the haystacks and the animals, and found within her own heart the only solace and love she was ever to know.

It was as if these women found a twin self who saved them from their abused consciousness and chronic physical loneliness; and that twin self is in all of us, waiting only to be summoned.

To prepare my class to comprehend God in this way, I requested they read narratives of these captured black women and also write narratives themselves, as if they *were* those women, or women like them. At the same time, I asked them to write out their own understanding of what the inner voice, "God," is.

It was an extraordinary class, Lucy! With women of all colors, all ages, all shapes and sizes and all conditions. There were lesbians, straights, curveds, celibates, prostitutes, mothers, confuseds, and sundry brilliants of all persuasions! A wonderful class! And almost all of them, though hesitant to admit it at first—who dares talk seriously of "religious" matters these days?—immediately sensed what I meant when I spoke of the inner companion spirit, of "God."

But what does my class on God have to do with why I snubbed you at the ball? I can hear you wondering. And I will get on to the point.

Lucy, I wanted to teach my students what it felt like to be captured and enslaved. I wanted them to be unable, when they left my class, to think of enslaved women as exotic, picturesque, removed from themselves, deserving of enslavement. I wanted them to be able to repudiate all the racist stereotypes about black women who were enslaved: that they were content, that they somehow "chose" their servitude, that they did not resist.

And so we struggled through an entire semester, during each week of which a student was required to imagine herself a "slave," a mistress or a master, and to come to terms, in imagination and feeling, with what that meant.

Some black women found it extremely difficult to write as captured and enslaved women. (I do not use the word "slaves" casually, because I see enslavement from the enslaved's point of view; there is a world of difference between being a slave and being enslaved). They chose to write as mistress or master. Some white women found it nearly impossible to write as mistress or master, and presumptuous to write as enslaved. Still, there were many fine papers written, Lucy, though there was also much hair tugging and gnashing of teeth.

Black and white and mixed women wrote of captivity, of rape, of forced breeding to restock the master's slave pens. They wrote of attempts to escape, of the sale of their children, of dreams of Africa, of efforts at suicide. No one wrote of acquiescence or of happiness, though one or two, mindful of the religious spirit often infusing the narratives studied, described spiritual ecstasy and joy.

Does anyone want to be a slave? we pondered.

As a class, we thought not.

Imagine our surprise, therefore, when many of us watched a television special on sado-masochism that aired the night before our class ended, and the only interracial couple in it, lesbians, presented themselves as mistress and slave. The white woman, who did all the talking, was mistress (wearing a ring in the shape of a key that she said fit the lock on the chain around the black woman's neck), and the black woman, who stood smiling and silent, was—the white woman said— her slave.

And this is why, though we have been friends for over a decade, Lucy, I snubbed you at the ball.

All I had been teaching was subverted by that one image, and I was incensed to think of the hard struggle of my students to rid themselves of stereotype, to combat prejudice, to put themselves into enslaved women's skins, and then to see their struggle mocked, and the actual enslaved *condition* of literally millions of our mothers trivialized—because two ignorant women insisted on their right to act out publicly a "fantasy" that still strikes terror in black women's hearts. And embarrassment and disgust, at least in the hearts of most of the white women in my class.

One white woman student, apparently with close ties to

our local lesbian S&M group, said she could see nothing wrong with what we'd seen on TV. (Incidentally, there were several white men on this program who owned white women as "slaves," and even claimed to hold legal documents to this effect. Indeed, one man paraded his slave around town with a horse's bit between her teeth, and "lent" her out to other sado-masochists to be whipped.) It is all fantasy, she said. No harm done. Slavery, real slavery, is over, after all.

But it isn't over, Lucy, and Kathleen Barry's book on female sexual slavery and Linda Lovelace's book on *being* such a slave are not the only recent indications that this is true. There are places in the world, Lucy, where human beings are still being bought and sold! And so, for that reason, when I saw you at the ball, all I could think was that you were insultingly dressed. No, that is not all I thought: once seeing you dressed as Scarlett, I could not see you. I did not *dare* see you. When you accuse me of looking through you, you are correct. For if I had seen you, Lucy, I'm sure I would have struck you, and with your love of fighting this would surely have meant the end of our ball. And so it was better *not* to see you, to look instead at the woman next to you who had kinked her hair to look like Colette.

A black student said to the S&M sympathizer: I feel abused. I feel my privacy as a black woman has been invaded. Whoever saw that television program can now look at me standing on the corner waiting for a bus and not see *me* at all, but see instead a slave, a creature who *would* wear a chain and lock around my neck for a white person—in 1980!—and accept it. *Enjoy* it.

Her voice shook with anger and hurt.

And so, Lucy, you and I will be friends again because I will talk you out of caring about heroines whose real source of power, as well as the literal shape and condition of their bodies, comes from the people they oppress. But what of the future? What of the women who will never come together because of what they saw in the relationship between "mistress" and "slave" on TV? Many black women fear it is as slaves white women want them; no doubt many white women think some amount of servitude from black women is their due.

But, Lucy, regardless of the "slave" on television, black women do not want to be slaves. They never wanted to be slaves. We will be ourselves and free, or die in the attempt. Harriet Tubman was not our great-grandmother for nothing; which I would advise all black and white women aggressing against us as "mistress" and "slave" to remember. We understand when an attempt is being made to lead us into captivity, though television is a lot more subtle than slave ships. We will simply resist, as we have always done, with ever more accurate weapons of defense.

As a matter of fact, Lucy, it occurs to me that we might plan another ball in the spring as a benefit for this new resistance. What do you think? Do let us get together to discuss it, during the week.

Your friend,
Susan Marie

A Sudden Trip Home in the Spring

For the Wellesley Class

Sarah walked slowly off the tennis court, fingering the back
of her head, feeling the sturdy dark hair that grew there. She
was popular. As she walked along the path toward Talfinger
Hall her friends fell into place around her. They formed a
warm jostling group of six. Sarah, because she was taller
than the rest, saw the messenger first.

"Miss Davis," he said, standing still until the group came
abreast of him, "I've got a telegram for ye." Brian was Irish
and always quite respectful. He stood with his cap in his
hand until Sarah took the telegram. Then he gave a nod that
included all the young ladies before he turned away. He
was young and good-looking, though annoyingly servile, and
Sarah's friends twittered.

"Well, open it!" someone cried, for Sarah stood staring at the yellow envelope, turning it over and over in her hand.

"Look at her," said one of the girls, "isn't she beautiful! Such eyes, and hair, and *skin!*"

Sarah's tall, caplike hair framed a face of soft brown angles, high cheekbones and large dark eyes. Her eyes enchanted her friends because they always seemed to know more, and to find more of life amusing, or sad, than Sarah cared to tell.

Her friends often teased Sarah about her beauty; they loved dragging her out of her room so that their boyfriends, naive and worldly young men from Princeton and Yale, could see her. They never guessed she found this distasteful. She was gentle with her friends, and her outrage at their tactlessness did not show. She was most often inclined to pity them, though embarrassment sometimes drove her to fraudulent expressions. Now she smiled and raised eyes and arms to heaven. She acknowledged their unearned curiosity as a mother endures the prying impatience of a child. Her friends beamed love and envy upon her as she tore open the telegram.

"He's dead," she said.

Her friends reached out for the telegram, their eyes on Sarah.

"It's her father," one of them said softly. "He died yesterday. Oh, Sarah," the girl whimpered, "I'm so sorry!"

"Me too." "So am I." "Is there anything we can do?"

But Sarah had walked away, head high and neck stiff.

"So graceful!" one of her friends said.

"Like a proud gazelle" said another. Then they all trooped to their dormitories to change for supper.

Talfinger Hall was a pleasant dorm. The common room just off the entrance had been made into a small modern art gallery with some very good original paintings, lithographs and collages. Pieces were constantly being stolen. Some of the girls could not resist an honest-to-God Chagall, signed (in the plate) by his own hand, though they could have afforded to purchase one from the gallery in town. Sarah Davis's room was next door to the gallery, but her walls were covered with inexpensive Gauguin reproductions, a Rubens ("The Head of a Negro"), a Modigliani and a Picasso. There was a full wall of her own drawings, all of black women. She found black men impossible to draw or to paint; she could not bear to trace defeat onto blank pages. Her women figures were matronly, massive of arm, with a weary victory showing in their eyes. Surrounded by Sarah's drawings was a red SNCC poster of a man holding a small girl whose face nestled in his shoulder. Sarah often felt she was the little girl whose face no one could see.

To leave Talfinger even for a few days filled Sarah with fear. Talfinger was her home now; it suited her better than any home she'd ever known. Perhaps she loved it because in winter there was a fragrant fireplace and snow outside her window. When hadn't she dreamed of fireplaces that really warmed, snow that almost pleasantly froze? Georgia seemed far away as she packed; she did not want to leave New York, where, her grandfather had liked to say, "the devil hung out and caught young gals by the front of their dresses." He had always believed the South the best place to live on earth (never mind that certain people invariably marred the landscape), and swore he expected to die no more than a few miles from where he had been born. There was tenacity even in the gray frame house he lived in, and in scrawny animals on his farm who regularly reproduced. He was the first person Sarah wanted to see when she got home.

There was a knock on the door of the adjoining bathroom, and Sarah's suite mate entered, a loud Bach concerto just finishing behind her. At first she stuck just her head into the room, but seeing Sarah fully dressed she trudged in and plopped down on the bed. She was a heavy blonde girl with large milk-white legs. Her eyes were small and her neck usually gray with grime.

"My, don't you look gorgeous," she said.

"Ah, Pam," said Sarah, waving her hand in disgust. In Georgia she knew that even to Pam she would be just another ordinarily attractive *colored* girl. In Georgia there were a million girls better looking. Pam wouldn't know that, of course; she'd never been to Georgia; she'd never even seen a black person to speak to, that is, before she met Sarah. One of her first poetic observations about Sarah was that she was "a poppy in a field of winter roses." She had found it weird that Sarah did not own more than one coat.

"Say listen, Sarah," said Pam. "I heard about your father. I'm sorry. I really am."

"Thanks," said Sarah.

"Is there anything we can do? I thought, well, maybe you'd want my father to get somebody to fly you down. He'd go himself but he's taking Mother to Madeira this week. You wouldn't have to worry about trains and things."

Pamela's father was one of the richest men in the world, though no one ever mentioned it. Pam only alluded to it at times of crisis, when a friend might benefit from the use of a private plane, train, or ship; or, if someone wanted to study the characteristics of a totally secluded village, island or mountain, she might offer one of theirs. Sarah could not comprehend such wealth, and was always annoyed because Pam didn't look more like a billionaire's daughter. A billionaire's daughter, Sarah thought, should really be less horsey and brush her teeth more often.

"Gonna tell me what you're brooding about?" asked Pam.

Sarah stood in front of the radiator, her fingers resting on the window seat. Down below girls were coming up the hill from supper.

"I'm thinking," she said, "of the child's duty to his parents after they are dead."

"Is that all?"

"Do you know," asked Sarah, "about Richard Wright and his father?"

Pamela frowned. Sarah looked down at her.

"Oh, I forgot," she said with a sigh, "they don't teach Wright here. The poshest school in the U.S., and the girls come out ignorant." She looked at her watch, saw she had twenty minutes before her train. "Really," she said almost inaudibly, "why Tears Eliot, Ezratic Pound, and even Sara Teacake, and no Wright?" She and Pamela thought e.e. cummings very clever with his perceptive spelling of great literary names.

"Is he a poet then?" asked Pam. She adored poetry, all poetry. Half of America's poetry she had, of course, not read, for the simple reason that she had never heard of it.

"No," said Sarah, "he wasn't a poet." She felt weary. "He was a man who wrote, a man who had trouble with his father." She began to walk about the room, and came to stand below the picture of the old man and the little girl.

"When he was a child," she continued, "his father ran off with another woman, and one day when Richard and his mother went to ask him for money to buy food he laughingly rejected them. Richard, being very young, thought his father Godlike. Big, omnipotent unpredictable, undependable and cruel. Entirely in control of his universe. Just like a god. But, many years later, after Wright had become a famous writer, he went down to Mississippi to visit his father. He found, instead of God, just an old watery-eyed field hand, bent from plowing, his teeth gone, smelling of manure. Richard realized that the most daring thing his 'God' had done was run off with that other woman."

"So?" asked Pam. "What 'duty' did he feel he owed the old man?"

"So," said Sarah, "that's what Wright wondered as he peered into that old shifty-eyed Mississippi Negro face. What was the duty of the son of a destroyed man? The son of a man whose vision had stopped at the edge of fields that weren't even his. Who was Wright without his father? Was he Wright the great writer? Wright the Communist? Wright the French farmer? Wright whose white wife could never accompany him to Mississippi? Was he, in fact, still his father's son? Or was he freed by his father's desertion to be nobody's son, to be his own father? Could he disavow his father and live? And if so, live as what? As whom? And for what purpose?"

"Well," said Pam, swinging her hair over her shoulders and squinting her small eyes, "if his father rejected him I don't see why Wright even bothered to go see him again. From what you've said, Wright earned the freedom to be whoever he wanted to be. To a strong man a father is not essential."

"Maybe not," said Sarah, "but Wright's father was one faulty door in a house of many ancient rooms. Was that one faulty door to shut him off forever from the rest of the house? That was the question. And though he answered this question eloquently in his work, where it really counted, one can only wonder if he was able to answer it satisfactorily— or at all—in his life."

"You're thinking of his father more as a symbol of something, aren't you?" asked Pam.

"I suppose," said Sarah, taking a last look around her room. "I see him as a door that refused to open, a hand that was always closed. A fist."

Pamela walked with her to one of the college limousines, and in a few minutes she was at the station. The train to the city was just arriving.

"Have a nice trip," said the middle-aged driver courteously, as she took her suitcase from him. But for about the thousandth time since she'd seen him, he winked at her.

Once away from her friends she did not miss them. The school was all they had in common. How could they ever know her if they were not allowed to know Wright, she wondered. She was interesting, "beautiful," only because they had no idea what made her, charming only because they had no idea from where she came. And where they came from, though she glimpsed it—in themselves and in F. Scott Fitzgerald—she was never to enter. She hadn't the inclination or the proper ticket.

2

Her father's body was in Sarah's old room. The bed had been taken down to make room for the flowers and chairs and casket. Sarah looked for a long time into the face, as if to find some answer to her questions written there. It was the same face, a dark Shakespearean head framed by gray, woolly hair and split almost in half by a short, gray mustache. It was a completely silent face, a shut face. But her father's face also looked fat, stuffed, and ready to burst. He wore a navy-blue suit, white shirt and black tie. Sarah bent and loosened the tie. Tears started behind her shoulder blades but did not reach her eyes.

"There's a rat here under the casket," she called to her brother, who apparently did not hear her, for he did not come in. She was alone with her father, as she had rarely been when he was alive. When he was alive she had avoided him.

"Where's that girl at?" her father would ask. "Done closed herself up in her room again," he would answer himself.

For Sarah's mother had died in her sleep one night. Just gone to bed tired and never got up. And Sarah had blamed her father.

Stare the rat down, thought Sarah, surely that will help. *Perhaps it doesn't matter whether I misunderstood or never understood.*

"We moved so much looking for crops, a place to *live*," her father had moaned, accompanied by Sarah's stony silence. "The moving killed her. And now we have a real house, with *four* rooms, and a mailbox on the *porch*, and it's too late. She gone. *She* ain't here to see it." On very bad days her father would not eat at all. At night he did not sleep.

Whatever had made her think she knew what love was or was not?

Here she was, Sarah Davis, immersed in Camusian philosophy, versed in many languages, a poppy, of all things, among winter roses. But before she became a poppy she was a native Georgian sunflower, but still had not spoken the language they both knew. Not to him.

Stare the rat down, she thought, and did. The rascal dropped his bold eyes and slunk away. Sarah felt she had, at least, accomplished something.

Why did she have to see the picture of her mother, the one on the mantel among all the religious doodads, come to life? Her mother had stood stout against the years, clean gray braids shining across the top of her head, her eyes snapping, protective. Talking to her father.

"He called you out your name, we'll leave this place today. Not tomorrow. That be too late. Today!" Her mother was magnificent in her quick decisions.

"But what about your garden, the children, the change of schools?" Her father would be holding, most likely, the wide brim of his hat in nervously twisting fingers.

"He called you out your name, we go!"

And go they would. Who knew exactly where, before they moved? Another soundless place, walls falling down, roofing gone; another face to please without leaving too much of her father's pride at his feet. But to Sarah then, no matter with what alacrity her father moved, foot-dragging alone was visible.

The moving killed her, her father had said, *but the moving was also love*.

Did it matter now that often he had threatened their lives with the rage of his despair? That once he had spanked the crying baby violently, who later died of something else altogether . . . and that the next day they moved?

"No," said Sarah aloud, "I don't think it does."

"Huh?" It was her brother, tall, wiry, black, deceptively

calm. As a child he'd had an irrepressible temper. As a grown man he was tensely smooth, like a river that any day will overflow its bed.

He had chosen a dull gray casket. Sarah wished for red. Was it Dylan Thomas who had said something grand about the dead offering "deep, dark defiance"? It didn't matter; there were more ways to offer defiance than with a red casket.

"I was just thinking," said Sarah, "that with us Mama and Daddy were saying NO with capital letters."

"I don't follow you," said her brother. He had always been the activist in the family. He simply directed his calm rage against any obstacle that might exist, and awaited the consequences with the same serenity he awaited his sister's answer. Not for him the philosophical confusions and poetic observations that hung his sister up.

"That's because you're a radical preacher," said Sarah, smiling up at him. "You deliver your messages in person with your own body." It excited her that her brother had at last imbued their childhood Sunday sermons with the reality of fighting for change. And saddened her that no matter how she looked at it this seemed more important than Medieval Art, Course 201.

3

"Yes, Gramdma," Sarah replied. "Cresselton is for girls only, and *no*, Grandma, I am not pregnant."

Her grandmother stood clutching the broad wooden handle of her black bag, which she held, with elbows bent, in front of her stomach. Her eyes glinted through round wire-framed glasses. She spat into the grass outside the privy. She had insisted that Sarah accompany her to the toilet while the body was being taken into the church. She had leaned heavily on Sarah's arm, her own arm thin and the flesh like crêpe.

"I guess they teach you how to really handle the world," she said. "And who knows, the Lord is everywhere. I would like a whole lot to see a Great-Grand. You don't specially have to be married, you know. That's why I felt free to ask." She reached into her bag and took out a Three Sixes bottle, which she proceeded to drink from, taking deep swift swallows with her head thrown back.

"There are very few black boys near Cresselton," Sarah explained, watching the corn liquor leave the bottle in spurts and bubbles. "Besides, I'm really caught up now in my painting and sculpting . . ." Should she mention how much she admired Giacometti's work? No, she decided. Even if her grandmother had heard of him, and Sarah was positive she had not, she would surely think his statues much too thin. This made Sarah smile and remember how difficult it had been to convince her grandmother that even if Cresselton had not given her a scholarship she would have managed to go there anyway. Why? Because she wanted somebody to teach her to paint and to sculpt, and Cresselton had the best teachers. Her grandmother's notion of a successful granddaughter was a married one, pregnant the first year.

"Well," said her grandmother, placing the bottle with dignity back into her purse and gazing pleadingly into Sarah's face, "I sure would 'preshate a Great-Grand." Seeing her granddaughter's smile, she heaved a great sigh, and, walking rather haughtily over the stones and grass, made her way to the church steps.

As they walked down the aisle, Sarah's eyes rested on the back of her grandfather's head. He was sitting on the front middle bench in front of the casket, his hair extravagantly long and white and softly kinked. When she sat down beside him, her grandmother sitting next to him on the other side, he turned toward her and gently took her hand in his. Sarah briefly leaned her cheek against his shoulder and felt like a child again.

4

They had come twenty miles from town, on a dirt road, and the hot spring sun had drawn a steady rich scent from the honeysuckle vines along the way. The church was a bare, weather-beaten ghost of a building with hollow windows and a sagging door. Arsonists had once burned it to the ground, lighting the dry wood of the walls with the flames from the crosses they carried. The tall spreading red oak tree under which Sarah had played as a child still dominated the church-yard, stretching its branches widely from the roof of the church to the other side of the road.

After a short and eminently dignified service, during which Sarah and her grandfather alone did not cry, her father's casket was slid into the waiting hearse and taken the short distance to the cemetery, an overgrown wilderness whose stark white stones appeared to be the small ruins of an ancient civilization. There Sarah watched her grandfather from the corner of her eye. He did not seem to bend under the grief of burying a son. His back was straight, his eyes dry and clear. He was simply and solemnly heroic; a man who kept with pride his family's trust and his own grief. *It is strange*, Sarah thought, *that I never thought to paint him like this, simply as he stands; without anonymous meaningless people hovering beyond his profile; his face turned proud and brownly against the light*. The defeat that had frightened her in the faces of black men was the defeat of black forever defined by white. But that defeat was nowhere on her grand-father's face. He stood like a rock, outwardly calm, the com-fort and support of the Davis family. The family alone defined him, and he was not about to let them down.

"One day I will paint you, Grandpa," she said, as they

turned to go. "Just as you stand here now, with just"—she moved closer and touched his face with her hand—"just the right stubborn tenseness of your cheek. Just that look of Yes and No in your eyes."

"You wouldn't want to paint an old man like me," he said, looking deep into her eyes from wherever his mind had been. "If you want to make me, make me up in stone."

The completed grave was plump and red. The wreaths of flowers were arranged all on one side so that from the road there appeared to be only a large mass of flowers. But already the wind was tugging at the rose petals and the rain was making dabs of faded color all over the green foam frames. In a week the displaced honeysuckle vines, the wild roses, the grapevines, the grass, would be back. Nothing would seem to have changed.

5

"What do you mean, come *home*?" Her brother seemed genuinely amused. "We're all proud of you. How many black girls are at that school? Just *you*? Well, just one more besides you, and she's from the North. That's really something!"

"I'm glad you're pleased," said Sarah.

"Pleased! Why, it's what Mama would have wanted, a good education for little Sarah; and what Dad would have wanted too, if he could have wanted anything after Mama died. You were always smart. When you were two and I was five you showed me how to eat ice cream without getting it all over me. First, you said, nip off the bottom of the cone with your teeth, and suck the ice cream down. I never knew *how* you were supposed to eat the stuff once it began to melt."

"I don't know," she said, "sometimes you can want something a whole lot, only to find out later that it wasn't what you *needed* at all."

Sarah shook her head, a frown coming between her eyes.

"I sometimes spend *weeks*," she said, "trying to sketch or paint a face that is unlike every other face around me, except, vaguely, for one. Can I help but wonder if I'm in the right place?"

Her brother smiled. "You mean to tell me you spend *weeks* trying to draw one face, and you still wonder whether you're in the right place? You must be kidding!" He chucked her under the chin and laughed out loud. "You learn how to draw the face," he said, "then you learn how to paint me and how to make Grandpa up in stone. Then you can come home or go live in Paris, France. It'll be the same thing."

It was the unpreacherlike gaiety of his affection that made her cry. She leaned peacefully into her brother's arms. She wondered if Richard Wright had had a brother.

"You are my door to all the rooms," she said. "Don't ever close."

And he said, "I won't," as if he understood what she meant.

6

"When will we see you again, young woman?" he asked later, as he drove her to the bus stop.

"I'll sneak up one day and surprise you," she said.

At the bus stop, in front of a tiny service station, Sarah hugged her brother with all her strength. The white station attendant stopped his work to leer at them, his eyes bold and careless.

"Did you ever think," said Sarah, "that we are a very old people in a very young place?"

She watched her brother from a window of the bus; her eyes did not leave his face until the little station was out of sight and the big Greyhound lurched on its way toward Atlanta. She would fly from there to New York.

7

She took the train to the campus.

"My," said one of her friends, "you look wonderful! Home sure must agree with you!"

"Sarah was home?" Someone who didn't know asked. "Oh, *great*, how was it?"

"Well, how was it?" went an echo in Sarah's head. The noise of the echo almost made her dizzy.

"How was it?" she asked aloud, searching for, and regaining, her balance.

"How was it?" She watched her reflection in a pair of smiling hazel eyes.

"It was fine," she said slowly, returning the smile, thinking of her grandfather. "Just fine."

The girl's smile deepened. Sarah watched her swinging along toward the back tennis courts, hair blowing in the wind.

Stare the rat down, thought Sarah; *and whether it disappears or not, I am a woman in the world. I have buried my father, and shall soon know how to make my grandpa up in stone.*

SOURCE

It was during the year of her first depressing brush with government funding of antipoverty programs that San Francisco began to haunt Irene. An educational project into which she'd poured much of her time, energy and considerable talent was declared "superfluous and romantic" by Washington, and summarily killed; Irene began to long for every amenity the small, dusty Southern town she worked in did not offer. With several other young, idealistic people, she had taught "Advanced Reading and Writing" to a small group of older women. Their entire "school" was a secondhand trailer in back of a local black college; the books they used were written by the teachers and students themselves. The women had a desire for learning that was exciting; the town, however, was dull; its main attraction a grimy, only recently desegregated movie theater with an abandoned appreciation for Burt Reynolds. Irene daydreamed incessantly of hilly streets, cable cars, Chinatown and Rice-o-Roni. Of redwood forests and the Pacific Ocean.

She decided to visit a friend from her New York college days, Anastasia Green. Anastasia now lived in San Francisco, and frequently wrote, inviting her to visit, should she ever make it to that fabled city.

Anastasia was tall and willowy, with cautious, smoky topaz eyes, hair the color of unpolished brass, and a mouth that seemed much smaller than her teeth, so that when she smiled the planes of her face shifted radically to accommodate a sudden angularity in a face that had seemed round. This irregularity in her features was not grotesque, but charming, and gave to Anastasia's face a humor she herself did not possess.

While Irene knew her on the East Coast, Anastasia went through two complete external changes: The first was from the "Southern Innocent" (she was from Pine Lake, Arkansas), wide-eyed, blushing, absurdly trusting—but not really—to the New York SuperVamp. Tall boots, of course, slickly bobbed *blackened* hair, heavily made-up eyes (brown and black make-up, a rather Egyptian effect), against skin that by contrast seemed to have been dusted with rice powder, and, in fact, had been. The second change was to a sort of Faye Dunaway, whom she—with her peculiar smile—some-what resembled, or what she referred to as her "little English schoolboy look." Hair lightened and cropped close to her (it was now revealed) *round* little head, bangs down to her eyebrows, skirts up to her ass. And always a swinging purse and absurd snubtoed shoes. In this getup she didn't walk, she *tripped* along, and one was not surprised if, when she passed trippingly by, "Eleanor Rigby" popped into mind.

It was while in this disguise that she fell in love with a man named Galen, who was as addicted to the theater as Anastasia was to travel. After college, Galen left the East Coast for the West, where he hoped to become an actor. He convinced Anastasia to come along. From letters, Irene knew that Galen had dropped out of the picture, so to speak, while doing TV commercials in Los Angeles. Anastasia, already rinsing her hair in vinegar and staying out in the sun, had pressed north.

TV documentaries about the flower children of the sixties carried many shots of people who looked like Anastasia-in-San Francisco. Gone was the vamp, the English schoolboy. Instead, she appeared in clogs, a long granny dress of an old-fashioned print and sleazy texture, with a purple velvet cape. The kinkiness of her hair was now encouraged, and formed an aura about her beige, unpowdered face. She was beaded and feathered to a delightfully pleasant extreme.

"It's great to see you!" the two women said almost in unison, embracing and smiling, amid the anxious and harried looking travelers at the airport.

With Anastasia were a young man, a young woman, and their baby. The baby's name was very long, Sanskrit-derived, and, translated into English, meant Bliss. The man's name, arrived at in the same fashion, meant Calm, and the woman's name, Peace. All three adults giggled easily and at everything, absent-mindedly fingering small silver spoons that hung around their necks.

Not knowing what the spoon signified, Irene was amused by it. Unisex jewelry, she thought, had finally hit the mark.

There was a van, painted all the colors of the rainbow, so that simply riding along felt *vivid*. The adults were soon chanting and singing; the baby was kicking and cooing. They crossed merrily over the bridge into Marin, to which Anastasia and her friends had recently moved. From there they would "strike" day trips into San Francisco.

"Source would love Irene," said Peace or Calm.

"He sure would!" Anastasia agreed, turning to give Irene's arm a squeeze. "I've told them you're one of the least rigid people I know."

Happy as Irene was whenever there were strange creatures to observe or meet, she did not hesitate—silently, of course—to agree. Who would *not* love me? was her attitude. The trauma of having lost the educational project had not damaged an essential self-saving vanity.

"Who is 'Source'?" Irene asked languidly, because by now the van was filled with mellow *sinsamilla* smoke.

"Wait and see" said Anastasia, mysteriously.

They lived in a large, rambling house on a hillside in Marin. The rooms were light and airy and filled with sunshine, Indian prints, seashells, rocks, paper mobiles, and lacy straw mats. From every window there was a view: the bay, sailboats; Tiburon, across the Bay.

"How do you manage all this?" Irene asked, glancing in a cupboard stacked high with bags of granola.

"Food stamps and relief," said Anastasia, with a slight shrug. It was the kind of shrug Irene was seeing a lot. There was . . . dissatisfaction in it; there was also acceptance. Missing—and, suddenly, it seemed to Irene—was defiance.

Bliss and her parents, Calm and Peace, disappeared into a separate part of the house. Anastasia and Irene sat down at the kitchen table.

"In parts of the country," Irene said in a voice modulated to show this meant nothing whatsoever to her, "the amount of assistance people get is less, by design, than they can live on."

Anastasia leaned forward, and in an equally nonpartisan tone said, "It is *much* better to be on welfare in a rich place than in a poor one. Not only do rich people here dress the way we do—if anything they're more tattered and less stylish—but they are *so* rich it delights them to support us in our poverty."

Irene laughed, dutifully.

"How is your teaching?" asked Anastasia. Like many of Irene's friends, she never read the newsletter that Irene and her group published, in which they discussed in detail methods of teaching older people, under- and miseducated young people, or what they called among themselves, just as society did, "the Unteachables." Only they said it with an informed sense of humor, not yet having encountered an absolute "unteachable."

For a moment, Irene debated with herself whether to respond with more than "okay." In stories, in literature, such work as she did sounds romantic, as well as idealistic. The reality, day to day, is different. In Irene's case there was, first of all, the incredible brain-broiling heat of the Southern summer, when the majority of her students—all women in their late forties, fifties and sixties—could attend classes from one to three weeks at a time. The trailer they used was not air-conditioned, and there were flies. Sometimes classes were crowded, and composed of people who—from years of being passive spectators in church, required only to respond in shouts or "amens"—found it difficult to take an active part in their own instruction. They doubted their own personal histories and their own experience. The food—donated by the local college whose backyard they were in—was bad. Bologna and pork and beans and yellow wilted slices of lettuce. Oversweetened lemonade that attracted mosquitoes. And there was the smell of clean poverty, an odor Irene wished would disappear from the world, a sharp, *bitter* odor, almost acrid, as if the women washed themselves in chemicals.

Teaching was exciting only sporadically, when student or teacher learned something. Often no one seemed to learn anything. In desperation Irene would sometimes show films, because whatever the films were about, they seemed to threaten her students less than Irene's constant insistence that they acknowledge their own oppression, as blacks *and* as women. From films like "Birth of a Nation" there would be an immediate rise; from a film like "Anna Lucasta" a stunned and bewildered silence. At first, anyway.

"It's not going well," Irene said, as Anastasia put a filter into the Chemex, spooned in coffee, and poured on boiling water. Through the low-slung kitchen window Irene saw the fog sliding into the garden, a cat napping on a rock, and a round terra-cotta urn of herbs on the back steps. There was a peace and unreality about the house.

"You wrote me about your school," Anastasia said as non-committally as possible, as they sipped mellow black coffee and munched on homemade carrot cake.

There was a side of Irene that Anastasia did not like. It was the side that seemed unnecessarily obsessed with the dark, seedy side of life. They'd once discussed Anastasia's inability to get involved in projects that interested Irene, and Anastasia had shrugged and said, "You're into pain!" They had laughed, but Anastasia realized Irene thought her incapable of deep emotion, and so, in a way, talked (or wrote) down to her. Since this spared her a lot of *Sturm und Drang*, she thought this was okay, and didn't complain. She accepted the shallowness this attitude assured.

It didn't occur to Irene that Anastasia could empathize with her commitments, and their college friendship had been based largely on a shared love of movies and jazz. Though she feigned a good-humored acceptance of Anastasia's easy-going life style, and her reliance on personal fashion to indicate the state of her mind, on a deeper level, she felt contempt for her, as a person who chose to be of limited use.

"It ended for lack of funds," Irene said.

"Who funded it?" asked Anastasia, politely.

Irene sighed, and began in a rush. "In the beginning, there *was* no funding." The two women could not help grinning in recognition of the somehow *familiar* sound of this: they had both been brought up in the church. "In the beginning, there *was* no funding," repeated Irene. "The women wanted to learn before they 'got too old' and they simply talked—and in some cases shamed—younger women into teaching them. Then there was a grant from the government that paid those like me who came from outside. The trouble with government funding, of course, is that it is so fucking fickle . . . With the war going on in Vietnam, and bombs to be bought, government could hardly be expected to care that a few dozen *old* black women still believe in education."

"I thought you said in your letters that some of the women are white," said Anastasia, resting her chin on the back of her hand, and gazing steadily at Irene. She liked to look at Irene, liked her sometimes *fierce* brown eyes, liked very much the dark richness of her skin—but she could never say so.

"Oh yes," said Irene, "some of them are. Three, in fact." When white people reached a certain level of poverty (assuming they were not members of the Klan, or worse, which they very often were), they ceased to be "white" to her. Like many of her quasi-political beliefs, however, she had not thought this through. She was afraid to, and this was one of the major failings in her character. If she thought this through, for example, she would have to think of what becomes of poor whites when (if) they become rich (and how could she waste her time teaching incipient rich, white people?) and what becomes of blacks when they become middle class; she was already contemptuous of the black middle class. In fact, for its boringly slavish imitation of the white middle class, which she considered mediocre in its tiniest manifestations, she hated it. And yet, technically, she was now a part of this class.

If she began questioning these things, she would have to question her own place in society and how she was going to be a success at whatever she did (she had few doubts about her capabilities and none about her energy) but at the same time avoid becoming bourgeois. She enjoyed so many bourgeois pleasures, and yet she loathed the thought of settling for them. Just as jazz was her favourite music because it held the middle class in abeyance, *Steppenwolf* was the novel that, since college, had most enduringly reflected her mind.

"Can the women go back to learning the way they did before the funding?" asked Anastasia.

"One day they might," said Irene. "I don't know. A funny

thing happened to them, and to me, around the funding from government. At first it lifted our spirits, made us believe someone up there in D.C. cared about the lives of these women, the deliberate impoverishment of their particular past. And the women settled down to learn in that belief. As amazingly as the funding began, though, it ended. We had just had time to get used to more than we had before when suddenly there was nothing at all. We had 'progressed' to a new level only to find ourselves stranded. To go back to the old way would feel like defeat."

As Irene talked, she thought of one of the women in her class who particularly moved her, and who resisted learning to read because everything she was required to read was so painful. Irene had had to coax her back to class after the first day. On the first day, the woman, whose name was Fania, had expressed a strong desire to learn to read. She was a stout, walnut-colored woman who wore her hair in braids that crossed at the back of her neck and, in her ears, small gold loops. Her embarrassment at not knowing how to read was so acute that, in admitting it, she kept her eyes tightly shut, and in the course of making a very short statement of her condition, she undid both braids and managed to get the earrings tangled in her hair.

Like so much that is deeply tragic, this sight was also comic. Realizing how she must appear to the class, and to Irene, Fania had blushed darkly and offered a short puzzled laugh at herself. It was a look and a laugh that Irene never forgot.

Irene had had much success teaching reading by using the newspapers. She found nonreaders related quickly to news about what was going on in their midst, and that often too they recognized certain words—like names of towns, stores, and so on—with which they were already familiar. Each time they "read" a word they already knew, they were encouraged.

For Fania, Irene had chosen a rather innocuous item about the increasing mechanization of farm labor, which was the kind of work most of her students knew well. She thought the words "fertilizer distributor," "automatic weeder," "cotton picker" and the like would be easy. They were long words, true, but words used every day by the women, as they passed by plantations where this new machinery was already in operation.

Irene read quickly over the short news item, to rob it of any surprise. Surprises in any form, she had discovered, inhibited these would-be readers.

" 'Way, Georgia: Sources at the Department of Agriculture predict that in less than ten years, farming as our state has known it for generations will no longer exist. Widespread use of fertilizer distributors, automatic weeders and cotton pickers will virtually wipe out the need for human labor. Thousands of tenant farmers who have traditionally farmed the land, have already been displaced. Crop prices—including those for soybeans and peanuts—are expected to continue to rise. It is expected that automation will increase profits and stimulate the growth of other industries that are beginning to relocate in the South because of the abundance of energy, in terms of both the environment and the ever-populous, non-unionized, labor pool.' "

Fania had stammered, choked, pulled at her earrings and her braids—but in the end had simply refused to learn to read that the only work she'd ever known would soon not exist.

While Irene talked, Anastasia fingered the colorful straw place mat in front of her. As so often happened when she talked to another black person, the world seemed weighted down with problems. "You can't improve anything, you know?" she said. "You can't change anything. I've learned that from Source."

Irene waited. Anastasia seemed inspired.

"Source got me and my folks together again. You won't believe this, but we write to each other now at least once a week. Hey, let me show you . . ." Anastasia rose and disappeared into another room. She returned with a bundle of letters. She peeled off a letter from the bundle and spread the pages on the table. She changed her mind about reading aloud to Irene, who was looking at her, she felt, skeptically. She pushed the letter toward Irene, who glanced quickly over it.

Anastasia's parents had once been Baptists; they were now Jehovah's Witnesses. There was a lot in the letter about continuing to love her and even more about continuing to petition Jehovah God in her behalf. From the letter, prayers were going up from Arkansas by the hour. The hair rose at the back of Irene's neck, but she forced herself to remain calm.

Irene had met Anastasia's family once, by design, she always thought, on Anastasia's part. Irene lived for a time in a terrible D.C. slum, and represented, therefore, a kind of educated lunatic fringe to those friends who thought poverty in and of itself was dangerous to visitors. While her parents were in town, Anastasia asked to stay with Irene, though in fact she was at that time living with her friend Galen. Her parents had driven up in the longest pink Lincoln Continental Irene had ever seen. Her father and brothers had braved the trashy street to come up to Irene's flat, but her mother had waited in the car—doors locked and windows rolled up tight—until Anastasia and Irene were brought out to her. Her gray, stricken eyes clutched at Irene's. Why? Why? they asked, while her mouth said how pleased she was they had finally met. "What is she afraid of?" Irene had asked Anastasia; "What *isn't* she afraid of?" Anastasia had replied.

Anastasia's brothers were amber-skinned and curly-haired, with the slouching posture and menacing non-language of other boys their age. They were fifteen and sixteen. Anastasia's father was an olive-skinned, crinkly-haired man whose intense inner turmoil and heaviness of spirit caused an instant recoiling; on his face, one felt a smile would look unnatural.

This father now wrote of God's love, God's grace, God's assured forgiveness, and of his own happiness that his daughter, always, at heart, "a *good* girl," had at last embarked on *the path of obedience*. This path alone led to peace everlasting, in the new and coming system of the world.

"*Obedience*," thought Irene. "*Peace Everlasting*! Holy shit!"

"I wanted to do good, too," said Anastasia, and laughed. "Of course all the 'doing good' is really for yourself, nobody else. Nobody ever does anybody else any good. The good they do is for them. Altruism doesn't exist. Neither do good works."

"Wait a minute," said Irene, a clenched fist resting on the letters in her lap. "I believe in movements, collective action to influence the future, and all that. Basically, I believe somebody is responsible for the child."

"People should understand," said Anastasia, speaking very fast and somewhat blindly, Irene felt, as if she were speaking with her eyes closed, so that for a moment she reminded Irene of Fania, "that when they suffer it is because they *choose* suffering. If you suffer in a place, leave."

The baby was awake now and Irene was holding him. His thick hair smelled of incense. His slender fingers probed her nose.

"You can't leave a baby," Irene said.

"Men do it all the time."

"Women stay because they don't want to be 'men.'"

'And men go because they don't want to be women—that half of the human race that never realizes it has a choice."

"But who will look after the children?"

"Someone will," she said, "or won't." She looked into Irene's face.

"It's all the same." She shrugged. "That's the point."

The baby's mother came into the room. She had a face the color of a pink towel, a stout figure and blue eyes shaped like arrows. Spiritual striving was most apparent in her

speech; over her harsh new York accent she'd poured a sweetness that hurt the ears.

"It's a beautiful baby," Irene said, as she plucked grapes
off a bunch on the table and began plopping them into her
own and the baby's mouths,

"Thank you," she cooed. "We're giving him to Anastasia.
She loves him so much and is such a good mommy. We're
going to South America."

"When?" asked Irene.

She shrugged. "Sometime."

"Was that hard to decide?" Irene wanted to know.

"Source teaches us that all children belong to everyone, to
the whole world."

"But not to anyone in particular?"

She sang, "That's right," and swept out of the room.

"We have to take you to meet Source," said Peace, who
came in next and rummaged through the grapes. He was
emaciated, far taller than the refrigerator and wore his long
straw-colored hair in a ponytail tied with a bright green cord.
A brilliant red birthmark, shaped like a tiny foot, "walked"
across his nose.

Source lived in a large apartment house very close by. One
of his daughters, a thin, sad-eyed girl in her teens, her long
black hair shining against her sallow brown skin, showed
them up to his flat. After admitting them she kept her gaze
below their knees.

Anastasia, Peace, Calm and Bliss had brought an offering
of wine and money, which they placed on a table near
Source's feet. Source himself was seated in the lotus position
on a round bed shoved against the wall of the otherwise bare
and dingy room. The guests were offered cushions on the
floor. A second daughter padded up silently, her eyes as sad
as the first's, and poured the wine into glasses which she
handed to each of them. She also lit a stick of incense. Soon
the room was hazy with smoke and the air heavy with the
sweet, oppressive smell.

A third daughter came and stood at her father's left hand, which he periodically raised and sent her scurrying into the other rooms for something he wanted.

"It is possible that all swamis look alike," Irene was thinking. Source was a pale, grayish brown, with dark glittery eyes and graying dark hair parted in the middle and hanging about his shoulders. He wore a white robe that he used, as he talked, to cover and uncover his bare feet. It was a slow, flipping motion that relaxed and in a way hypnotized his audience.

Irene was determined not to think any of the prejudicial things she was thinking, and adjusted her face to show interest, concern, anticipatory delight.

Source's voice had a whine and a drone somewhere in it, however, and this made it objectionable. He was saying how the first time he met Anastasia, whom he called in Sanskrit, Tranquility, she looked exactly like Kathleen Cleaver, "dressed all entirely completely in black" (he was to use triple qualifiers frequently). "Her hair like an angry, wild, animal bush. And her skin pale pale pale, like that one. Militant, you see?" He laughed, fluttered the fingers of his left hand in the air beside his nose, and the sad-eyed daughter standing beside him shifted the pillow behind his back.

Anastasia was laughing, fingering her spoon and occasionally sniffling and rubbing her eyes, which were red and glassy.

"Well"—she shrugged—"I thought I was black."

"Nobody's anything," said Source, as to a dense child, and Anastasia shrugged again.

Source called out sharply. There was a flurry of movement in the kitchen, and his other two daughters came and stood next to the one who had remained beside the bed.

"Nobody's anything," he repeated. The daughter began to write down his words. Through her rather bedraggled sari it was clear she was pregnant.

"I used to live in Africa, in Uganda," continued Source, "and the Africans wanted to be black black black. They were always saying it: black black black. But that is because Africans are backward people. You see? Indians do not go about saying, 'We are brown brown brown,' or the Chinese, 'yellow yellow yellow.' '

"No," said Irene, "they say they are Chinese Chinese Chinese and Indian Indian Indian."

However, it was out of line to speak while Source spoke. He continued as if she had not interrupted.

"Africans are strange creatures. I will tell you a story that really happened in Africa. An African . . ."

It was such an ancient racist joke, Irene had not heard it since she was a small child. "The African" in it as stupid, lazy, backward and unmotivated to improve as any colonialist could wish. Tranquility, Peace and Calm and even the baby—whose vicariously stoned response to the world was a look of slack wonder—giggled.

"Where are you going?" asked Tranquility, as Irene rose.

"I'll meet you on the street," Irene said.

On the way back, Peace and Calm talked disjointedly of ego and humility and how they now, since knowing Source, had none of the former and lots of the latter. It was hinted that Irene might likewise be improved.

"Is the pregnant daughter married?" she asked coldly.

"Why should she be?" asked Calm.

"She has Source," sniffed Peace.

Which was precisely what Irene feared, but she decided against pursuing it.

"Who supports Source?" she asked.

"We all do," they said proudly. "Source is too precious to waste his life working."

A moment later, Tranquility said, "He's a teacher, like you. Teaching *is* his work."

"I'm sorry," said Anastasia next day. "But we have decided you have to go."

"What?" asked Irene.

"You disapprove of us."

"I don't understand you."

"Listen," said Anastasia. "I've finally got my life together, and it's all thanks to Source. I understand I am nothing. That is what Source was testing you to see. You still think you are Somebody. That you matter. That Africans matter. They don't," she said. "And if they are nothing—if nobody's anything—it is impossible to humiliate them."

"But he's a racist; he treats his daughters like slaves."

"He is above all that. You *don't* understand. *Right*. But see, if nobody's anything, everyone is equal. That's clear enough, isn't it?"

"Clear enough, but impossible."

"Before I had my breakdown I didn't understand either. I wanted to *be* Kathleen Cleaver. I met her once at a party in New York before *she* was Kathleen Cleaver. She had long straight, light-colored hair, like mine, *just* like mine, and she sat in a corner all evening without saying a word. Not one. Men did all the talking. Months later, she changed. Suddenly she was doing the talking because the men were dead or in jail. She cursed a lot, she dressed in boots and sunglasses and black clothes and posed for photographers holding a gun. I did all that. I even found a revolutionary black man to live with who beat me—and thought nothing of forbidding me to talk to what he considered 'strangers,' even though they were my friends.

"My parents came from Arkansas and got me. They had me locked away in a 'rest' home. It was a long time before I could see their point of view.

"When I was a child I wanted to change things. When the sit-ins started I wanted to join. I wanted to integrate schools and lunch counters. But I was so *fair*, and I'd never even seen my own hair unstraightened; mother started having it straightened when I was three, for God's sake ... But my color wasn't the problem. Oh *God*, I'm so *bored* with color being the problem. It was my undeveloped comprehension of the world. My parents already *had* the Truth, which is why they love Source so much, as much as I do. They knew nobody's anything, that color is an illusion, that the universe is unchangeable. Source teaches us nothing can be changed, all suffering is self-indulgence and the good of life is, basically, indifference to it—pleasure, if that is possible."

"The good of life is *indifference*?"

"They released me into Source's care. They help support him, financially. It works out."

The baby, hungry, was crying and crawling over the floor. Irene walked over to him and picked him up. His mother flew into the room and snatched him from her arms.

"We try to protect him from bad vibes," she said.

"*Bitch*," said Irene, under her breath, then she turned again to Anastasia, who was trembling from the righteousness of her stand.

"Anastasia," Irene said, "I didn't come all this way to criticize your life. I came all this way because mine is lying kaput all around me, remember?" She knew she wasn't wrong about Source, but what did he matter? she thought. "Perhaps I was wrong about Source. Perhaps you are right to defend him. This is a bad time in my life to have someone like that sprung on me, actually. I was predisposed not to like him; maybe he sensed this . . ." She rambled on, but Anastasia was not listening. She imagined Anastasia, Peace and Calm meeting in the dead of night to plan just this scene between them. It seemed to her that only the baby, Bliss, had welcomed her, from the start.

"Your life is what you make it," Anastasia said, stonily.

"But that's *absurd*. Not everyone's life is what they make it. Some people's life is what other people make it. I would say this is true of the majority of the people in the world. The women I teach didn't choose to be illiterate, didn't choose to be poor."

"But *you* chose to teach that kind of people. Why complain?"

"*That* kind of people?"

"Miserable. Hopeless in this incarnation."

Irene laughed. "You make me think of Kissinger, who said, 'This is not Africa's century.' "

Anastasia did not smile.

"I didn't mean to complain," Irene said, humiliated at the thought.

"If you suffer in a place, *leave*," Anastasia said with conviction, and, Irene thought, a great deal of smugness.

"If you suffer in a *condition*?"

Anastasia lifted her spoon.

It was now years later for almost everyone. It was certainly years later for Irene, who was astounded one day to find herself discussing teaching methods with a group of Native American and white women educators in Alaska.

"As soon as I heard you were coming," said Anastasia, who now lived near Anchorage, "I told my man, 'I have to go see her; she's an old friend!' "

They were sitting in a bar that on clear days boasted a perfect view of Mt. McKinley, a hundred miles away. Alas, clear days were apparently rare, and Irene had seen nothing of Alaska's legendary mountains but their feet. But even these were impressive.

"You've forgiven me, I hope, for throwing you out," said Anastasia.

"Oh, sure," said Irene. She was looking at the other people in the bar. She liked Alaska. She liked the way the people looked as if they had come, that very month, from someplace else. The damp weather, however, though not cold—as she had expected it to be—made her long for the sun, for fireplaces, for a less penetrable selection of clothing than she'd brought.

Anastasia had snared her directly from the stage, where Irene had sat beside a Native Alaskan woman who talked of the failing eyesight of Alaskans, who were reading print, over long periods, for the first time.

"Native Alaskans always took perfect vision for granted," the woman had said. "Then comes this reading. This television. This shopping where everything is labeled with words for more reading. Everybody needs glasses now to see anything at all." She was wearing huge aviator glasses with purple lenses. She yanked them off and blinked at the audience. It was a long pause, during which she dropped the assertive stance of her statement and seemed, somewhere inside herself, to fold. "There's a basic distrust maybe," she continued softly, "about acquiring knowledge in a way that can make you blind. This has to be behind many of our older people's reading problems."

Irene didn't doubt it for a moment.

Anastasia had taken Irene's arm and stood close beside her while Native Alaskan educators pressed her hand warmly. "So good to see you!" they said, as if they had been waiting for her. "So happy you could come all this way up from the Lower 48!"

"When I heard you were coming, and that it would be a conference about Natives, I thought I'd be the only white chick around. But I see I'm not."

Irene did not blink at this.

And now they sat at the bar, with its famous absent view of Mt. McKinley. Irene felt drained from the panel discussion. Thinking of the woman in the aviator glasses, she was also depressed. She finished her first Irish whiskey and ordered another. When she looked at Anastasia, whose hair was now in braids and held by leather thongs with feathers, and whose eyes literally danced, it was as if Anastasia were receding, receding, receding, into the blurred landscape. But this was a momentary and maudlin vision, which Irene had another gulp of her drink to squelch.

"So," she said, "nobody's anything."

"I heard you were happily married," said Anastasia, ignoring Irene's remark.

"We *were* happy. I'm almost sure we were happy. You know happiness is being able to assume you are happy. Anyway, he left me."

"I *love* being white," Anastasia said, plunging in and screwing up her face in a mock excess of delight. "Ask me why."

"Why?" said Irene.

"Because as a black person I had no sense of humor!" She laughed, and her funny face and her laughter meshed.

"I can't deny that," said Irene. "Besides, passing for white is so—so—*color*ful." She meant, really, that it was passé.

"No, no," said Anastasia. "That's *Imitation of Life*—and what was that other tacky movie? *Pinky*? Not even a Jessie Fauset or a Nella Larsen novel, where being white is such a to-do about what colors now look good against your skin. There *were* shades of *Autobiography of an Ex-Colored Man* in the beginning—you know, could a potentially *great* black woman find happiness as a mediocre white one?—but that passed." She laughed. "Anyway, I'm not passing; I'm just through trying to correct other people's opinion."

Irene, staring directly into Anastasia's eyes, felt the strangest sensation. Those eyes now looked out of a white person. What did that mean?

"I loved being married," said Irene, lowering her gaze to her glass. "I was finally calm enough to look about me without panic." She shrugged. For years of her marriage there had been so little panic she'd fallen asleep. So that if you asked her what she did between 1965 and 1968, she would probably recall only that those three years amounted to one day, really, and that on that day one of her neighbors had invited her to go fishing, and she had declined.

"That's *it*," said Anastasia, "sort of. When you're not living with someone it's like all sides of you are exposed at once. Right? But when you are living with someone at least one side of you is covered. Panic can still strike, but not on that one side." She wanted to emphasize how this was especially true in the case of race. That, having put race aside as a cause of concern, she could now concentrate on whatever assaults were in store for the other facets of herself. But of course Irene would say she had not put aside race, only chosen a different side of it to live on. Blacks who had not had her experience were rarely inclined to appreciate her point of view; though she understood this, she still thought it spoke of limitation on their part.

"What happened to Source, Peace and Calm, Bliss and Co.—South America? Do you have the baby here with you?" Irene asked, looking about the bar as if she expected to see Bliss crawling under the tables in their direction.

Anastasia looked glum. Her cheeks, Irene noticed, sagged when she wasn't smiling. But this was no worse than what the years had done to Irene's own face.

Anastasia had switched to Mai Tais; in her mind, Alaska and Hawaii were very close—they were so distant from the other forty-eight states. She said, sullenly, taking a sip from her small, overdressed drink (in addition to the traditional umbrella, there were tiny snowshoes), "I have a permanent tremor under my eye now—you know that? I've had it since living in San Francisco. It comes and goes. Now that I've mentioned it, watch for it. It is sure to make its appearance before long."

Her right eye, underneath the eye, really, began to quiver.

"I *hate* that," she said, clapping her palm over it. "I don't know *where* they are. They may have gone to South America, for all I know. I don't know *what* happened to Bliss." She giggled.

"*Some*thing happened to bliss," said Irene, and giggled also. The two of them whooped, thumped their glasses on the table and rumbled their feet underneath. A solicitous waitress inquired if there were something she could do.

"Find out what happened to bliss!" they said, laughing up at her and ordering doubles.

"After a couple of years I began to fall apart again," said Anastasia. "Facial tic, constant colds, diarrhea, you name it. You should have seen me. My hair looked like brass *wire*, my skin had more eruptions than Indo*nesia*. My *teeth* were loosening ... If I was so tranquil, why was this happening? I hadn't slept a whole night since I couldn't remember when, either.

"But I didn't want to leave Source, oh no! Listen, *average* sex, but with great dope, a little music, somebody above you to intercede with God, and the world outside your im*mediate* premises fails to interest."

"*Hum*mmmm," said Irene.

"Leave Source? Not on your life! Or *my* life, as the case was. Enter my parents—as screwed up as I was myself, but a mite put out that I was in the habit of talking to myself as easily as to strangers on the street." She shrugged. "Back to Arkansas. A few months of house arrest, no dope, church music (listen, the only reason Jehovah's Witnesses can sing is they've ripped off so many Baptists) and the realization that neither black nor white had ever known what to do with us in Arkansas. That we were freaks. And that it was my parents' ambivalence, as much as anything, that had driven us all nuts. They were, horrified if my friends were poor and black, disappointed in my taste if they were black and middle class, and embittered if they were white; where was my racial pride?

"I married the first man who signed up from Arkansas to work on the Alaska pipeline. Found a job. Divorced him. *Voilà*."

Irene thought of Fania, whose interest in reading had finally been sustained by the slave narratives of black women so similar, she felt, to herself, and who would have read with keen interest the story Anastasia was now telling.

Was your mother white?

Yes, she pretty white; not white enough for white people. She have long hair, but it was kinda wavy ...

Were your children mulattoes?

*No, Sir! They were all white. They looked just like him . . .
then he told me he was goin' to die . . . and he said that if I
would promise him that I would go to New York, he would
leave me and the children free . . . . He told me no person
would know it (that I was colored) if I didn't tell it.**

"Did I ever tell you about Fania Evans?" asked Irene. "No?
She was one of the women I tried to teach to read the
newspaper. I had trouble because she refused to learn to
read anything that hurt her. The world being what it is, this
left very little news."

"Oh yes, I think I remember something about her," said
Anastasia, in the spirit of the conversation. She didn't
remember a word. "But wait a minute," she said, "let me
really bring you up to date. The man I live with now is an
Indian, an Aleut. Did I tell you that?"

"You probably tried to," said Irene, "but no saga of sexual
superiority, womanlike tenderness or rippling muscles,
please."

"He does have it all," said Anastasia, happily, "but I won't
mention it."

"Thanks," said Irene.

"We live in a small fishing village where the only industry
is smoking salmon. That's all the women there know how to
do. But as a white woman—" she grinned across the table at
Irene, who at that moment was feeling unpleasantly sour, "or
should I say as a non-Native? Anyway, they didn't expect me
to know how to smoke salmon. When I did it along with
them, they were delighted. It was as if I'd evolved. They don't
know this yet, but I'm on my way to being them." She paused.
"I think really that Source was a fascist. Only a fascist would

* Rev. H. Mattison, *Louisa Picquet, the Octoroon: A Tale of Southern Slave Life* (New York, 1861), as quoted in *Black Women in
Nineteenth-Century American Life*, edited, with an Introduction,
by Bert James Lowenberg and Ruth Bogin (The Pennsylvania State
University Press, University Park, PA., and London, 1976).

say nobody's anything. Everybody's *some*thing. Some*body*. And I couldn't feel like somebody without a color. I don't think anyone in America *can* . . . Which really *is* pathetic. However, looking as I look, black wasn't special enough. It required two hours of explanation to every two seconds of joy." She paused again. "And it *was* two seconds."

"Gotcha," said Irene. She was so drunk by now that she understood everything Anastasia said as if she'd thought it herself. But she also forgot it at once.

"Now, tell me about Fania *Who*sis? I want to know all about her," said Anastasia.

"No," said Irene, "I'm too drunk."

"I'll order coffee," said Anastasia. "I also have to go to the toilet."

"So do I," said Irene, feeling her stomach muscles rebel against her control-top panty hose.

When they returned, a pitcher of coffee shaped like a moose's head awaited them. Irene was still mopping her face and neck with a wet paper towel, and Anastasia was taking a small container of honey from her handbag. She did not eat sugar.

For ten minutes they drank the strong coffee in silence. Eventually, their heads began to clear.

For the first time, Irene was aware of the people in the booth directly behind them. *Fifteen years ago*, a man's voice said, *they weren't allowed in places like this. No dogs, Eskimos or Indians Allowed. That's terrible*, a woman's voice replied. *Especially since it was their country*, a young man spoke, sneeringly. *But we developed it*, said the young woman, in sisterly explanation. *Oh, sure*, said the young man. *How can a woman say something so stupid? You've been developed yourself, only you're so dumb you think you like it*. The older woman's voice, attempting to keep the peace, spoke up, changing the subject. *Is it really all that much bigger than Texas? Oh, way bigger*, said the older man with pride.

All Irene had known about Alaska she'd read in an Edna Ferber novel. Now she had learned about gigantic turnips, colossal watermelons, marijuana that was not only legally grown, harvested and used, but that regularly grew twenty feet tall in the hot, intensely productive summers. She had learned that parkas were way beyond her budget and that mukluks made her feet sweat. The Eskimos and Indians she saw on the street looked like any oriental San Franciscan. Now her mind stuck on *fifteen years ago*, and her own witnessing of similar signs coming down in the South. But the signs had already done their work. For as long as she lived she knew she would be intimidated by fancy restaurants, hotels, even libraries, from which she had been excluded before.

"It's nice to look at you. To tell you I *enjoy* the way you look." Anastasia reached over and caressed Irene's cheek. Then she got up, bent over Irene, and very deliberately gave her a kiss, pressing her lips firmly against the warm, jasmine-smelling brown skin. "I always envied you, before," she said.

"It's supposed to be the other way around," said Irene, smiling.

"It was so *miserable*, growing up, not resembling any of my friends. Resembling, instead, the people they hated! And oh, black people were so con*fused*. They showed me in every way they envied me because my color and my hair made things 'easy' for me, but those other people, with hair and skin like mine, they despised, and took every opportunity to tell me so. And another thing, I'm really rather homely, even funny-looking. But I was convinced very early that I was a beauty. I was never permitted an accurate reflection of myself."

"Why do I think you must have enjoyed it, at least a little?" asked Irene.

"Of course I was glad to be the 'princess' for a long time," said Anastasia. "I don't deny it. But never without *such* feeling of guilt. Why was I picked to be Snow White, Cinderella, and any other white lady in distress, when *all* my classmates were better actresses? Why did the boys *flock* to me, in high school, when I couldn't dance, was afraid to make jokes, and had a mother who let them know the darker shades of black were not acceptable? Oh, finally I got so *tired* of black people, that was why I decided to go to college in the North. They finally seemed to me—merely thoughtless, and selfish, and so fucked up over color it was embarrassing. Then in the sixties they started crying 'freedom!' but certainly this wasn't for the likes of me."

"You already had your freedom," said Irene. "The freedom to go either way."

"To be *thrown* either way, you mean," said Anastasia. "Even you got in on the throwing."

Like most people who have come to believe they are better than they are, Irene resented the notion that she could be intolerant. She sat up very straight to listen to this.

"Remember Styron's *Nat Turner*?" asked Anastasia.

"Vaguely," said Irene, who had worked diligently over a decade to erase the book from memory.

"Well, I remember it very well. One of our professors had the nerve to teach it to our class, and when you couldn't make him see what an insult Styron's *monster* was to the memory of the real Nat Turner, you were so mad you wouldn't speak to anyone on campus for days. That was when you started to drink a lot. And you were this shining example of sober, intelligent black peoplehood, too!" Anastasia laughed. "Not only drunk every evening, but *nastily* drunk. Throwing *up*, starting *fights*, calling people *names*. And they couldn't really *expel* you; you were the only really *dark* black student they had. And they *adored* you. But you said that was shit because they could *not* adore you and teach Styron's version of your history at the same time. Which made absolute sense to me."

"Hyprocrites, the whole bunch," said Irene.

"And so were you. You *loved* being adored. Being exceptional. Representing the race. I knew, from the backhanded way *I* was treated, that they were hypocrites. I mean, they knew *I* was black, I just didn't *look* black. I never got any of the attention you got, and I could have used some, because those white folks were just as strange to me as they were to you. But you thought everything was *fine* until the hypocrisy touched you."

"Oh, if only we didn't have to live with what we have been," thought Irene, feeling a surge of self-disgust. What Anastasia said was basically true; but even worse was the realization that she had viewed Anastasia in the same "back-handed" way her professors had. In fact, *she* had never been able to consider her entirely black, and in subtle ways had indicated a lack of recognition, of trust.

"We had gone for a walk, to help clear your head," Anastasia was saying. "I understood what you were feeling because, wonder of wonders, *I* felt the same way. I followed you back to your room—do you realize you were the only student in the whole school who *had* a private room? Remember what you said to me?"

She hadn't *wanted* the private room, was all she could think, but that was not the answer to the question. Irene thought and thought. She couldn't remember. She had been assigned the private room because she was "different," *that* she could remember.

"As we were going into your room, I said, 'God, I know *just* how you feel.' And you turned, right there in the doorway, and you blocked me from coming into your room, and as you closed the door very slowly in my face, you said, very distinctly, and as if you'd thought about it for a long time, 'How could you possibly?' '

Irene felt as if live coals had been thrown down her back.

"Wait, wait a minute," she said with relief, having found a straw to clutch. "Styron's book wasn't even out then. That was two or three years later!"

Anastasia looked at her, and pushed her palms against the edge of the table in front of her.

"So?" she said. "It was the same book with a different name. There's at least *one* racist best seller published a year."

Irene groaned. "I was *drunk*."

"Not good enough," said Anastasia.

"No."

Anastasia was glad she was finally able to say these things. All her life she had felt compelled to take and take and take from black people, anything they gave. Compliments and curses with the same benign, understanding silence. After all, she was exempt from their more predictable suffering, and must not presume to assert herself. Now that was over, and it felt good.

She realized that something was shifting, in her talk with Irene. They were still linked together, but it was not, now, the link of race, which had been tenuous in any case, and had not held up. They were simply two women, choosing to live as they liked in the world. She wondered if Irene felt this.

"You were my objective correlative," said Irene. She struggled over each word, as if she would unmask her own confusion in this matter, or else. "You see, my great fear in college was that I could hardly avoid becoming an ordinary bourgeois success. I was bright, energetic, attractive, with never a *thought* of failure, no matter *what* sociologists say. Those students who were destined, within ten years, to know the names of the designers of their shoes and luggage, to vacation in Europe once a year and read two best sellers every five—while doing a piss-poor job of teaching our children—scared the hell out of me. That life, and not the proverbial 'getting pregnant and dropping out of school,' represented 'the fate worse than death.'

"Your dilemma was obvious. You, even *objectively* speaking, didn't know who you were. What you were going to do next; which 'you' would be the one to survive. At the same time that I condemned you for your lack of commitment to anything I considered *useful*, I used you as the objectification of my own internal dilemma. In the weirdest way, your confusion made mine seem minor by comparison. For example, I understood that the episode with Source was a short cut, for you, to the kind of harmonious, multiracial community that you could be happy in, and which I also believed possible to create in America. But politically this is a shaky vision. It was, in a way, *convenient* for me to think *how much more* shaky your 'dope & guru' program was. I was looking toward 'government' for help; you were looking to Source. In both cases, it was the wrong direction—*any* direction that is away from ourselves is the wrong direction."

"Ah, ah," said Anastasia, shaking her head from side to side, though the "ah, ah" was affirmative. "I was attracted to you because your destiny seemed so stable. Whatever else, you would remain a black woman. Black women, even the bourgeois successes, don't desert."

"Can't desert. Some of them certainly would if they could."

Anastasia laughed, as did Irene.

Anastasia now felt smug. Whatever *she* was, she thought, her child, which she hoped to have someday, would be a Native American, once more and at last at the beginning of things.

"You know," she said thoughtfully, rising and collecting her things, because although it was still disconcertingly bright outside, it was after midnight, "Source made us use his name as our mantra during meditation, so there'd be no part of our consciousness he was excluded from. But you know how mantras are: at first they sound like someone's name and you keep getting that person in your mind. But soon the name becomes just a sound. For me, the sound became a longing and then a direction for my life." She shrugged. "I knew I had to merge this self with something really elemental and stable, or it would shatter and fly away." She smiled, thinking of the man she loved.

"You're happy to be going home to him, eh?" said Irene.

"Positively *ecstatic*," said Anastasia, beaming.

"Write," said Irene. "I've missed you."

"You *have*?" asked Anastasia.

Irene hugged her with a hug that was not an embrace of shoulders; she hugged her whole body, feeling knee against knee, thigh against thigh, breast against breast, neck nestled against neck. She listened to their hearts beating, strong and full of blood.

As they left the bar they passed a group of tourists who were pointing off merrily into the distance. Irene and Anastasia looked in the direction they were pointing and began to smile. They thought they were finally seeing the great elusive mountain, a hundred miles away. They were not. It was yet another, nearer, mountain's very large feet, its massive ankles wreathed in clouds, that they took such pleasure in.

The Women's Press is Britain's leading women's publishing house. Established in 1978, we publish high-quality fiction and non-fiction from outstanding women writers worldwide. Our exciting and diverse list includes literary fiction, detective novels, biography and autobiography, health, women's studies, handbooks, literary criticism, psychology and self help, the arts, our popular Livewire Books for Teenagers young adult series and the bestselling annual *Women Artists Diary* featuring beautiful colour and black-and-white illustrations from the best in contemporary women's art.

If you would like more information about our books, please send an A5 sae for our latest catalogue and complete list to:

The Sales Department
The Women's Press Ltd
34 Great Sutton Street
London EC1V 0DX
Tel: 0171 251 3007
Fax: 0171 608 1938

Also of interest:

Alice Walker
Her Blue Body Everything We Know
Earthling Poems 1965–1990 Complete

Pulitzer prize-winning author Alice Walker has been writing
poetry since the summer of 1965. This is her first complete
volume, containing many previously unpublished poems, plus new
introductions to those previously collected. Bringing valuable new
insights and reflections, this beautiful, definitive volume offers a
unique look at a remarkable writer's development and provides a
fascinating retrospective on the political, social and spiritual issues
of the last three decades.

'One cannot read Walker and remain unmoved.'
Books and Bookmen

**'One of the most important, grieving, graceful and
honest writers ever to come into print.'** June Jordan

Poetry £9.99 pbk/£15.95 hbk
ISBN 0 7043 4322 3 pbk/0 7043 5061 0 hbk